CLASSIC IN THE CLOUDS

CLASSIC IN THE CLOUDS

A Case for Jack Colby, Car Detective

Amy Myers

This first world edition published 2012
in Great Britain and 2013 in the USA by
SEVERN HOUSE PUBLISHERS LTD of
19 Cedar Road, Sutton, Surrey, England, SM2 5DA.

British Library Cataloguing in Publication Data

Myers, Amy, 1938-
  Classic in the clouds.
  1. Colby, Jack (Fictitious character)–Fiction. 2. Antique
  and classic cars–Fiction. 3. De Dion-Bouton automobile–
  Fiction. 4. Automobile rallies–England–Kent–Fiction.
  5. Detective and mystery stories.
  I. Title
  823.9'14-dc23

ISBN-13: 978-0-7278-8223-3 (cased)

All Severn House titles are printed on acid-free paper.

Severn House Publishers support The Forest Stewardship Council [FSC], the
leading international forest certification organisation. All our titles that are printed
on Greenpeace-approved FSC-certified paper carry the FSC logo.

Typeset by Palimpsest Book Production Ltd.,
Falkirk, Stirlingshire, Scotland.
Printed and bound in Great Britain by
MPG Books Ltd., Bodmin, Cornwall.

AUTHOR'S NOTE

Jack Colby and Frogs Hill are based not very far from where I write, but it takes more than one person to bring Jack to the printed and electronic page. I could not record his cases without the help of my husband James whose expertise as a classic car buff has been the lynchpin of this series. It has, as always, been a pleasure to work with Severn House, in particular Rachel Simpson Hutchens and Piers Tilbury, and Dorothy Lumley of the Dorian Literary Agency has once again been a stalwart supporter of Jack Colby (and me).

My thanks are also due to the De Dion Club (www.dedionboutonclub. co.uk) and to David Burgess-Wise and Nicholas Pellett in particular; also to Colin Stephens and his team at Gowers Garage in Lenham for their help over a knotty problem. Any mistakes are through no fault of theirs. Amongst printed sources, I consulted in particular Luigi Barzini's *Peking to Paris, The Mad Motorists* by Allan Andrews, *Brighton Belles* by David Burgess-Wise and *A Celebration of the First Races for Motors in Great Britain* by Nicholas Pellett.

Jack Colby operates in Kent, situated between London and the Channel, and the majority of the locations for the action of this novel are real. For plot purposes, however, a few fictional villages, buildings and organizations have also played their part. The famous Peking to Paris 1907 challenge is, of course, fact and is still making headlines; its counterpart in this novel, however, is fiction.

In addition to appearing on my website (www.amymyers.net), Jack Colby also has his own website and – even more dear to his heart – a blog about classic cars. Both can be found on: www.jackcolby.co.uk

ONE

Major Stanley Hopchurch wasn't nicknamed the 'Mad Major' for nothing. I'd heard of him but never met him, so when he telephoned me at the farmhouse one evening it was a surprise, to say the least. When I heard what he had to say, I assumed it was a joke. Even mad majors weren't this mad.

An assertive cough to open proceedings and then: 'Jack Colby?' he barked. Without waiting for my confirmation the Major swept on. 'Good. Heard the rumour that one of the De Dions is kicking around somewhere in Kent?'

'What De Dions?' I asked cautiously, conscious that my pasta was congealing on the plate. De Dion Boutons are few and far between and classic cars rarely 'kick around'.

His impatience grew. 'The two that took part in the Peking to Paris rally.'

'The rerun in 2007?' I asked.

'Good grief, no!' he roared at me. '*The* rally, race – whatever you like to call it. The one in 1907.'

Now I knew why he was called the Mad Major. I didn't have all the facts ready and waiting but I was quite sure that none of the four cars that made it all the way to Paris in that historic event would be 'kicking around' anywhere near me. I opened my mouth to speak but apparently it wasn't my turn.

'You call yourself a car detective, don't you? Pay you for your time.'

This sounded more interesting. 'For doing what?'

'Tracking it down, man,' he barked. 'I want it found. Meet you at Treasure Island at ten tomorrow morning.'

'*Where*?'

'Carter's place. Harford Lee. Can't miss it.'

*   *   *

Life at Frogs Hill comes out on the pleasant side when the pros and cons are weighed up. It certainly beats the oil trade, which was formerly enriched by my presence. Now I live in the old family farmhouse and Frogs Hill Classic Car Restorations are carried out in one of the barns, suitably converted and dubbed The Pits. Frogs Hill sits on the Greensand Ridge by the North Downs and surveys the lush Weald of Kent beneath it. Only two things mar this existence: one is the need to pay the hefty mortgage; the other is that apart from Len Vickers and Zoe Grant, who run the restoration business for me, I live in the farmhouse alone and am currently nursing a bruised heart.

Nothing could be done about the latter, but for the former I have to follow up every opportunity to balance the books. Len and Zoe won't let me near any of their precious hands-on restoration work, so their boss has to eke out their contributions by other means. I don't in fact 'call myself a car detective', as the Mad Major worded it – that was Zoe and Len's withering description of the odd jobs I do for the Kent Police Car Crime Unit or for anyone else who cares to hire my services. My staff – if I might dare to use that term – think it a hilarious joke that I have to work to keep the Pits' roof over their heads, and of course my own.

They were working overtime (by special favour on their part as they were totally absorbed in the engine compartment of an Austin Healey) so abandoning my cold pasta I walked over to the barn where the familiar combined smell of grease and oil cast its usual enchantment over me. Len and Zoe were even deeper under its spell because they didn't even hear me come in.

'Either of you know Stanley Hopchurch, Major or ex in Her Majesty's Army?'

Zoe's head briefly popped up above the Healey's bonnet (she had recently abandoned her former red spikes of hair for a sleek dark-haired approach). 'No,' she stated and went back to work.

'Bentleys,' muttered Len, eyes intent on banishing a blue-bottle that seemed to have designs on the Healey's cylinder head.

'Drives them? Works for them?' I patiently enquired.

Len is a man of few words, especially at the moment as a mate of his – a brilliant car restorer – died in a freak accident a week or so ago. Len had worked with him on the racing scene in the late sixties and they had kept in touch ever since. I had met Alfred King once or twice, liked him and admired his work. Len had taken his death hard. Nevertheless he did stop work to consider my question, wiping his hands on the greasy cloth he favours, and came up with the answer.

'Stuck in the 1930s. Don't know why. Before he was born. Model of the Brooklands race track in his garden,' he informed me. 'Races Bentley Boys round it. Sammy Davis, Tim Birkin in the four and a half litre, the Dunfee brothers – all the greats. Thinks he's right back there with them.'

This did not sound encouraging. I'd every admiration for Woolf Barnato and his fellow 'Boys' and indeed for model cars, but racing them in one's garden is a step too far for me. Still, who am I to talk? I go into Dad's Glory Boot whenever I want a quiet think. (More about that later.)

'Know anything about something called Treasure Island at Carter's place in Harford Lee?' Although I'd been back in the UK some five or six years now and had been brought up here, there was still a lot I had to learn about Kent. It's a county of hidden surprises. Down every lane you'll find an unexpected turning or two. Follow one and who knows what you might find.

Fortunately, Len did know about Treasure Island. 'It's a car collection. Knew the old man, Henry Carter. Nice old chap. He began it, but he went years ago. Met his son once or twice, but he's gone too, a year or so back. The jaw is that his son has plans for it. He's the fellow who bought that Iso Rivolta that you fancied.'

And couldn't afford, I remembered ruefully. 'I'm off there tomorrow. What sort of collection is it?'

Len had shot his bolt, however. 'Dunno. You'll find out. Weirdos the lot of them.'

*   *   *

Kent in springtime – any time really – is a fantastic place
to be. Apple blossom and bluebells still abound despite all
mankind can do to divert fruit trees and woodland to its own
idea of development. It was still only mid April but the
bluebells were beginning to take an interest in blooming,
and I was looking forward to the drive. I decided to take
my Gordon-Keeble out for an airing rather than my daily
driver. Its 1960s majesty might be appreciated by the Mad
Major.

From Piper's Green – the closest village to Frogs Hill – it
is an easy drive to Canterbury and a pleasant one, especially
on the route I chose, which climbed the Downs past Charing
towards land which Julius Caesar might have travelled during
his brief invasion. From Shalmsford a road winds along a
ridge of the Downs through open countryside giving the
sensation of driving along the top of the world. It's true
the various delivery vans that came face to face with my
Gordon-Keeble on this single track road weren't quite as
enchanted with the road as I was, but they obligingly made
way for us. The Gordon-Keeble's quality shines out.

On such a day as this, I decided not to think too hard about
what might lie ahead in respect of the Mad Major and the De
Dion Boutons in the 1907 rally-cum-race – or *raid* as the
French call it, which is, I suppose, a mix of the two: an adventure trip starring cars. I'd had a quick check on the Internet
and in the book collection in Dad's Glory Boot. This is an
extension of the farmhouse where he kept his famous collection of automobilia, everything from Giovanni oil paintings
to saucy postcards (both featuring cars, of course), and from
ancient cranking handles to steering wheels touched by the
hands of the famous.

I now knew that the winner of the rally, an Itala, was safely
in a museum and so was the Spyker, but I could find no record
of what had happened to the other two cars that succeeded
in reaching Paris, the ten h.p. De Dion Boutons. The last
mention of either of them, according to the available books
on the subject, Dad's invaluable handwritten notes in them,
and the *Times* archive he had consulted, seemed to be in late
1907 at the London Olympia motor show of 1907, where the

London De Dion company advertised one of them as being on display. Nothing after that. I wasn't entirely surprised. In those heady early days of motoring there were so many long-distance races going on that it was doubtful whether sticking the cars in a museum was top priority for the manufacturers and drivers.

My newly acquired knowledge made me uneasy, however. To me this project was way up in the clouds of unreality. Suppose the Major really was serious, however, and truly believed there was something to this rumour? It still seemed to be highly unlikely that over a hundred years later there could ever be a positive identification of one of the missing two De Dion Boutons.

Harford Lee is a wooded rural hamlet along a lane off a B road to Canterbury, which makes it *very* rural. No shop, only a pub – and that, being before ten o'clock in the morning, was closed. A girl was hanging out tablecloths to dry in the garden however, and so I stopped to ask directions for Carter's 'place' and Treasure Island. She looked puzzled.

'There's a gentleman lives out at Burnt Barn Bottom,' she said doubtfully. 'Think he's called something like that.'

'That might be it.' I wasn't all that confident, however, especially when she directed me back the way I'd come, then to find a gate, go through it and along a lane, and take the first right after a mile or two.

I was even less confident when I found the gate and the lane that lay beyond it. I began to regret bringing the Gordon-Keeble as I met one pothole after another. The road surface deteriorated the further I went towards Burnt Barn Bottom, so I forgot about impressing the Mad Major and decided to walk the rest of the way. My precious car had suffered enough in the cause of my car detective work and I had promised it an easy life from then on.

I'd walked about another quarter of a mile before I heard a car behind me. It was a 1950s Bentley Continental and someone who could only be the Mad Major poked his head out of the window. Motoring cap, moustache, mid sixties. Maybe he was the son of a Bentley Boy.

'Jack Colby?' he barked.

I nodded.

'That your Gordon-Keeble?'

I agreed it was.

'Not bad.' A tone of condescension nevertheless. 'Jump in.'

I duly jumped, and – with both hands clutched on the wheel as though he were at Brooklands – the Major charged along the lane and driveway, then past the side of a large early-Victorian red brick house, then past what must be its walled garden and round to its rear. We came to a gravelled area, sheltered by woodland on both sides, with, so far as I could see, fields and woodland at its rear. It was dominated by several huge and unsightly corrugated iron sheds in the middle – which had probably given rise to the Island part of its name and were the result of the Burnt Barn that had preceded them.

The Major drew up outside the largest of them, where waiting for us was a slightly built man of medium height and about my age in his mid-to-late forties, together with a younger woman in her mid thirties who looked much more interesting.

She had a warm smile that reached her soft eyes, tumbling curly auburn hair and an air that indicated she was welcoming you into her life – on a friendly basis, not sexual. Well, not yet. She was quite tall and I liked the way she moved forward immediately, hand extended.

'Helen Palmer,' she said as I shook the hand. No rings on the other one I noted. Not that that was a foolproof basis on which to proceed. And proceeding seemed a good idea to me.

'Julian Carter.' Her companion took her place at the hand-shaking ceremony. 'Helen, Stanley and I are the trustees of the trust. You know about that?'

'Not yet.' But I'd like to, as it involved Helen.

Julian was not as welcoming as Helen, nor as extrovert as the Major. He was the quiet, intense and perhaps wary sort, and was staring at me as though he wanted to sum me up before deciding whether he wanted me to interrupt his day.

What I did recognize immediately from years of experience was that he was the stuff of which fanatical car collectors are made. After all, it was he who had snaffled up that Iso Rivolta. He had the look of a hunter who would let nothing stand in his way between desire and achievement. Was it he or the Major who was on the scent of the De Dion Bouton? I realized uneasily that I had stopped thinking of this quest as a joke.

'Army training.' The Major glared at me. 'Thought I'd explain the trust to you as we do the recce.'

Forget the army. I was still at sea. 'This De Dion Bouton,' I said firmly. 'Are you hoping to buy it for Treasure Island?' I wasn't sure whether this was the official name for the collection or not, but I tried it out.

It seemed I'd cast a casual firebomb into the arena. Julian and the Major both tried to speak at once, and Helen gave something between a gasp and a giggle.

'Both of us want it,' Julian said coolly. 'Stanley heard this snippet of information about its being in Kent and insisted on paying you to find out whether it is true.'

What about Helen? I wondered. She seemed to be excluded from the 'both'. I was still at sea, but paddling fast. 'But it is for the Treasure Island collection?' I persisted.

Helen, I noted, was keeping very quiet.

'Certainly,' Julian said after a short pause. 'And we need it urgently.'

'Because you want to display it as soon as possible?'

'Yes, but it's for the rally.'

I was really flummoxed now, but before I could flee to a saner world, Helen stepped in. 'Suppose we introduce Jack to Treasure Island and then explain our plans.'

The voice of calm – and a smile that could win a convalescing heart like mine. It was needed because then she threw open the door to Aladdin's cave.

I've seen a lot of classic car collections and museums in my time, and I love them all, from the huge, all-encompassing ones like Beaulieu and Haynes to smaller specialist ones such as the Morgan museum at Rolvenden. There are also plenty of 'fishing' stories about privately owned barns with

rumoured splendours behind their closed doors, whether they
be cherished possessions or sad wrecks mouldering away
unloved. But never, never, had I seen a collection housed
like this.

At first I thought I'd entered another Glory Boot like Dad's.
What hit me immediately was the sheer colour of the place.
The inside of this outwardly drab greyish shed was painted a
vivid red, both the barrel ceiling and all the walls of this warm
shell. Within their red cocoon cars glowed welcome – or did
their best to do so. It was a maze with cars jumbled up with
photos, models, books – you name it, I could see it. Each car
on display seemed to have its own shell area painted in a
different colour: a vivid blue, a green, a primrose yellow, giving
the effect of an enormous jigsaw puzzle. A second look told
me that some of the paint needed redoing, that several of the
cars were well past their due date for restoration, and the whole
place needed a face lift. But that first impression still had me
gasping.

Helen shot me a sideways look. 'It's a bit – um . . .'

'Impressive,' I supplied tactfully. 'What exactly is it a
museum *of*?'

'Memorable Motors,' she told me. 'Each car is set in context
of what it's memorable for. A famous owner, a race winner,
a getaway car for a famous theft. That sort of thing.'

'Motors represent history, *people's* history,' Julian said with
owner's pride. 'Cars are the people who loved them.'

I could see now that within each car area, the differing
colours provided a backdrop to the automobilia displayed with
the car.

'The cars each have their own story explained,' Helen said
proudly, pointing to a 1946 Riley 1 ½ litre that been used, she
told me, as the getaway car in the famous raid on Beechwood
Castle. The board I could see at its side was covered in large
copperplate handwriting – no impersonal computer-generated
labels for Treasure Island.

'Are all these from your grandfather's collection?' I asked
Julian.

'He began it, my father added to it, and I intend to do the
same.'

'I hadn't heard of it,' I said, puzzled. 'Is it open to the public?'

'My grandfather never wanted that,' Julian replied – it seemed somewhat unwillingly. 'He loved it too much.'

That ticked a few boxes. The avid collector spirit is alive and well in the car field just as art collectors hanker after treasures that lie squirrelled away.

'My father turned it into a charitable trust just before he died,' Julian continued, 'so that it should be opened for all to appreciate. Times change, so that's what we shall now do when the money is available.' He didn't look happy about it though.

'Have a look round,' Helen suggested and I was only too eager for a solitary wander. I made a beeline for a Bristol 406 Sedan, but got seduced by a Lea-Francis on the way, and then by – well, let's say, every single car I could see. The story-boards – for want of a better word, although it made me think of my lost Louise, whom I'd met on a film set[1] – carried tales of the rich and famous, the notorious, and the unknown, such as the mother who had bought a Ford for her son's twenty-first birthday, which waited four years for him to return from the First World War. He won a posthumous VC at Zeebrugge and the car was never used. Louise would have found that as poignant as I did.

'So that's why you want to display the De Dion Bouton, if there's any truth to the rumour you heard,' I said to the Mad Major when I finally forced myself to return to them.

'There *is* no doubt about it.' The Major glared at me. 'How are you getting on?'

I forbore to point out that it was less than sixteen hours since he had 'commissioned me' and for half of those, as is usual with mankind, I had been asleep. 'It seems to me there's quite a lot of doubt, but I'm putting the word out to my contacts.'

'Fat lot of use that will be,' the Major snorted.

Julian lost his cool too and panic antennae shot out all round him. 'We need discretion. Everyone in the world will be after it.'

---

[1] See *Classic Calls the Shots*

'True, but unless you hope to buy it from a scrap merchant, that will happen anyway.'

Julian flushed and his eyes took on the manic look again. 'I have to have first crack at it.'

I noted the 'I'. Was I dealing with the trust or with Julian Carter, car collector? Could there be a lack of 'full disclosure' here?

'I don't want the whole world chasing after it,' Julian added shortly.

I changed tack. 'You said the rumour was already going around, Major. When did you first hear it?'

He stared at me angrily. 'I want the car, not an inquisition.'

It had seemed a reasonable question to me. What on earth was going on here? 'For Treasure Island?'

'Of course,' Julian said stiffly. 'The jewel in the crown.'

Helen gave me an amused look and I was reassured – almost. 'The De Dion would certainly be a draw,' I agreed, 'but don't be too confident I'll find it. What if I don't? Given the way that false rumours can fly around that's more probable than finding it. A car that hasn't been heard of for over a hundred years is more likely to remain hidden than to suddenly pop up on the radar. And you know that rare cars like early De Dions are worth real money, and with the pedigree of the one you're after it would go through the roof.'

'I'll pay your time,' the Major barked impatiently. 'And if you find the car, I'll double it.'

That seemed fair enough – if I took the job. I was still thinking about it though. Why me? Because I was known to be a chump?

'Tell me,' I said firmly, 'just why you believe it's still to be found. A vague rumour isn't much to go on.'

Boxed into a corner, Stanley managed some sort of reply. 'One of the two was definitely around in the 1960s.'

Well, that was a help. Halfway there. Only another fifty or so years in which it could have vanished again. 'How do you know that?' I asked, when he stopped right there.

'I was attached for a few months to the British Embassy in Paris,' he continued unwillingly. 'Heard enough about it then to convince me it was still around. After all, the Itala and Spyker are.'

'The 1960s are a long time ago,' I pointed out, 'and that was in France, not Kent. Where did you hear this recent rumour?'

'Does that matter?'

I thought maybe I'd entered John Cleese's Department of Silly Walks. 'Yes. Could you try to remember and explain why it's so *urgently* needed?'

All three trustees of the future Memorable Motors museum looked at me as though *I* were crazy, and not them.

'It's for the rally.' Julian looked shocked that I should ask.

That word 'rally' again. Fortunately Helen read my face correctly. 'Didn't you tell him about that, Stanley?' she said crossly.

The Major cleared his throat. 'It's urgent because we've only got four months. We're rerunning the Peking to Paris rally in August.'

This time I was left speechless. Helen giggled. 'It's taking place here, Jack, not in Asia. We're doing it on the cheap.'

'Here?' Call me stupid, but Peking to Paris does involve Asia.

'It's going to be fun,' she assured me. 'We've mapped out a weekend route starting at Dover, which is our Peking – now Beijing, of course – and ending two days later in "Paris". That's going to be Canterbury, or perhaps here at Harford Lee. Overnight stops at "Urga" in Mongolia on the far side of the Gobi Desert, and Tunbridge Wells which is Omsk in Russia on the original rally. Then we return to "Paris" by a different route. Every town and village will be decked out in period costume accordingly, and serving appropriate foods.'

I was trying to take all of this in. 'What's the reason behind it, apart from fund-raising?' I asked weakly.

'Fun,' she promptly replied – and I warmed to her even more. Pipe dream? Fantasy? Helen seemed quite serious about it, however, and though I had put Julian and the Major down as fantasists, I did believe in her.

'We're allotting each town and village an appropriate

name from the route that the original rally took – and the hazards they faced too. Romney Marsh is the Gobi Desert, for instance.'

I had to laugh, which pleased them all. All the same I wondered what the thus honoured Kent villages would think of their new identities. 'Do the places concerned *know* what's going to hit them?'

'Of course.' Helen looked slightly annoyed at my all too obvious scepticism. 'We've been planning it since last autumn and have done the basic work clearing it with the traffic police and contacting parish and borough councils. And before you ask, we want as many classic cars and clubs to enter as possible, although the police have set a limit of sixty cars. And they don't have to fall through bridges and get mixed up in floods as they did in the real rally. We're just about to start the serious publicity – so you can see how the De Dion Bouton would fit in so nicely.'

It was crazy, but could indeed be fun. Looking at Helen, it seemed certain it would be – except for my nagging suspicion that where Julian and the Mad Major were concerned it wasn't going to be all plain sailing. I felt there was something I hadn't yet got the hang of. 'Who's agreed to take part so far?'

'Most of the motor clubs in Kent and East Sussex have agreed in principle. After all, it's for charity. One half goes to each town's local charities, and the rest to us. Our charity being Treasure Island and the project of opening it to the public.'

I had to ask: 'Suppose the million to one chance comes off and you do get the loan of the original 1907 De Dion, are you hoping it will actually take part in the rally?' That surely had to be too much to hope for.

'No,' Julian said promptly. 'Display only as the centrepiece. After I've bought the car, of course.'

This all sounded optimistic, to say the least. I could see trouble ahead. Big time. 'It would cost the earth.'

'Then I shall pay the earth – somehow,' Julian patiently replied. 'Do you think I'd let my grandfather's – and my – dream go without giving all I've got to fulfil it? It was hearing

his father talk about that race and reading the books about it
that set my grandfather off on a lifelong hunt for memorable
cars – and in particular for those two De Dion Boutons. One
of them he had to have, but he could never track one down.
Now I'm going to do it for him.'

If Julian could afford to pay for the De Dion (even
'somehow') why, I wondered, was it necessary to organize an
event to raise funds for the museum? It was understandable,
I reasoned. Cash in hand is one thing; running a museum is
a long-time commitment and thus quite another. Was the aim
of the rally to flush the De Dion out of hiding? I dismissed
the idea. They said they wanted the car before the race, not
as a result of it.

I saw Helen's hopeful eyes and I formally accepted the job
from the Major. It occurred to me as I drove away, however,
that I still felt uneasy about it. I couldn't figure out why this
was at first, but then it came to me. The Major had never told
me where he first heard the rumour. It had not reached me,
so it could hardly be widespread as yet. He had avoided
answering me. And why, if it was Julian who was so dead
set on buying the car, was it the Major who was commissioning me?

The other thought that occurred to me was that I hadn't
seen inside the other two sheds, only Treasure Island itself.

I returned to Frogs Hill still pondering whether I'd been
wise to take the job on. Although I'd been honest about my
chances of success, and although it was possible I might
track down the source of the rumour, I knew I didn't stand
much chance of getting any further than that, especially
given that the Mad Major was hardly being cooperative. I
suspected that if Helen hadn't been involved I wouldn't be
going this far. There were too many unanswered questions,
I hadn't much taken to Julian and the Mad Major was off
his rocker. That was just for starters. I argued that Helen
seemed sane and that therefore she must believe there was
a chance. If so, I needed to get going on the rumour front
and for that I should pull in some favours. That, like charity,
would begin at home.

Zoe and Len. Zoe hadn't been her usual self recently, but one avenue might be through Rob Lane, her boyfriend, partner, chum – I never know which with Zoe. A layabout from a wealthy family, he's an odd companion for otherwise practical fancy-free Zoe, and incidentally he and I have a chequered relationship. We don't get on. He barges in and I throw him out whenever I can.

I drove the Gordon-Keeble tenderly back to the rear garage at Frogs Hill where it lives together with my other classic, the 1938 Lagonda. How can I afford two classics when I'm broke? They are a part of the reason for it. Like beautiful women, they can be costly.

Then I went over to the Pits to find Zoe decoking the cylinder head of the Austin Healey. When I mentioned asking Rob to put out feelers for me, the answer was clear to my astonishment.

'No,' she said shortly.

'But—'

'He's found another dumb floozie.'

I did a double-take, recognizing a bruised heart with a fellow feeling. 'Not "another", Zoe. You're not a dumb floozie.' Privately I was overjoyed. It was an enormous bonus if Rob had vanished for good from her life.

'No,' she agreed. 'I'm just a mug.' And she promptly went back to work on the Healey as a subtle hint that the conversation was over.

Len didn't look in a chatty mood either, so I returned to the farmhouse to put out calls to my usual contacts – none of whom was likely to be in the market to make a rival bid for a De Dion Bouton from 1907. They might know a man who was, however, so I took care to explain they were to listen for, not spread, the rumour. Reliable? Well, maybe. I decided I'd give Harry Prince a miss since he's the one contact (of a sort) who might be the exception to the 'listen only' guidelines. He made his cash by gossip.

This accomplished, I went into the Glory Boot to have another look at Dad's books. I knew he'd had a first edition of Barzini's *Peking to Paris*, the story of Prince Scipio Borghese's winning experiences in the Itala – Luigi Barzini, a journalist, had been in the Itala with him. This book had, Dad had told me, seized the public's imagination all over the world and thus, in Dad's opinion, was largely responsible for putting the Peking to Paris race into folklore. One of the De Dion drivers had written his story too, but as luck would have it Dad hadn't bought a copy, perhaps because, I then discovered, it was never translated into English. However, there were other books about the rally-cum-race – or *raid* as *Le Matin* newspaper intended it to be when they first launched the idea of the Peking to Paris challenge – and even several sketch maps of the route.

As usual in the Glory Boot, I became absorbed in what I was doing and it was late evening by the time I returned to the farmhouse living room. The landline was ringing as I did so. Ever hopeful that it might be my lost love Louise declaring that she couldn't live without me, I sprang to answer it, but it wasn't her. She was following her wandering star in an acting career, something she couldn't combine with Frogs Hill (and me). The call was from Dave Jennings of the Kent Car Crime Unit, who commissions me for the freelance work that I do for the Unit. Work that's vital, as I explained, for keeping at bay predators (like Harry Prince) who think they'd like to buy me out. I get on well with Dave, though he can be a funny old stick at times.

'Did you know Alfred King?' he asked.

'Yup. Great friend of Len Vickers. Len was very cut up about his death. I liked him too. He was a good guy. Why—?'

'Am I ringing you?' Dave cut in. 'Answer. Maybe something odd about his accident.'

'Coroner's query or police?'

'Neither. Judged straightforward. The car lift fell on him.'

I hadn't known the details and I blenched. 'So why the doubt? Accidents can happen to the best of us.'

'Not if the nut locking the hydraulic ram into position has been loosened.'

'Is that fact?'

'Fact that it was. Not fact that it was deliberate. Looks like a moment's inattention, but the widow isn't happy.' A pause. 'There's a lot of four-by-fours vanishing all of a sudden. Could be there's a new kid on the block and he's trying his muscle. Want to sniff around?'

I knew Dave's shorthand. A new gang working Alfred King's area. Had Alf been blocking its path?

'I'm on for it, Dave.'

'Right. Funeral's next Monday. Might be a good starting point.'

TWO

'Turn right at the roundabout.' Zoe broke the silence unnecessarily. Sitting next to me in the passenger seat and clad in dark skirt and jacket, she seemed smaller and almost vulnerable compared with the Zoe I usually see at work in the Pits. Surely she could see that losing Rob was a plus not a minus? Then I thought of the train of disastrous ladies I could count in my own past, each of whom had seemed 'right' at the time, and decided to be more sympathetic.

I know the road to Eynsford, where Alfred King had lived and worked, and my Alfa daily driver could find it without any help from me, let alone from Zoe. It's an attractive village at the heart of the picturesque Darent Valley, and the river runs right through its centre. Its beauty made our journey here for his funeral seem all the worse.

Zoe and Len had taken it for granted we were all travelling here together, which was flattering. I wasn't surprised, of course, that Len was attending the funeral – only by the fact that he wasn't surprised that *I* was. Maybe it was my imagination, but that did not look good. Did he too think something was amiss with the 'accident'?

It wasn't my imagination. He climbed out of the Alfa when we parked in Eynsford, and caught me off guard by planting himself in front of me with folded arms.

'Alf wasn't the sort to leave that nut loose.'

'It can happen,' I said cautiously.

'Not to Alf. That's why you've come here.'

It wasn't a question, and there should be no hedging. 'It's a possibility.'

Len looked at me scathingly. 'There's proof and there's knowing. Knowing's all I need. Just find the bastard, eh?'

Zoe and I watched as he stalked off ahead to St Martin's church. In his funereal dark clothes, he looked an unfamiliar figure to the one we're used to, clad in ancient overalls with smudges of oil everywhere, but just as in the Pits, I knew he meant business.

'He's not going to let it go, Jack,' Zoe observed. 'Can you do anything?'

'My damnedest OK?'

'It'll do.'

Eynsford represents many different ages in its origins and architecture. In Dad's Glory Boot is an old calendar from the Fifties displaying what was then a quintessential English village beauty spot: Eynsford's small stone bridge over the River Darent, the green swathe of grass bordering it, the picturesque Plough pub and a row of old cottages beyond it – oh, and for car lovers, a splendid 1953 Humber Imperial. All that can still be seen (except the Humber perhaps), and when you add a ruined Norman castle and a Roman villa within walking distance – what more could one ask?

And yet in this tranquil place violent death had come to Alf King. He worked in a small complex of buildings along Lea Lane, off the main street that runs through the village. His restoration business, like Frogs Hill, wasn't the sort that demanded a main road presence. A killer bent on murder would be unlikely to drop in on the off chance of finding a car up on the lift and Alf there alone. Had someone loosened the nut just to the point where the next person to put pressure on it would bring the whole lot tumbling on top of himself, including the car that Alf was proposing to work on? That someone would have to know exactly what they were doing in order not to go a step too far and bring it down prematurely or not at all.

I recalled Len telling me that Alf had a youngish lad working for him – so how could a potential killer be certain that it wouldn't be him who was the victim, not Alf? Unless of course, it was the apprentice who loosened the nut, or that the apprentice *had* been the intended victim. I stopped myself. This was sheer fantasy at the moment. Then I remembered Dave's new kid on the crime-scene block whose existence was as yet hearsay and whose name was unknown. That was stretching fantasy even further, based on the insubstantial notion that Alf might have got in the way of somebody's plans for increasing the Kent car crime rate. No one else would surely have any other reason to kill Alf – and no casual thief was going to dream up such a scheme for murder.

As we crossed the road and went into the church, I thought about Len's 'knowing' and 'proving'. Proving was the police's job, but if they had nothing to go on, it would be my job at least to 'know'.

St Martin's was crowded, as the full car park had suggested. Alf was obviously a popular local man as well as having a lot of grateful customers. Somewhere in the midst of this crowd, was there a 'new kid'? If so, I wouldn't be able to pick him out amongst the mass of men present. No disrespect to Zoe, but there tend to be fewer women mechanics than male, and the male car restoration community seemed to be present in force. Unfortunately it included Harry Prince, I noted. More happily, I glimpsed Helen Palmer and wondered what brought her here.

Alf's family had chosen to hold the after-service gathering at his home, an old farmhouse deep in the countryside on the far side of Eynsford, beyond the hamlet of Lullingstone. That too has a castle much loved by Queen Anne who frequently descended on the family for visits. Her former bathhouse by the river can still be seen, though I wouldn't fancy it myself.

It was warm and dry enough for us all to gather in Alf's garden; the numbers had decreased as not everyone at the service had chosen to drive on to the crematorium let alone return to Eynsford for the gathering (such as the 'lady' in the silver VW Polo who had practically run me down in her haste to depart from the village car park).

After the cremation, while we looked at the floral tributes to Alf, I had noticed a couple of sturdy guys who seemed to be watching rather than grieving. It's a fine distinction but that's the impression I received, despite its summoning up images from James Bond films. They hadn't come back to the house, either. Alf's family had laid on a combined late lunch and tea buffet with sandwiches, cakes, coffee and tea, with I think some alcohol around for those who wished to seek it out. Tea and coffee seemed much more appropriate, however, and I think Alf would have approved.

I doubt if he would have approved of Harry Prince though, as he rolled up to me carrying a scone and a mug of tea just to keep him going until his next blowout. As I've said earlier, Harry is already the opulent owner of several local garages and is bent on adding Frogs Hill Classic Car Restorations to his empire. Not to mention my farmhouse – and in particular the Glory Boot. He's had his eye on that for many a long year, but is happy to take the rest of the 'estate' with it. He awaits my mortgage payment day as figuratively as I do in practice. One hint that I am in default and he'll be in with an offer within minutes.

'Good to see you, Jack. Sad day, eh?'

It was, and we talked soberly for a few minutes about Alfred King. I wasn't that surprised Harry was here, because he has a finger in more pies than Little Jack Horner, and Alf could well have been another candidate for Harry's Christmas wish list. Not now. Alf *was* the business. His death saddened me all over again. Quite apart from his loss to his family, which judging by today's gathering was immense, but with him went all that knowledge. Gone – and a good man too. The classic car business can't afford that kind of loss.

That over, Harry eyed me speculatively. 'Rumours flying around, Jack.'

'About Alf?' I asked innocently. Any dirty work and Harry could well know of it or at least the reason for it. He's not the sort to get too far into the deep end himself.

His eyes sharpened. 'Should there be?'

'About buying the goodwill,' I said blandly.

He smirked. 'Waiting for Frogs Hill, Jack. I reckon it could be any time now.'

He was right and wrong. My finances were indeed on a knife-edge sharper than a chef's, but not in a million years would I sell to Harry. Not that he's all bad. Very few folks are, and Harry has occasionally done me a good turn – albeit probably in his own interests.

'The buzz is you're looking for a De Dion.'

Harry's turn to look innocent and mine to be surprised at the speed he'd heard about it. On second thoughts, it was hardly surprising, I realized. 'Chinese whispers, Harry, that's all.'

'You don't stand a chance, Jack. The story about that De Dion has been going the rounds for months, and it's gathering speed.'

'Must be fire to the smoke, eh?'

He smirked. 'You don't stand a chance.'

'For once, Harry, I probably agree with you. Even the weirdest tittle-tattle sometimes turns out to be fact. Thought I'd poke around.'

'Taking part in this rally to raise money for Carter's old crocks?'

'Aren't you?' I countered sweetly.

'Not my style. I'll put a quid in the box. Not –' he tapped me playfully on the shoulder – 'that that's going to go far in buying that De Dion.'

'Every little helps.' As he seemed about to leave me, I added casually, 'How do you know it's for sale?'

He dropped the scone, which fell to the grass unheeded. 'Just a turn of speech, Jack.'

'Here's one for you, then. Heard anything about a new crowd around, specializing in four-by-fours?'

Harry struggled to regain his poise (but not the scone). 'Jack, Jack,' he said, forcing a laugh, 'forget it. And you know me. Fountain of good advice.'

'What's the water quality like today?'

'You will have your joke, Jack. Well, here's something for you, but it's no joke. Did you see a couple of chaps at the graveside – standing back a bit?'

'Yes.'

'Then forget them – and quick. *And* anyone you saw them talking to. They're out of your league. Leave this one to Dave Jennings.'

'How can I do that?' I enquired plaintively. 'Me, with a mortgage to pay. Just a hint, Harry?'

Harry looked mutinous, then undecided, but finally hurled at me: 'Connor Meyton.'

I said he was a good guy sometimes. The name meant nothing to me, but I stowed it away for future reference.

After Harry had scuttled away, I decided to pick my own companion this time. So I walked over to Helen Palmer, who looked as pleased to see me as Harry, although I hoped for different reasons. She was clad in a grey jacket and skirt which made the red in her hair stand out like a Pre-Raphaelite's dream. Now was not the place to tell her that, but I hoped it would come.

'How did you know Alf?' I asked, after we had greeted each other.

'He was a friend of my father's – he restored one of his cars.'

'One of?' I enquired politely.

She grinned. 'I suppose that does sound somewhat lofty. He's a retired policeman with a Fiesta and an old Karmann Ghia. Satisfied?'

'Eminently. I like Karmann Ghias. Did Alf do work for Treasure Island too?'

She looked taken aback. 'I think Julian and Stanley knew him slightly, but so far as I know he wasn't their main car restorer. They use Parr & Son in Canterbury. Anyway, restoration hasn't been at the top of the trust's priorities so far. Getting it at least in better shape in time for the August rally is. After that, we can think about the Pompeii and Herculaneum disasters.'

I blinked. 'Archaeological digs?' I ventured.

'Ah. None of us mentioned the sheds?'

'I'd have remembered.'

'Pompeii and Herculaneum are our names for them, just as Julian and Stanley have adopted the village nickname of Treasure Island. They do tend to gloss over their existence, however. They're so called because they contain unknown buried treasures – in the car field, of course.'

'Ready and waiting with my spade,' I said hopefully. This sounded good.

'I only work there part-time so I'll give you a ring when I can fix a time for you to see them. It's best to come when Julian and Stanley aren't around. The Major is sensitive on the subject and Julian pretends it doesn't exist.'

Even more interesting, but Helen was clearly eager to change the subject. 'How are you doing on the De Dion Bouton front?'

'Still digging. I'm trying to keep enquiries low-key as requested, but I've had to put it out to contacts who'll broadcast it to friends of friends quicker than Facebook.'

She studied me for a moment and smiled. 'I like your profile.'

'I'm not on Facebook.'

'I didn't mean Facebook.' She didn't say it as a come-on and I didn't take it that way. 'I watched you in church and talking to that – er – plump man over there.' She indicated Harry, who was deep in conversation with a slightly built man of middle height, who looked fairly nondescript – and yet Harry seemed nervous from the way he was shifting from foot to foot.

'You're looking worried,' Helen added, jerking me back to giving her my full attention. 'Thinking about Alf? I hope so. I was very fond of him.'

'His death is very tough for my chief mechanic, Len – over there.' I pointed him out to her. 'He was close to him, which means that I take his death personally too, although I hardly knew him.'

Helen stared down at her mug of tea. 'Doris – his widow – doesn't believe it was an accident,' she said. 'I spent yesterday afternoon with her and she was quite sure about it.'

So that story would be spreading shortly if not already. Helen was unlikely to be the only person besides the police to whom Doris King had voiced her suspicions. No need for me to keep it too far under wraps, then. 'Does she have any evidence?' I asked.

'Best to talk to Dean Warren – he worked with Alf. He's here somewhere. Mid twenties, tallish, darkish, Latin-lover type.'

'Wouldn't he have told Doris or the police if he knew anything definite?'

'Perhaps he has. Alf thought the world of Dean. I only met him a couple of times, but I wasn't that struck. I—'

'Didn't like his profile,' I finished for her.

'Quite. Now,' she said in revenge, 'about this De Dion Bouton. What do you honestly think the chances of finding it are?'

'Slightly worse than nil.'

'I'd agree, only the rumour doesn't seem to be going away. The Mad Major—' She caught herself with a quick look at me. 'Stanley mentioned it at New Year but the story seems to have hotted up because he then heard that it might be for sale, which is when Julian *really* picked up on the story.' She paused. 'Why are *you* here, Jack? Because of Len?'

'Because of Alf's death.'

She gave me a straight look. 'Officially? I heard you work for the Kent Police.'

'*Car* crime,' I said. 'Not officially on suspicious deaths.'

'Semi-officially then,' she supplied and I didn't quarrel with it. 'Doris would like to know that.'

'She will – if there's anything to tell her. Otherwise it could do more harm than good.'

She nodded. 'Understood. Talking about doing good, though, I'd better do my social duty over there on Doris's behalf.' She indicated an elderly woman in her mid-to-late sixties, whom I remembered seeing in the church because she had been sitting next to the woman who nearly ran me over in the car park. She looked pleasant enough, with a touch of the Miss Marple about her with her grey hair, pink complexion and rounded figure. The shrewd eyes, as we approached, suggested that she might also have some of Miss Marple's intelligence and common sense too. The table she was sitting at was full of teacups and goodies, and she looked at it rather wistfully as if she would really prefer to repel intruders and get on with the cakes.

Helen however was the kind of person who could unfreeze even the coldest shoulder with ease and banish diffidence with a single smile. She certainly banished Brenda Carlyle's, as 'Miss Marple' turned out to be named, and we were quickly ensconced at the table with our own ration of cakes.

'Mrs King tells me you knew Alf,' Helen said. 'Was he a close friend?'

'Not really. My friend knew him better, but she had to leave right after the service. He did some work on an old car of hers.'

'Do you like classic cars yourself?' I asked.

'Oh yes – well, I'm not *knowledgeable* about them, but I like the stories behind them. I have a little house in France and my neighbour talks about cars to me, about how people loved them. It seems so sad that they get sold to strangers when they die. My husband had an old Morris Minor and he loved it so much, but I had to get rid of it when he died.'

'You'll have to come to see our museum, when it's open,' Helen said. 'That's centred on classic cars and the stories behind them. We're holding a rally in August to raise funds for it.'

'I heard about that from the parish council,' Brenda said. 'The route is running near where I live.'

'Come and watch it if you can. There's a faint possibility we might have one of the actual De Dion Boutons that ran in the 1907 rally.'

'Really?' Brenda looked startled. 'But that's surely very unlikely. They'd be in museums like the other two cars. Where is it?'

'No idea. Just a rumour doing the rounds,' I told her.

'We doubt if it will come to anything, but you never know. I like impossible challenges,' Helen said cheerfully.

We left Brenda to her cakes, and moved back into the main gathering. 'Is that what attracts you to work for the trust?' I asked Helen. 'Or is that because you're a car buff yourself? Or both, come to that.'

'The first, I think,' Helen said frankly. 'I like cars – and I like the stories behind them. But mainly I enjoy tackling difficult projects. Part-time at least. The rest of the time I do something sane and ordinary – I'm a freelance accountant.'

'Is that enjoyable too?'

'Yes. I enjoy tying up the loose ends and getting things right – and then I go to Treasure Island and go berserk trying in vain to move impossible obstacles.'

'Or not so impossible.'

'I like your confidence. Are you as certain about investigating Alf's death?'

'More.' Was I? If determination equalled success, then I was.

'You need to speak to Doris. Have you met her yet?'

I hadn't. I could see her sitting at a table on the far side of the garden with two couples and various teenage children coming and going. Her family, I guessed. She was looking confused and in any case this was not the time or place to bombard her with questions about Alf. I asked Helen to mention I would get in touch some other time.

Meanwhile I decided that Dean Warren would be a more fitting target to tackle first, and I went in search of someone who fitted Helen's description of him.

It wasn't hard.

Zoe was with him. In fact she was so close to him she could have been welded to him. It took me aback because I'd never seen her in a clinch before – and this was as close to one as the circumstances would permit. Dean was indeed a Latin-lover type, and looked completely at home with a girl looking adoringly at him. I took against him immediately although I might have been prejudiced. Zoe had already proved how bad a romantic picker of men she can be, and here she was heading for the same situation. I tried to tell myself I should not judge by appearances, but failed.

'Dean, this is Jack Colby,' Zoe reluctantly introduced me. 'I work with him.'

Two brown eyes stared firmly into mine. I'd been going to describe them as frank but then changed my mind. Not sure why. He seemed harmless enough, but overconfident, as if he was convinced he was the next Ferdinand Porsche.

'I've heard of you,' he informed me. 'And Zoe's been telling me more.'

I wondered what this might have been, but murmured something appropriate, and then added, 'Alf's death must have been a great shock for you.' I meant it. 'Did you find him?' If so the sight that greeted him must have been a gruesome experience.

'No, I'm always off on Wednesday afternoons. If I'd been there it might not have happened. As it was, I got a phone call from the police that evening. Some delivery chap found him.' Dean looked so genuinely distressed that I realized I'd misjudged him.

'The nut could have gone at any time,' I pointed out. That was so, whether it was accident or murder. I made a mental resolve to institute a double-check system by two people in Frogs Hill before our car lift was used. We have every procedure we'd been able to think of in place at present, but a double-check of them would do no harm.

'It could have been you, not Alf.' Zoe shivered.

'I know. That's what makes it so bad.' Dean looked even more forlorn. 'I keep thinking Doris wishes it had been.'

'She's far too upset to be thinking anything of the sort,' Zoe replied practically.

I quickly changed the subject. 'What will happen to the business now?' Not strictly my affair but it could be relevant.

He hesitated. 'Not sure yet. I hope to take it over. I know a chap who might come in with me.'

'Not Harry Prince?' I asked with foreboding.

'No.'

Well, that was good news. I temporarily put conspiracy theories on hold. 'How long did you work with Alf?'

'Four years or so.' Another hesitation. 'I heard you'd been asking around about De Dion Boutons.'

'True enough.' Who had told him that? I wondered. Zoe?

'Alf was interested in De Dions. He worked on one or two before I joined him.'

'What did he say about them?'

'Nothing much. He only got talking about them a couple of months back because some chap had come in asking if he could bring his De Dion along. I never saw him and it turned out to be a no-show. Alf told me there were some in the London to Brighton rally most years and that De Dions had started off motor races in Britain in the 1890s when they were only motorized pedal cycles. Know that?'

I told him I didn't – which pleased him. 'I'd be interested to see his records of the cars he worked on,' I said.

Dean started to say something but then looked over my shoulder. I sensed someone approaching. 'Here's my new potential partner,' he said.

I turned round to see the nondescript man who had been talking to Harry Prince. He came straight up to me.

'I heard you'd been asking about me, Jack.'

'Have we met?' I asked.

'We have now. My name's Connor Meyton.'

THREE

So much for Connor Meyton being nondescript and self-effacing. There was always the chance that Harry was wrong and that this wasn't the new kid on the car-crime block, but Harry doesn't get jittery for nothing. I sized Meyton up – and remembered a chap rather like him whom I'd run across in my oil days. Thanks to him my company lost the biggest concession that had appeared for many a year. All in a day's business? Not when half my mates on the geological survey disappeared without trace – or in the case of one of them with only bloody traces evident. His death was put down to bandits, but the grin on the guilty joker's face had told me a lot – and so did his future upward career path.

'Were you a friend of Mr King's?' Meyton asked me when Dean left us together. The eyes were snake-like and the tongue darted hither and thither as if in search of food (in my case I hoped only information). I was sure that Meyton knew exactly who I was. I didn't want to chat about Alf's death and Len's distress with him, so I simply replied, 'Yes. And you?'

'Yes as well. I met young Dean when I brought a car in and he introduced me. A good business, don't you think?'

'Alf's knowledge is going to be missed.'

'I've a pretty good team to bring to the party.'

Interesting. He was taking it for granted I knew about his aims for King's Restorations, but how much more did he know about me? And even more pertinent, how much did Alf know about Connor Meyton? If he'd known too much about his four-by-four operations, that could have provided a motive for the loosening of that nut – especially as Meyton could have known it was Dean's half day off if he was already courting Dean's goodwill.

'My line is four-by-fours,' he added blandly. 'New and classic.'

In the oil business you learn how not to blink and it's a

skill that comes in handy. 'A fashionable line,' I replied. 'Not a fan myself. An Alfa's good enough for me.'

'And a Gordon-Keeble, I've heard.'

Something in his voice made me cold, very cold. If he targeted my Gordon-Keeble . . . Keep still, very still, I told myself. Like animals faced by a snake. Play it deadpan.

'Right,' I said.

'I gather De Dion Boutons are more your style. And a very special one. Peking to Paris?'

I managed to look pleased. 'Right again. Peking to Paris. Where did you pick that up?'

'The word goes round. It might have been from Alfred King.'

Play it his way for the moment. 'Any ideas on where it is – *if* it is?'

'Do you have a client for it?' he whipped back. 'I doubt if the Car Crime Unit would be in the market.'

He was good. It isn't general knowledge that I work for Dave, because neither of us broadcasts the fact, but it can hardly be a secret in car circles. What is secret is my list of contacts, which I go to some lengths to protect for obvious reasons. Connor Meyton was slithering into my affairs expertly camouflaged.

'Are you in the market yourself for this De Dion?' I joked. 'Not exactly a four-by-four, is it?'

He played it deadpan too. 'I might be.'

A cheery approach needed now. 'I thought so. Dean Warren said that Alf King had been talking to him about De Dions. Someone had come in a month or two back claiming to have one to restore but it never appeared. That must be why.'

A cool hard stare. 'You work out near Pluckley, don't you, Jack? Piper's Green. Place called Frogs Hill? I'd be interested to see it one day.'

It came over as a threat.

When I'd left Frogs Hill that morning I'd assumed that the Mad Major's curious quest and Alf King's death were in separate compartments of my working life, but I was beginning to wonder if that was the case. Could the two be connected

in any way? It was a wild leap from one to the other and I
knew I should not hare off down that route too far or I might
miss the correct one. If I did, then doing a U-turn might be
tricky. Nevertheless I wasn't going to ignore the possibility.

I could see Dean once again with Zoe and her body language
clearly sent out a signal that no one should interrupt this nice
chat again. So I interrupted it.

'Hi there,' I said breezily. 'Great chap, Connor Meyton.
Enjoyed talking to him, Dean. I gather he's interested in De
Dions too. Just like Alf.'

Dean flushed, shifting awkwardly as though wondering
whether he should be off. Zoe glared at me. Neither of them
spoke, though, so I pressed home my earlier attack. 'These
De Dions that Alf worked on . . .' I paused for the moment
of maximum impact. 'Any chance of seeing those records?'

Dean seemed to find the grass at his feet fascinating.
'Maybe.'

'I'll have a word with Mrs King and ask if I can look through
them then. You never know, it might turn something up.'

No comment from Dean. So now, as the Americans say, we
were cooking with gas.

We drove back to Frogs Hill almost in silence, Len because
he was too choked to speak, Zoe because she was dewy-eyed
over Dean, and I because I was reluctant to break into their
thoughts. I used some of the journey home, when I wasn't
negotiating the finer points of the motorways, to assess my
two tasks and decide how I would take them forward. The
call to Doris was top of the list because I didn't want Connor
Meyton vetoing my visit. I had briefly paid my respects to her
at the funeral but I doubt whether it registered. If not, I couldn't
decide whether Helen or Dave was my best way of smoothing
my path with her.

Apart from inspecting all the old barns and garages of
Kent, there wasn't much more I could do for the Major's
commission, save further investigation as to what might have
happened to the two Dion Boutons after the Olympia Motor
Show of 1907. I could, however, pursue Alf's death. Having
heard the tributes to him at the funeral and seen the grief

his death had caused I was determined to push forward on that front.

Both Len and Zoe lived near Pluckley, which apart from Piper's Green is the nearest village to Frogs Hill. I dropped Zoe off first, hoping thereby to have a quiet word with Len, reasoning that he might not wish to speak in front of Zoe. I pulled up outside his home and went straight to the point. 'Anyone you can think of who might have wanted Alf dead, Len?'

He knows the car trade grapevine as well as I do, but some gossip might have reached him that hadn't come my way yet. Len promptly postponed his exit from the car, almost as though he had been waiting for this. 'No, Jack.'

It isn't often Len calls me by my name. That involves one more word and he doesn't usually waste them, so I realized how deeply he felt about this. 'No one I can think of. Couldn't be cash involved. He earned peanuts, took too long over his jobs to charge properly for them.'

His voice was full of disapproval – which was ironic considering that Len does exactly the same and has taught Zoe to follow suit.

'What about the business?'

'Also worth peanuts without him at the helm. Agree?'

'Yup. So if he was killed it was more likely because of something he knew.'

Len winced. 'The bastard.'

He got out of my car and I sat there while he marched up to his front door. It occurred to me that I might have played into Dean's hands by asking for those records. He, not Meyton, was in the best position to loosen any nuts to a lethal position, even if it had been at Meyton's instigation. What reason would Dean have for wanting to kill the golden goose? Unless of course the golden goose had discovered something amiss with Dean or his work. Such as his collusion with Connor Meyton? Too far, too soon, I realized. Start thinking again with a clean slate.

What could Alf know that would in some pervert's mind require his death? And did it have anything to do with the De Dion I was chasing? There were still a fair number of

De Dions around, and Alf could have worked on any of them, *if* Dean was speaking the truth. The shadow of Connor Meyton made me wary of any such assumption. It could be complete coincidence that Meyton was interested in De Dions *and* Alf's garage.

It was not until the next morning that I could get Dave's all clear on approaching Doris. I received it, but decided it might be good procedure as well as enjoyable to ring Helen and ask her to smooth the path with Doris first, especially as it was only a theory that Alf might have worked on the De Dion Bouton.

When Helen's warm voice answered I felt guilty about this strategy but she agreed she would contact Doris to give me a clean bill of health. Then I put my foot in it.

'As soon as she feels up to it. Today if possible.'

A pause. 'So you're officially investigating Alf's death?'

'I am.'

Another pause, then: 'Whoever did it, make sure you *get* him.'

The second time I'd been told that. Alf had a lot of friends. Helen arranged for me to see Doris that afternoon, a fact Zoe leapt on when I mentioned it in the Pits. It turned out that just by chance she wouldn't mind dropping in on Dean, and so she would drive me over to Doris's, wait there and then take me on to King's Restorations.

'Any ulterior motives around?' I asked.

The sweet old-fashioned little girl blushed. Then she stopped blushing and retorted: 'Go by yourself then.'

'Together, dear Zoe.'

'Done – with dinner afterwards if Dean doesn't ask me.'

'Done.' That suited me admirably and I forbore to ask how I would get home if she was wined and dined by Dean.

Doris was on her own when I arrived at the house – a different experience today, with the garden quiet. There was no sign of her family although there were two cars parked in the driveway. She looked stronger than she had yesterday, which was a relief.

'Helen says you're from the police,' she ventured.

'I am.' I produced my credentials but she waved them away.

'If Helen says you are, then you are,' she said simply. 'It's about Alf then. Not really this De Dion Bouton you're asking about.'

'Both in fact. Alf's records might produce the answer, which is why I'd like your permission to see them. There might just be a dissatisfied customer or two.'

Doris looked at me sternly. 'Helen says you knew Alf and Len Vickers works for you. You know there would be no dissatisfied customers. But I want you to look at them, just in case it gives you any clues. He would never have been so sloppy over the lift. *Never.*' Her lips quivered.

I assured her that I would do my best to find out what had happened, and we became good friends.

'I'll ring Dean and tell him you can look at whatever you want,' she offered.

'I'd prefer to go unannounced,' I told her.

Another stern look. 'Alf thought the world of Dean. He's a *nice* young man.'

'Then he has nothing to fear,' I said diplomatically.

When Zoe and I arrived at King's Restorations it didn't look as if it was exactly humming with work, although I could see Dean through the open door of the workshop busy with an MGB engine. I steeled myself to go inside to talk to him, and I suspect Zoe did the same. Inside was the car lift that had killed Alf. It looked innocuous enough in its down position, but all too easily I could picture what had happened that day.

Dean saw us looking at it. 'Waiting for the firm to give it an overhaul,' he said almost defensively. He too must be continually remembering what had happened. 'My new partner says he'll replace it with something newer though. Sounds good to me.'

'Are you . . .?' Zoe began, but couldn't continue.

'Using it?' Dean picked up. 'No way. Only taking jobs that don't need it.'

She looked at him with starring eyes and I could almost see the chemistry working. Time to get real.

'About those records, Dean,' I said firmly.

'Records?' He looked at me blankly.

'We talked about them at the funeral.'

Truculence replaced defensiveness. 'I'll have to ask Mrs King.'

'If you wish. I've already spoken to her however, and told her I'm working with the police.'

'Police?'

Either that or the fact that Zoe was fluttering her eyelashes at him suddenly persuaded him that nothing would be too much trouble. He put on a good show, leading us to the office with swaying hips, as if he'd just triumphed in a bullfight. I recognized an old coat of Alf's still hanging on the door and I was glad that Len had not come with us.

Dean heaved out several large boxes full of files – no computer software for Alf obviously. Opening one at random I could see all the entries were in Alf's neat handwriting. Each tax year was allotted a box of its own with neatly labelled files of expenses, income bank statements and so on. Everything I needed – if I had known what I was looking for. Any mention of De Dion Boutons of course, but what else? I'd no idea, but sometimes ideas come best off their own bat. I settled down to the task, while Zoe entertained Dean, or vice versa. Zoe looked the keener as Dean shot worried glances in my direction every so often. He looked even more worried when I told him there was a box missing.

'Which one?' he asked.

'Tax year 2006 to 2007.'

'I've only worked here three years. Maybe Alf took that year's records home.' Dean clearly thought this exonerated him, but not in my book. I was fairly sure Doris would have told me if that was Alf's habit.

'Mr Meyton's going to need it.' Dean seemed anxious about this.

Unless he already has it, I thought grimly. 'Has he moved in here yet, or is he going to wait until it's official?'

'Doris doesn't want him to have any of the books until the lawyers give their say-so. That was my idea,' he added with a touch of pride.

Zoe clearly thought this a masterpiece of business planning and it must have given him confidence to bluster. 'Look, what's this all about?' he demanded. 'Why are the police interested?'

And why are you sweating with nervousness? I wondered. 'Lots of shady people around these days,' I told him. 'We just need to check everything's in order when a death's involved.'

'Alf was as straight as a die,' Dean said uneasily.

'It wasn't Alf I was thinking of,' I said.

'*Me?*' Dean went white.

I tried to look shocked. 'I meant customers, suppliers, gangs . . .'

He said no more, and I continued to skim through the files that detailed the cars that Alf had worked on. It was an impressive list. Together they could have formed a great museum and it made me all the sadder that Alf was no longer here to carry out his loving work.

To my initial excitement, I found two De Dions listed. One was a fifteen h.p. invoiced in 2002, and the other was a post First World War model. Neither could be the one I was after. The remote possibility that the De Dion Bouton of my quest had passed through Alf's hands was ruled out – unless of course it was listed in the missing box file.

'You wouldn't have the invoices for 2006 on computer, would you?' I asked Dean hopefully.

'Alf did it all manually.' There was a note of smugness in Dean's voice. 'I computerized the system a couple of years back although he still used the manual system – if you call it that.'

Looking at the precision of Alf's bookkeeping, I could indeed call it a system and a good one, but it had yielded nothing save for that missing year.

'Fancy an Indian tonight, Zoe?' I heard Dean ask in a caressing voice as I prepared to leave. He was back in a field where he felt at home.

The last straw. Without my lift home, I'd be taking the train back to Ashford, forking out for a taxi to Frogs Hill and dining on a ready meal. Great.

'Thanks, Dean. Can't make it tonight though,' Zoe said in the most offhand voice I'd ever heard her use.

Sometimes I think I don't understand women – particularly

as Zoe started up the old wreck she calls a car with a pleased smile on her face.

A week later, my contacts were still only bringing in rumour, not hard information, about the De Dion Bouton. Admittedly Easter had intervened, but the criminal world doesn't observe niceties such as that. My last hope was that the Mad Major's restorers, Parr & Son, might have an idea of where and when they'd first heard this story. They do good work and are well established so it was worth having a shot at it. What's more, that meant I could ring Helen and get an invitation to those mysterious sheds. I'd tried her over Easter in the hope that work could be combined with pleasure, but only voicemail greeted me on the landline and I had no mobile number for her.

She seemed pleased to hear from me on the Tuesday following the bank holiday however, and suggested my coming over the next day. She was showing someone round Treasure Island in the afternoon but in the morning she and I could poke around Pompeii and Herculaneum to my heart's content.

'Should I clear it with Julian?' I asked.

'I'll tell him, if you like. As I said, he's sensitive about them.'

'Does he have a wife or family?'

'Neither. I think there's a son somewhere but Mrs vanished long ago clutching her toddler. Julian works from home, surveying consultancy, so he's out a lot of the time. But even he knows the sheds have to be dealt with sometime. He just doesn't want to face it and nor does Stanley. Fantasists both of them. Look at it this way: you might have some idea how to tackle their problem so you'll be doing them a favour.'

I was hooked. Pompeii, Herculaneum and Helen too. What more could I ask?

Answer: a more fruitful visit to Parr & Son. The weathered Len-look-alike who appeared when I rang the bell informed me he was the Son and that Parr senior had long departed. Pete Jones had no problem remembering the Mad Major. He was a frequent visitor, I was told, as was Julian. Nor did he have any problem remembering the story about the De Dion. They'd all had a good laugh about it. Where had it come from? Ah now, bless me, my non-informant chuckled, now you have me. He couldn't remember. He thought the Major told them – or did they tell him? There'd been some chap in here . . . Perhaps it was he who told them. Or had they thought it up themselves as a good joke? Whichever, they knew they'd talked about it and laughed their socks off.

'Did you pass the story on?' I asked.

His answer: why not? It was a joke, wasn't it? What exactly was the joke? Well, now, he recalled, it involved Kent, De Dion Bouton and Peking to Paris 1907. Big deal. To cut the story short, the race was over, as far as Parr & Son was concerned.

When I arrived frustrated at Treasure Island, Helen was wonderfully comforting. Dressed in jeans and T-shirt, she exuded warmth as she dispensed instant coffee and words of solace. 'Is it so very important to trace the source?' she asked.

'Yes,' I said gloomily. 'If you find the centre of the whirl-pool you'll understand why it's whirling.'

'So you hope the De Dion really is around in Kent?'

'Yes, but I'm tired of chasing this will o' the wisp.'

'Perhaps seeing Pompeii and Herculaneum might help. Perhaps the De Dion's in one of them.'

'Temptress. Lead on.'

'Prepare to gasp,' she warned me when we arrived at the locked doors of Pompeii.

I prepared.

In vain, however. *Nothing* could have prepared me for the vision before me when Helen opened the door.

There's a wonderful novel by Carlos Ruiz Zafón that opens with a cemetery of forgotten books. Here before my eyes lay a cemetery of forgotten cars. Dust lay on them all so thick that I couldn't even tell the colour of most of them. A few were only the bare bones of chassis frames picked clean by vultures; from another I could see a lone steering wheel sticking up like a hand beseeching help, and empty seats echoed the loneliness of this derelict collection. These poor carcasses could not even have had the dignity of driving here under their own steam – and some of them might indeed have been steam powered. There was a double door large enough and high enough for them to be dumped ignominiously by low-loader and crane. Nothing but huge piles of car wrecks met my eyes, some halfway up their neighbour's bonnet, others piled on top of one another. These forgotten classics looked as if they were waiting in some motor-car limbo for someone to decide their fate, be it heaven or hell.

All these cars had been loved – once. They looked so pitiful I felt like crying. They seemed to be pleading that they had a former life. The glory has departed, I thought. Wasn't there a word for that?

'Ichabod,' murmured Helen at my side.

I took her hand. 'You read my mind.'

'Hard not to feel that way faced with this, isn't it? I hate the sheds.'

'Is Herculaneum as bad as this?' I asked. Goodness knows how many cars lay in this forgotten place. Seventy-odd? Eighty? More? Perhaps the De Dion itself really was here.

'Worse,' Helen replied. 'It's heaps of *bits* of cars.'

I couldn't face that. 'Some other time,' I muttered. 'Tell me how this came about.'

'They're all cars that Grandfather Carter and Father Carter bought, but didn't restore,' she told me sadly. 'Grandfather Henry ran out of money. Eyes bigger than his bank balance. Dad Carter simply went on buying and closed his eyes to the same problem, although he did set up the charitable trust. Julian inherited it and he too shut his eyes until we were forced to discuss it at a trustees' meeting after his father's death.'

There was no clear path through this heap, but Helen and I got into the spirit of the thing and scrambled around like kids. I managed to edge my way along one wall to have a closer look at something. I wish I hadn't. I found a rare 1924 Jowett, only just about identifiable and beyond restoration. The sheer horror of it drove me back to Helen.

'Could there possibly be a slim chance that the De Dion Bouton *is* in this lot?' I asked. There was no way I could fight my way through to check that for myself.

'No. That's the one thing we can be sure of,' she said to

my relief. 'Mrs Grandfather Henry was a great record keeper and listed each car as Grandfather drove it triumphantly home or had it dumped here. Usually the latter I gather. His son did the same and Julian doesn't dare buy any more unless they're in decent nick.'

'Are the entries fully catalogued with source and any claims to fame?'

'I doubt it. I suppose that's part of my job, isn't it?' She pulled a face.

I remembered from Zafón's novel that the privileged few allowed inside the cemetery of forgotten books went from shelf to shelf and browsed until one particular book cried out to be read. Here though? Could one browse through the cars or the heaps of automobilia that waited so patiently to be found? I thought how much Dad would have loved this place, and wondered if he had seen it. I couldn't believe so, because the sheer thrill of it would have led him to talk to me about it. I was his only outlet, because my mother hadn't been so keen on cars and automobilia – perhaps because her chance of a normal life with holidays tended to vanish with each new acquisition.

'Is the August rally to raise money for sorting and restoring this lot as well as Treasure Island?' I asked Helen. It would have to be a highly successful fund-raising effort to make any dent on the sheds.

'Not even Julian and Stanley would dare push for that. The rally money is only for opening the museum to Joe Public, insurance, staff wages, security stuff, accounting, loos, snack bar – that sort of thing.'

I gave one last despairing look at the heaps in front of me. 'Are you absolutely *sure* there are no De Dion Boutons or any wreckage in the other shed? Did Stanley check what lists there are?'

'I don't know if *he* did, but Julian and I went through them and clambered around in here when the rally idea first came up.'

'Whose idea was this rally? The Major's?'

Helen shrugged. 'How do ideas get born? No one person was responsible for this one. At the initial trustees' meeting

I'd been talking of fund-raising events and suggested some kind of rally. Julian joked that we should organize one of those Peking to Paris revivals they hold from time to time. Stanley said why not hold our own here, Peking to Paris. Romney Marsh could be the Gobi Desert, etcetera, and Canterbury could be Paris. And then it went on from there.' She turned those warm brown eyes on me and smiled.

Two ideas were born to me that very moment and they were all my own. Firstly I was going to find Alf King's killer as well as getting to the truth of this De Dion story. Secondly, that I wanted to take Helen to bed – and preferably soon.

Neither was accomplished that afternoon, but I left her with the two ideas still firmly in my sights. From the kiss she returned as I left, I thought the second idea might be in hers as well.

The next day I paid another visit to Doris. She had been staying at her daughter's home over Easter, but still seemed shaky – not unnaturally as only ten days had passed since the funeral. She was eager to see me, though, and had even baked teacakes for me. We got on like a house on fire. It wasn't hard to imagine her home life with Alf – nor how much the manner of his death weighed on her.

I told her about the missing records for 2006 but she shook her head when I asked if he could have left them at home. 'Alf never did that. I wish he had worked at home. I'd have seen more of him.' A hesitation, then: 'So you are treating it as murder,' she said bravely.

I explained that I wasn't from the Serious Crime Directorate but had been asked to look into her claim because I knew about cars and car crime, but that we hadn't reached any conclusion yet. I could see she understood right away. She seemed very much like Alf, in fact. I could imagine them chuckling together at the odd ways of the world, contented and comfortable.

'Did you share Alf's love of cars?' I asked.

'No. I never could see what made cars so special for him although some of them are nice enough to look at. He and I just agreed to differ. After all, he could never tell one plant from another but to me they're all special because they're growing. Cars aren't alive.'

'Nor are great works of art,' I pointed out. 'And yet they can change people's lives. Cars can do that too.'

She sighed. 'I expect you're right. It's just that Alf's met his end by cars – it's so terrible, *terrible*. I'm sorry.' She mopped her eyes. 'I'm not sleeping too well.'

'That's natural.'

'Yes.' A silence fell. Then: 'Do *you* believe it was an accident?'

'It seems an odd one to happen to someone as experienced as Alf but—'

'Don't say accidents happen,' she interrupted firmly. ''Course they do. But I think someone wanted him dead.'

I tried to go gently but there was no real way round it 'Why could that be, Doris?'

'I can't think. I'd like to help but I can't. Who would want to hurt him?'

I plunged in. 'Did he ever suggest he was being threatened, or that anything was wrong at work?'

She stared at me. 'Never.' Her eyes filled with tears but I had to press on now.

'Do you remember anything odd about 2006 that would explain the missing records?'

'No. Dean might though. He wants to buy me out with a partner. The lawyers are waiting for me to decide, but I can't think what Alf would have wanted so I'm taking it slowly.'

I took her hand in both of mine. 'Don't rush. Take it very gently.'

'It's hard, Jack.' A pause. 'You said 2006?'

'Yes. Any odd customers or cars?'

She tried to please me but had to admit, 'He had so many. Some customers came to the funeral. Alf would have liked that.'

'Regular customers?' Could that be a line to follow up? I wondered.

'Some. There was one lady at the funeral. Her late husband brought several cars to Alf and after his death she brought one too. She used to come to see us every so often after Alf worked on her car, but not recently. Came to the funeral with her neighbour Brenda.'

I clutched at this fleeting point of contact. 'I met Brenda here after the funeral. Who was the customer?'

'Victoria I think her name was. I saw her in the church with Brenda, but she didn't come on to the crematorium or back here.'

Another forlorn hope flickered and died. Then I remembered Brenda's startled look at the mention of a De Dion Bouton while we were talking at the funeral and hope flared up again. 'Do you have either of their addresses or surnames?' It was probably nothing but any port in a storm was better than the open sea in which I was currently floundering.

'No, Jack. I'm sorry. Brenda told me she'd read the announcement about the funeral in the newspaper. Is it important?'

'I doubt it.' I smiled at her. 'But I'm going to find out anyway.'

Glory be, I rejoiced as I drove away. Forlorn hope or not, it was greatly helped by one of the few quirky talents I have: an uncanny photographic memory where car licence plates are concerned. Any other figures I fight to retain, but put a number plate before me and it's lodged with me for good. Somewhere, that is . . .

I concentrated. I saw that VW Polo coming towards me again – I'd jumped aside and turned round with shock, so I had two opportunities at seeing the number plate. I only needed one. I relived the scene in my mind and conjured up that plate again.

The magic letters and numbers. The number plate. It was there, before my eyes. *I had it.*

And soon, thanks to Dave, his team and the Swansea registration office, I'd have the owner's name and address.

FOUR

'Alfred King? What about him?'

The female voice at the end of my phone line was querulous, crotchety and possibly cranky. Nevertheless Victoria Drake was the current owner of the car that had nearly run me down, and might have some useful information about Alf if her dealings with him had included a car in the year of the missing records. Especially – although I scarcely dared hope as much – if a De Dion Bouton had been that car.

After convincing her that I wasn't selling double glazing or insurance, I explained that the Kent Police Car Crime Unit needed to check whether Alf could possibly have been involved, unwittingly, in a crime network past or present. We were therefore checking his customer register in which she figured.

'Am I supposed to be part of this supposed crime network?' she snapped back.

'No, Mrs Drake, but organized crime is increasing in this field and we need to eliminate any suspicion that Mr King's death was no accident. For instance there's a current rumour that there is a valuable classic around and as Alf—'

Funny how even over the phone one can pick up vibes in the silences. I'd hit a nerve. I broke off immediately, not knowing whether to curse myself for mentioning it or rejoice at a possible bull's eye.

'I drive a Polo and do not possess a De Dion Bouton.' Her icy voice broke the silence.

Bullseye. I had not yet suggested she did.

'Then may I ask which car Alf King restored for you?'

'Just how far has my privacy been invaded, Mr Colby?'

Definite hostility now, so now more fencing. I was going to take this five-barred gate blindfold at one leap. 'Your name and a De Dion Bouton were in his records for 2006.'

I waited for another furious retort but it did not come. She must be thinking very carefully indeed, which was good news.

'I inherited a wreck of a De Dion Bouton from my late husband,' she replied at last. 'After his death, I had it restored by Mr King. I no longer possess it. Goodbye, Mr Colby.' Then a click and the line was dead.

And that was that.

Or so Victoria Drake obviously believed. I had different ideas.

Victoria Drake lived on the outskirts of Lamberhurst, south-east of Tunbridge Wells and Goudhurst. It's a striking village and I know it both for its vineyard and for its proximity to the magical gardens and house of Scotney Castle. Her address was Elmtree House, Shoulder Mutton Green, so called from its eponymous shape, though the name had lost its 'of' over the years. It is a hamlet off the Goudhurst road, and it seemed to me that a reconnaissance trip there would do no harm at all.

Brenda Carlyle had claimed Victoria as a neighbour, although that isn't a precise term in rural England. I once met an old chap who owned a castle and who claimed that his nearest neighbour – who also owned a castle – was fifty or sixty miles away in the next county. This being in England, not in the Australian outback, it was an interesting remark as his definition of neighbour was obviously the nearest person with whom he exchanged social visits. That way of life is passing now, but all the same Victoria Drake's 'neighbours' might not necessarily live in the next-door house. Anyway, I wanted to see the lie of the land before I tackled either lady again. As Victoria had stated that she no longer owned the De Dion Bouton, I checked with Swansea registration office to see if one were registered to her. Nothing turned up, and my online research revealed no trace of any early De Dion Bouton being sold by or to Victoria Drake in the last twenty years.

I had longed to drive my Lagonda or the Gordon-Keeble on today's trip but had reluctantly decided that being

inconspicuous would be advisable. The journey from Frogs
Hill to Lamberhurst is so spectacular it lifts the heart. After
rounding the two sharp bends into Goudhurst one descends
through the village to magnificent views of the Weald lying
beneath. The landscape here presents a gentler face than does
the sharper Downland of eastern Kent, and as my Alfa passed
the village duck pond the ducks seemed to be lining up to
quack welcome at this gateway to the Weald.

I passed the entrance to Finchcocks, another majestic house
hidden in the heart of the countryside, this one devoted to
keyboard music; then I looked for the turning to Shoulder
Mutton Green. The green is still common ground open to all,
although the houses bordering it would, I guessed, be far from
common.

There was no pub or shop or church in this hamlet to give
me a legitimate reason for stopping, and I was well aware that
any unusual arrivals in a place this size would be sure to be
noted by someone. I drove slowly past the row of houses
which did not in fact look particularly grand, but they were
early Victorian and therefore large compared with today's
offerings in the way of housing. So were the gardens in front
of the houses and I imagined the rear ones were even larger.
I couldn't see much of Elmtree House itself, because the trees
and shrubs in front of it had grown so high that they shielded
most of it. If the closed gateway was anything to go by,
however, it needed repainting.

Did the De Dion Bouton live behind those trees in a high
security garage? My guess was no. If Victoria Drake did still
own it, it was probably not for sale, and nor would she be
disposed to let the world know about it. If it was too close at
hand, tradesmen, guests, casual callers might all spread the
story.

I remembered spotting a postbox on the green, which would
give me an apparent reason for wandering back for another
look at the house. I parked the Alfa further up the road, took
an old envelope out of the glove compartment and sauntered
along with this legitimate mission in hand. We sleuths are
adept in such cunning schemes. Dad knew someone who had
been a real-life spy in the 1930s and his chief strategy to avoid

detection had been to slink past his prey with his hat pulled down over his eyes.

I could only see one garage from the gateway to Elmtree House as I walked back to the Alfa. It was closed and Mrs Drake's silver Polo stood outside it. Could there be another garage anywhere? Possibly, but I still thought she would store it further away. Where though? I'm no psychologist but I did my best. In a barn or garage for sure, but not *too* far away. I remembered Brenda Carlyle reacting to my mention of a De Dion Bouton at the funeral, and she was a neighbour. I could be way out, but Victoria Drake's husband must have loved the car and he would want it reasonably nearby to keep an eye on it. Victoria was unlikely to have moved it after his death.

Satisfied with this reasoning, I continued walking towards my Alfa. Elmtree House was the last in the row of these detached Victorian houses and next to it on the far side was a driveway to a farm. A narrow road skirted the bulge of the green, but further up opposite where I was now standing there was another driveway. In the distance I could see more farm buildings. My money (although admittedly I haven't got much) would be on the De Dion being in one of those two farms. I did not dare investigate further, because although the countryside might seem quiet and devoid of human life, it's a safe bet that a whole army of unseen eyes can be focused on you, and I did not want Victoria Drake forewarned of my presence.

The best of plans go awry. As I reached my Alfa I ran straight into Brenda Carlyle, ostensibly on her way back from the farm with some eggs. I say ostensibly because the bag she was carrying looked empty.

'I thought I knew that car,' she beamed. 'You're Mrs King's friend, aren't you? We talked at poor Mr King's funeral.'

'You've caught me out,' I admitted ruefully and I hoped disarmingly, while I fished in the Alfa for my credentials. 'I have to confess I'm from the Kent Police Car Crime Unit, and I'd hoped for a chat with your neighbour Mrs Drake. She didn't want to talk to me on the phone so I thought I'd come over here in the hope she might relent if she saw I wasn't a

Policeman Plod. Nothing sinister – I just need to know more
about Mr King's business life.'

'Oh.' She looked the picture of a village worthy from Miss
Marple's St Mary Mead. 'Victoria can be difficult.'

A window of hope? Brenda was clearly dithering over
whether to help or hinder me. 'I know Mr King did restore
her De Dion Bouton some years ago.'

I prompted her. 'What's happened to it now?'

'Is this to do with the Peking to Paris rally?' Brenda
enquired, unexpectedly sharply. Then her cherubic face
blushed, as she saw my astonishment. 'We were talking about
that at the funeral . . . I wonder . . .'

'Yes?' I said encouragingly when she paused.

'If you just wanted to talk to Victoria about that . . . I might
be able . . . Not today, of course. I'd need a day or two.'

She needed seven to be precise, and during that time several
things had happened. Firstly, I'd reported to Dave my theory
that Alfred King's death and the rumour about the 1907 De
Dion Bouton might be linked. He didn't think much of it.
Connor Meyton and his racket were the line he preferred me
to follow up. Secondly, I also had to report to the Mad Major.

'Interim report only,' I explained.

He wasn't easily deterred. 'Come on, man, spit it out.'

'I have tracked down a De Dion Bouton, but I don't know
whether it's the one you're after. I'm hoping to find out shortly.'

'Whose is it?' he shouted down the phone.

Time to be firm, although it was an interesting reply. 'I have
to do it my way. Clash of interests.'

He ranted and raved, but calmed down in the end. The third
development came a few days later, and was even less
welcome. I looked out of the farmhouse window early one
morning and saw Zoe drawing up in a cloud of smoke.
(Physician, heal thyself, as they say.) So far all was as usual.
What was not as usual was that I saw her *running* and not to
the Pits but towards the farmhouse, waving a newspaper. A
newspaper that looked suspiciously familiar. I had a horrible
feeling it was the *Kentish Graphic* and Wednesday was its
publication day.

In her eagerness Zoe almost fell through the door as I opened it. 'Seen this?'

I hadn't. It wasn't the lead story, but not far off it. It was a splendid picture of an early De Dion Bouton and above it a huge caption blared out: 'Have you seen this car?'

I grabbed the paper from her to look more closely and my appalled eyes took in the fact that a donation would be made to a charity for any information leading to the discovery of a mysterious De Dion Bouton said to be the actual one that ran in the Peking to Paris rally. It ended with the news that it was thought to be in Kent and that the *Kentish Graphic* was hot on its trail. I didn't even need to look at the reporter's name. I knew it already.

It was Pen Roxton.

She and I go back a long way, and most of it has been a troubled path. I like Pen. Who could fail to be charmed by her quivering sharp nose, her lanky blondish hair and wiry pushy figure busy pushing itself into other people's business? Indefatigable is Pen. Harsh words or criticism roll off her quicker than water from a penguin. I had as much chance of knocking this story on the head as finding the Contal tricar buried in the sands of the Gobi Desert. That had been the fifth contender in the 1907 rally, but its driver had had to abandon it at this early stage.

However, did I want to knock the story on the head? I was being paid to find the De Dion Bouton and Pen's story might help. I say 'might' because with Pen nothing is certain except that she'll be there exactly when you don't want her. She claims this is because she's very good at her job. I maintain it's because thinking round a story never occurs to her. She says she's paid to produce, not think.

'Thanks, Zoe.'

'Saw the word De Dion on the placards so I went in to buy one for you.'

I glanced at it. 'Any mention of Alf King or Dean?'

'No. Should there be?' she asked warily.

'Not if I can keep it out, and even if I can't, not yet.'

'Want me to ask Dean about this?' A mite too casual.

'Why not?' I can do casual too. 'Are you seeing him soon?'

'Dinner tonight.'

'There or here?'

'Halfway. He lives at West Malling.'

'Married?'

She shot me a disdainful look and marched away, leaving me feeling ashamed of myself. There had after all been no Mrs Dean at the funeral, and even though Greek-god types aren't my first choice for Zoe, they're a whole lot better than Rob Lane. At least this one had a job. Admittedly this was now likely to be with Connor Meyton. Greek gods have always struck me as being somewhat short on the IQ front. Of course, the business would be Doris's to sell but no doubt Dean was playing a role in it.

Zoe stopped short in her progress to the Pits and called back to me. 'Forgot to tell you – sorry. Jack. Had a call on the Pits phone for you yesterday when you were out. Helen Palmer.'

I glared at her. 'What did she want?'

'To know if you were married. I said yes, with six kids.' Zoe went off giggling.

Helen was on voicemail, so I gritted my teeth and rang Pen. Not a pleasant task. When I said I like her, I meant it – but that's at a distance. Dealing with her when she has her nose to a story is a different matter.

'Thought I'd be hearing from you, Jack,' her inimitable voice squeaked at me.

'Nice story, Pen,' I purred. 'Where did it come from?'

'Does that matter?' She sounded hurt. 'I couldn't tell you even if I remembered. Which I don't.'

'The rumour's been going the rounds for a time now, Pen. It's hardly a scoop.'

'I'm the first to give it street cred. And I'll be the first to find that car. You betcha.'

'Or claim you are,' I countered. Sometimes Pen can be persuaded to do deals.

She considered this proposition. 'Possibly,' she conceded. 'I heard you'd been asking after the car's health.'

I wasn't going to be led by the nose, particularly by Pen.

'I'm on the trail, Pen,' I told her. 'Give me leeway and you'll be the first to know—'

'Done.'

'Unless,' I finished, 'it clashes with my police work.' Fool, *fool*, that I am on occasion, usually when Pen is around.

'So there might be a connection with Alf King's death?' she asked brightly. 'Heard you were at the funeral. Knew there must be a story.'

'Don't go there,' I warned her. 'Just don't.'

'You know me, Jack.'

'And, dear Pen, you know me.' I put just enough threat into my voice to make her realize I was serious. There are some boundaries that even Pen wouldn't cross – not out of delicacy or morals, just safety first for her own interests. Or so I comfort myself.

There was a brief silence, then: 'Working on the story with an old lag.'

'*What?*'

'Well, doubt if he's done stir, but looks as if he's kicked around a bit. Sports photographer from years back.'

'Does he live in these parts?'

'Woolwich way. In a pub most of the time. Arthur Orton's his professional name, known as Bob. He might tell you more. He's glad of a pint or a penny or two, whatever's on offer.'

'Thanks, Pen.'

'You owe me, darling.'

No sooner had I put the phone down than Brenda Carlyle rang me.

'Such good news, Mr Colby,' she trilled. 'Victoria has agreed to talk to you. If you would like to come to tea here tomorrow she will be present.'

'That's splendid,' I said warmly. I'd have preferred to talk to Victoria Drake alone, but this wasn't too bad a scenario. I might even get Brenda's support.

Unfortunately she continued hesitantly, 'Her daughter Patricia Morris and her husband Tom might also be coming. They're very interested in the Peking to Paris rally, so we can all chat about it.'

I inwardly groaned. A nice chat with half the world wasn't exactly what I'd had in mind, but nevertheless half a loaf was better than none – provided of course the truth wasn't masked by family considerations. Was it the rally or the De Dion Bouton that had caught the Morrises' attention, I wondered.

When I arrived the next day with my best bib and tucker on, I was prepared to find tea, scones and maybe a cup cake or two. Afternoon tea isn't a meal that figures highly in car detection work. One glance at TV documentaries demonstrates that the criminal life of the everyday copper in the vast run of true crime cases is either humdrum or vicious or both, often dealing with sad people who have lost or never found their way in life. Nevertheless there's a huge stratum of society, just as real and perhaps equally humdrum, that proceeds along more gentle channels. Brenda Carlyle and the Morrises were doing just that. I was therefore pleasantly amazed to find not stale cupcakes, but a whole buffet of the most delicious-looking French pastries I'd seen this side of Paris.

'Did you bring these over from France?' I asked.

'Oh no. I made them myself,' said this surprising lady. 'My neighbour in France showed me the way. The villagers said Monsieur Beaumont prepares the best eclairs in France, so ask him how to make them. So I did, and now I can make them too,' she said with simple pride. 'I do like France.'

That explained the prints and photographs on the walls, framed photos of the Loire and prints of Monet and Cézanne, even a Seurat. I was the first to arrive, and so I had had time to assess the room – and taste the delicious petits eclairs.

Such delights lasted only ten minutes or so and then the remaining guests arrived en masse, as if to underline a united family front. Their body language told me they were armed for battle and their set faces did not bode well for cosy chats.

'I'm Patricia Morris,' the daughter announced somewhat uncertainly. She was flanked by two men, not just the husband I had expected, and seemed dwarfed by them both in stature and confidence. She could only be in her early fifties but she looked and behaved older than that with clothes and hairstyle that owed nothing to fashion. The elder of the two men, obviously husband Tom, said he was pleased to meet me but did not look in the least pleased. He looked as if he was spoiling for a fight. Even his chin stuck pugnaciously out. The younger of the two was introduced by Brenda as 'dear Nick', their son. Dear Nick was a strapping lad in his mid twenties, who announced he'd taken the afternoon off because he liked cars. I wasn't sure if I was meant to express gratitude or not. Tom Morris was, I guessed, also in his early fifties, and Brenda had earlier conveyed the news to me that he had recently been made redundant. That explained not only why he was here on a weekday afternoon but also his bullish attitude. He was out to make me reap the whirlwind of an unjust world.

I've deliberately left Victoria Drake until last. The Morrises might have taken the lead in announcing themselves, but this was where the power lay. No doubt about that. Victoria looked in her early seventies, smartly dressed and definitely formidable. She was a medium-sized woman with short cropped grey hair, thirties style, and was clearly a woman who knew her own mind – as I had already found out to my cost. She might even be a match for Pen. So why had she found it necessary to bring her daughter and family as back-up? Was it because she wanted to be seen as in control – even though this was her neighbour's home? True, they would probably support her refusal to help me over the De Dion, but why would this sharp-eyed woman need such support? I already knew she was capable of telling me to get lost.

Brenda bustled around with coffee, tea and cakes, to which I could no longer give the attention they deserved, as it was evident that Victoria Drake was about to launch an assault.

'I only agreed to speak to you, Mr Colby,' she told me coldly, 'because of this story in yesterday's *Graphic*. Did you have anything to do with that?'

'No. The story about the Peking-to-Paris De Dion has been around much longer than my own connection with it.'

'That's pretty hard to believe.' Tom fired up like a Bugatti. 'Brenda was under the impression it began when she met you at Alfred King's funeral.'

'The rumours began months before that, but it is true,' I

said blandly, 'that the police for whom I work are interested in Alfred King's contacts, which include Mrs Drake because of her De Dion.'

'A car restored in 2006 is hardly likely to result in a death several years later,' Victoria commented acidly.

Nick Morris was craning forward, eager to get his own oar in. 'But if your car *was* the Peking-to-Paris competitor, Gran, you'd have told me, wouldn't you?'

Silence from Granny Victoria.

'Dad would have known, wouldn't he?' Patricia asked her mother. 'You told me it belonged to him, didn't you, Mummy? That's why we didn't know about it.'

Mummy turned her Gorgon-like stare on her daughter and Patricia promptly shut up.

'Where is this car, Victoria?' Tom barked at her. 'You need my help over this, especially if it is the right car. Let's get an expert in.'

'No,' Victoria replied calmly.

'But, Gran . . .' Nick began, only to be shouted down by Tom with the occasional cry from Patricia.

I let this interesting family situation go on for a while, until I could see a chink of light. I prepared to make it a beam.

'Of course,' I said blithely, 'if you still possess your De Dion Bouton, you would have a very valuable possession, Mrs Drake, and it would be even more valuable if it was indeed one of the original two rally De Dions. It would be excellent if it could be on display at the rally in Kent that's coming up in August. Is that a possibility?'

'It is not,' she barked instantly.

'Because you've sold your De Dion already?' Checkmate, I thought, and this was confirmed by the fact that all three Morrises were tensely waiting for Victoria's reply. Victoria ignored them, concentrating her attention on me.

'You seem to be an intelligent man, Mr Colby, and so you will by now have checked the records and found no trace of a sale. I therefore confirm that I still have *my* De Dion. There is no proof that it was the one that drove in the rally of 1907.'

'But, Gran,' Nick shot back, 'have you actually checked it out?'

'More tea anyone?' Brenda asked brightly, perhaps in the hope of saving her friend from any vultures that might be hanging around. Victoria was made of stern stuff, however.

'I don't need to check it out. Why should I? In fact, it belonged to my mother, and before I had it restored it was merely a wreck kept off the road. I believe she had inherited it from her own mother. It has no connection with France. None at all.'

I mentally reeled at this revelation that she had lied over saying it belonged to her late husband. And why bring France into the matter? Because it was a French car? 'Do you have any documents relating to its origin, Mrs Drake?' I asked. 'Did Mr King consider its previous history?'

'I have no documents,' Victoria said firmly. 'He and I merely discussed the restoration. He carried it out, returned the car to me and there the matter rested. It could have nothing to do with his death.'

The tone of her voice had finality in it, but she wasn't going to get away with that. I would get no further on Alf's death until I knew more about this De Dion. I did not believe her story, or rather I would qualify that to my not getting the full version. Judging by the way her daughter and son-in-law were shifting around, and her grandson fuming, they weren't happy either. Brenda seemed the most composed person present.

'What year is your De Dion?' I asked politely.

'It is an early one. I don't know the exact date.'

'May I see it?' I asked brightly.

'You may not.'

It was time to play dirty. 'I'm sure you've seen it,' I said equally brightly to the Morrises. 'Lucky people.' Before Victoria could shoot too many daggers at me, I added, 'If it were one of the two 1907 cars it would gain immense publicity at the rally and the value would shoot up.'

'Why keep talking about this rally? What's so special about it?' Victoria asked irritably, though rather more peaceably than I had expected.

'I explained that to you, Victoria,' Brenda cut in quickly. 'It's a mock recreation of the Peking to Paris rally for charity, but it will be held in Kent and Sussex.'

Victoria was not impressed. 'I believe you did mention it. I fail to see what purpose my De Dion would serve, however, as it is not one of the original cars.'

I was skating on thin ice. 'Even so, if it's roughly from the right period it would give a flavour of the original rally if it were on display. The money raised from it will go to good causes, some to local charities and some to opening a new classic car collection to the public, run by a charitable trust.'

Brenda clasped her hands together. 'That sounds lovely,' she said hopefully.

'Just think of how much the De Dion would be worth, Victoria,' Tom said eagerly.

Nick saw his opening. 'I'll *drive* it in the rally, Gran. You said it had been restored.'

I almost applauded and Patricia gazed at him as if she'd given birth to an Einstein.

Silence from Victoria herself, so I persevered. 'The trustees are eager to hire the car for display, properly insured of course, to attract donations. A buyer might even emerge through it, if you are willing to loan it to the trust. As I said if it was one of the two real cars from 1907 the price would shoot up – way over a million, I'd say.'

There's something about the word million that catches the attention, even in these days when the number of millionaires has shot up dramatically. I could see I had all the Morrises' full attention.

'Even if it's not the real car,' I added, 'it would still be worth a great deal.'

The silence continued. Patricia, Tom, Nick and even Brenda were looking interested, to say the least. Victoria was not. Every one of her muscles seemed to be uniting in a show of implacability.

'The car will not be displayed or take part in any rally of any kind,' she decreed.

'But—' This was a mistake on Nick's part. After so dogmatic a statement that word can only put people's backs up and convince them that they are in the right. I mentally kicked myself for letting it get to this stage.

'The answer is no, Mr Colby,' Victoria broke in coolly, as protest burst forth from her family. 'And,' she added, 'it will always be no. Whatever old wreck the trust finds to lure people to this rally, Mr Colby, it will not be my De Dion Bouton.'

FIVE

Woolwich is no longer the place that Henry VIII would have recognized in its shipbuilding days. Nor the one that Dad might have known post Second World War when it was still licking its wounds from the aircraft and Doodlebug raids and before the Royal Ordnance Factory came to the end of its glorious days there. Nevertheless the town still has the feel of history about it, and walking into the Red Bear pub was like stepping out of a time machine into a different age. I wasn't alive in the 1960s but Dad would have recognized this sort of pub. By that I don't mean the legendary glamorous swinging sixties, but the decade as the vast majority of people experienced it. Today the Red Bear had not opted for gastro food but remained a serious drinking facility, dark, small and smelling of beer and sweat. No longer smoke, but it was easy to imagine how once it would have been reeking of it.

Today at least the occupancy was solely male apart from the barmaid and, hard times or not, there were plenty of customers. Even if Bob Orton had not waved at me from the bar, however, I would have picked him out as my target. He was a wiry man, with a lined, almost weather-beaten face in his late sixties or early seventies, but his dashing cap and silk scarf, plus a touch of arrogance, indicated he reckoned he was still a big player on life's circuit. His eyes told me that too; they were sharp, which made him not only the good photographer I presumed he might still be, but a fitting soulmate for Pen Roxton.

'What can I get you?' he asked perfunctorily.

'Let me.'

The ritual completed with a whisky for him and a pint for me, we got down to business.

'Pen Roxton,' I said, opening the festivities.

'Darling girl,' he informed me. 'Knew her father. She's a chip off the old block.'

'He must have been quite something. The chip alone is more than I can cope with.' Nothing like badinage to get the conversation going.

'Had your ups and downs with her, eh?'

'Down mostly. Not that she can't be a good sort on occasion.'

'Know what you mean. So what can I do for you? She says you're with the police.'

'Right, but not on the De Dion Bouton story. She says she got that from you.'

The whisky level went down. 'The tale was going the rounds so I thought I'd make a bob or two.'

'And I take it you know more than has appeared so far?'

Oblique answer to this. 'Photography is my thing. Did quite a bit on motor racing, and the rumour popped up now and then years ago. No big deal though.'

'Was that in England or France?'

He blinked. 'France? No, right here in lovely old Britain.'

'Was there any back-up to the rumour?'

'Looked into it at the time, but didn't get much further. Story was that the car was bought as a wreck by some Frenchie's girlfriend as a present for him; he dropped her and she hung on to it. General feeling was it was in the south here.' He held out his glass hopefully. 'Heard about that rally coming up in August. That could flush it out if it's still around, eh?'

I agreed. 'Do you still work as a photographer?'

'Off and on.'

So he didn't. 'Still around the car world, are you?' I asked.

'For this story, mate, yes. Pen does the story, I give her the leads. This pub and a few more I know give me all I need without moving my hind quarters overmuch.'

I believed him. 'Where cosier than a hotbed of crime?' I joked.

The sharp eyes flickered. 'This one's straight. That's why I suggested it. You're a spare-time cop, Pen says. That right?'

'Something like that.'

'You're checking out Alf King?'

'Did you know him?'

'No, but I know about a chap who did.'

'Who might that be?'

'The buzz is that he works with Mick Smith, or did. Don't know Mick but I hear he runs a racket nicking cars to order. The name's Connor Meyton. Know him?'

'I met him once.'

'My advice is leave it at that, Jack.'

I drove back unimpressed. Pen's contacts usually have more bite, although his grapevine could be useful. Bob was the sort who would turn up a jewel the minute after you'd written him off. At the moment I could do with a jewel or two, so I decided to keep in touch.

When I returned to the Pits late in the afternoon, Zoe told me that according to Dean everything had gone quiet on the deal with Meyton to take over Alf's business. Neither Dean nor Doris nor her solicitors had heard a dicky bird, and whether by chance or design Meyton's phone was always on voicemail.

I didn't know whether to be glad or sorry. Zoe was in one of her truculent moods, so I left Dean out of it. 'Is Doris upset?' I asked her.

'Dean says not. She didn't take to Connor Meyton. I don't think Dean minds too much either. He says Meyton's too wily. Dean's hoping Doris will let him run it on her behalf,' Zoe added.

'Alone?' I was dubious about that.

'He'd have an assistant.'

'And who will that be? A babe in arms?'

'No. Me,' she shot back. At least she had the grace to look abashed as she said it.

Incoherent with shock, I struggled for words. Zoe was part of Frogs Hill, she knew that. She was well paid and I'd thought she was happy. 'But Len—' I croaked. What on earth would he say? He'd given years of training to Zoe.

'I'm only thinking about it,' she said hastily.

I hit on the first argument that came to mind. 'Bad plan to work with someone you fancy.'

A scathing look, but no reply.

I wanted to shout, 'Don't leave us, Zoe!' The words trembled on my lips, but I shouldn't, *couldn't*, say them. She had to make her own decision, but I hoped it would be on merit, not emotion.

'There's a Porsche 356 asking to be booked in,' I said briskly, hoping to tempt her into remembering home blessings here at Frogs Hill. 'Zoe has a special love of Porsches. Could you fit it in?'

Her eyes lit up. 'Can a Beetle crawl?'

We were back to normal, and I think we were both relieved.

I was so busy worrying about Zoe that I put aside Connor Meyton and De Dions until the next morning. I wanted to go over to Treasure Island to tell them I'd found the owner. Some days ago I had rung Helen to invite her to dinner but she had murmured some instant excuse about being already booked in a tone that told me she wasn't. There the matter had rested, perhaps because I had seen my old flame Louise's photo in the press a few times recently and had not yet hardened myself to the inevitability that it would always be this way, because Louise is an actor and a good one. If I was subconsciously drawing breath, however, I knew it was time to start living again.

I thought I would drive over in my Lagonda, which spends most of her time with my Gordon-Keeble. Before the apparent anomaly of my owning two such classics is too glaring I should point out that tight for cash though I am, there's no way I would part with either. It would be as bad as selling a mistress – not that I'd ever had such an arrangement, only a stormy marriage with a wife I'd have been glad to give away. That sounds harsh – but then only to those who hadn't met Eva.

Everything seemed to be humming in the Pits, and it seemed just another Tuesday at Frogs Hill – until I strolled round to the rear of the farmhouse to the barn-cum-garage where my two classics live. They're guarded with a good security system, but somehow it had overlooked the fact that an intruder had opened the doors. The intruder emerged just as I was developing my bull charge for the defence. I froze. It was Connor Meyton in person.

'Good morning, Jack.'

I tried to control myself, because I needed to be foxlike, not bullish, to contend with this slippery eel.

'Any particular reason you're here, Mr Meyton?'

'Oh, Connor, please.' He grinned. 'I couldn't resist having a peek at the Gordon-Keeble.'

'It's more usual to ask the owner first.'

He looked hurt. 'Rang the bell, Jack. No reply.'

I could have sworn he hadn't but I let it go. At least the cavalry had arrived in time to prevent too much dirty work – I hoped.

'Good alarm system you've got,' he added.

'Thanks for testing it. Seems I should be upgrading it though.'

He seemed amused. 'Don't bother.'

He was having a great time but just what was his game? Spying out good classics to pinch to order? Or was it just a threat not to get too close to his interests?

'How's the deal over King's Restorations going?' I asked.

He didn't seem fazed. 'Not really my style. Still thinking about it.'

'And Mrs King?'

'So is Mrs King. All's fair in business, Jack.'

'Not everything.'

He eyed me for a moment. 'Still after the De Dion?'

'Yes. And you? Someone was chatting to Alf about De Dions earlier this year. You?'

'Perhaps.' A pause. 'Anything in Carter's collection I'd like to see?'

At least he wasn't au fait with its nickname, which was a good sign. 'See, perhaps,' I replied. 'More active involvement, no.'

He laughed. 'You've got style, Jack. Nice little girl you've got working in that old barn of yours.'

The way he said it made my flesh creep. Was this camaraderie a ploy to get Zoe away from Frogs Hill or did he just know the way to get on my wick by the shortest possible route?

I decided to postpone my trip to Burnt Barn Bottom and Treasure Island, because Connor wasn't my only uninvited visitor that day. After he had finally left, I went back to the farmhouse for a phone session on behalf of the classic car business – and also to see whether any news had come in on the De Dion. I glanced through the window to see all three Morrises getting out of a Volvo saloon, which was so clapped out I thought they'd come for a restoration. My luck was out, however. Zoe came to greet them, dutifully conducted them to my door and bawled out 'Jack!' Then she left them – and me – to it. I was still fuming at the bombshell Zoe had thrown at me, not to mention the way Meyton had bypassed my security system, so I was hardly in a mood for chit chat. I pulled myself together when I realized that their arrival meant they must have a mission. It might even be a reprieve from Victoria, agreeing that the De Dion could be shown at the rally after all.

Ever optimistic, I ushered them into the living room, which is a far more comfortable place for chatting than my cubbyhole office, but more formal than the kitchen to which most of my friends automatically gravitate.

'Are you bearing good news from Mrs Drake?' I asked cheerfully as I put a tray of coffee mugs down on the table.

'No.' Tom glared at me – and the instant coffee. 'And knowing your mother, Pat, that's that.'

'Do you know why?' I asked as Patricia cringed. 'Could it be just the sheer effort of insurance, registration and so forth that's putting her off?'

'I wish it were so simple,' Tom said savagely. He was strutting round my living room like a city banker with a bonus. He was clearly going through the stage of believing he was still a big business man, which was natural enough in his circumstances. The corollary to it was that he thought he was doing me a favour by his mere presence. That suited me. Being underestimated is an advantage if it comes to a sparring match.

'She's just a stubborn old witch,' Nick contributed.

'Nick!' Patricia's shocked plea was ignored.

Tom took over Nick's line. 'She wants us all under her thumb. Anything we want she'll block.'

A family row was not going to help, and I hastily asked, 'Could anything make her change her mind?'

Patricia seized her chance. 'Yes,' she said eagerly. 'My

mother's very fond of Nick, so if the rally organizers were to formally ask him to drive the De Dion in this rally that might work.'

'That seems a good route,' I agreed. So it would be if the De Dion was drivable. 'But she still has the whip hand. For a start, do you know where the car is and what condition it's in?'

Mistake. I saw their expressions and realized why I was being honoured by a visit. 'We have a few ideas about that,' Tom told me loftily. 'We thought you might care to follow them up.'

There was a big snag here. 'It's Mrs Drake's car, so I couldn't do that.'

'But you were hunting for it.' Tom looked amazed.

'Only to find the owner and if she doesn't want it found, there's nothing I can do.'

'I'm her grandson,' Nick yelled at me. 'Mum's going to inherit pretty soon.'

'There'd be something in it for you,' Tom assured me.

Fellow conspirators with the Morrises? No way. I recovered my breath. It was one thing to scout around on my own initiative, but to be in cahoots with the owner's daughter and her husband was quite another. If I found the car and if it could indeed be one of the 1907 rally De Dions, what then? Would the Morrises want me to put on a stripy jumper and play burglar? Or would they ask a pro such as Connor Meyton to do it for them? I could see murky roads ahead, all of them leading to the end of my career with the Kent Police Car Crime Unit.

'Sorry,' I said firmly. 'Conflict of interest.' It struck me I might already have one if the Mad Major's commission and Dave's met face to face.

Patricia looked indignant. 'We only want you to find out where it is.'

'It's no use, Mum,' Nick said disgustedly. 'You're wasting your breath.'

And my time. I grabbed what was left of the situation. 'Not entirely. As I told Mrs Drake, if her De Dion could be proved to be the actual 1907 car its value is going to shoot up. But she would need to prove its provenance. Your mother said she inherited it through her family, so could you tell me whether there's any documentary evidence?'

'I thought we made that clear already. We've only just found out about this car,' Tom said angrily.

Patricia confirmed this. 'I heard nothing about it as I was growing up. After my stepfather died a few years ago Mum did say something about restoring an old wreck he owned but we heard nothing more. We only moved to Lamberhurst three years ago so we weren't seeing her on a daily basis. Nick's the car addict in the family.' She looked adoringly at her thickset bullish son. 'He's dotty about them. My mother only told us that this old car was a De Dion after she'd read the newspaper article. Then you came to see us. We've asked her to tell us more but she says she doesn't know anything more.'

Asked her? More probably pestered her, I thought. 'So first her line was that it belonged to your stepfather, but now that it was inherited through her family, which seems more likely.'

'Or perhaps it actually belongs to my real father, Robert Fairhill,' Patricia said gloomily. 'He likes cars.'

'Is it possible it was his?' I asked.

'I suppose so. I never met him. He was – well, a bit of a rascal, so my mother says. He lives in the States somewhere and she's not in regular touch with him, only if he comes over here. If it belongs to him, that could be why she's so funny about it.'

Possible, but it sounded like another false avenue to me. If it really did belong to him, why not tell us? It would be the perfect answer. Orton said the rumour had always been that it was in the south of England somewhere, as the current rumour also suggested. That tied in better with Victoria's ownership than with a far-off former husband. Inherited from her mother who inherited from hers. She would not have to keep the car's whereabouts and existence so secret if it belonged to someone else who clearly didn't care a damn about it.

'Has your mother given you any idea about where it's been all these years?' I asked.

Tom looked at me with great satisfaction. 'You can hardly

expect us to tell you, in view of the fact you've turned us down, Colby.'

I'd dug a pit and jumped inside it, I thought ruefully, as they left Frogs Hill in virtuous triumph. Then I consoled myself. I had one lead at least left. All roads – including Connor Meyton – seemed to meet at Alfred King.

It was too late to drive to Harford Lee by that time, but I dutifully rang the Mad Major instead. There was no answer, and I had no mobile number for him, and so with my conscience now clear I rang Helen. I thought her voice sounded a trifle frosty, but the phone can do weird things to voices, so I didn't take much notice. She told me there was a trustees' meeting that evening and I should come over right away to give a progress report to them all before the meeting began. It was to be held at Julian's home, Cobba House.

'Dinner after the meeting?' I ventured. 'I could hang around till it's over.'

'Thank you, no. Things to do – and I'm sure you're *busy*,' she added as a Parthian shot. I hadn't realized there were any Parthians about, so it took me by surprise. I clearly had not imagined the frost.

All in all, I was not in a jolly mood as I drove over to Treasure Island, even though Helen lay at the end of it. A sort of Helen of Troy as a reward if I fought the Trojan Wars first. Worth it? Yes, even though I had an increasing feeling that with both my commissions I was playing a different game to everyone else on the board. What's more, I was not even sure what the game was and there might well be invisible players in it. Then I remembered the cemetery of forgotten cars and cheered up. Pompeii and Herculaneum were surely worth fighting for and if the De Dion could play a part in the resurrection all the better.

Cobba House was a surprise, even though I was disappointed not to catch a glimpse of the Iso Rivolta I had coveted, only of a four-by-four Range Rover. For an obviously comfortably off man, he lived modestly. It had been his family home, I imagined, from the number of photographs and sporting awards I passed on my way through it, not all of them featuring cars.

I was ushered outside to a terrace with steps down to a lush
green, a scene so 1920s that I expected someone to bound up
crying, 'Anyone for tennis?'

No one did. Instead, three pairs of accusing eyes stared at
me. The Major's, Julian's and Helen's. She looked gorgeous
and summery in plain cream trousers and jacket which set off
that auburn hair magnificently. While I was appreciating the
view, she began the assault. I wasn't even offered a drink,
although glasses and bottles adorned the table in front of us.

'Your girlfriend tells us you've seen the De Dion and know
where it's kept, Jack. We'd like to know why we weren't told.'

In the face of disaster, tell the truth. 'Because I *haven't* seen
it and don't know where it's kept, but I do know who the
owner is. I've come here to tell you. Secondly—'

'That's not what your girlfriend claims,' she interrupted.

'*Secondly*,' I continued doggedly – but then did a double
take. 'What girlfriend? I don't currently have one.' Louise's
image popped up before me and was dismissed.

'We've met her,' Helen almost snarled. 'Blondish,
sharp-featured—'

'Pen?' I exploded. 'Pen Roxton is a journalist. She is not
and never has been my girlfriend.'

'She says she is.'

'She's a *journalist*,' I said wearily. 'Of course she would.
She wants a passport to you.'

Helen looked less certain. 'When she came to see Treasure
Island yesterday, she said you gave her the story about the De
Dion.'

'Not guilty. The only thing I gave her was hell when I read
it. I've known Pen for years and as a girlfriend never. She's
a career lady through and through. Actually,' I explained, 'that
story might not be all bad for us, and I've agreed to give her
severely limited help. It might bring the De Dion to light.'

'Or drive it underground,' Julian said nastily. 'If someone
snaps it up, it will be down to you, Colby.'

'*Not* me. The owner.'

Then it was the Major's turn to give me a bad time. 'That's
it,' he roared. 'I want to meet her.'

I noted that. 'At the right time, I agree, but—'

'That's now,' he interrupted again, banging the table. 'We're paying your wages.'

'And I'm doing the job.'

That stopped him in his tracks, and I saw I'd won a reprieve. Then Julian took over. 'What's your next step, Jack? If this De Dion is the real thing I don't intend to lose my chance of getting it. The rally is only three months away now, and if we stand any chance of getting that car we need to advertise the fact in plenty of time. Helen's done a great job on the organizational side, but the charity appeal needs to be integrated with it. We can't wait much longer to know if the De Dion is going to part of it.'

'What's the support from the car clubs like so far?' I asked.

'Not bad. We've volunteers aplenty, beforehand and for the three days of the event. We're holding the finale of the rally here, rather than in Canterbury as originally planned, so that we can give everyone a tour of Treasure Island. So we all – especially you, Jack – need to get our skates on. How's the situation looking?'

'Bad, at present. The owner's a Mrs Victoria Drake and so far she's refused point-blank to cooperate.'

'Why?' the Major yelled.

'Not known. There's a suggestion mooted that she might relent if the De Dion was actually driven in the rally and by her grandson Nick.'

'Did she say that?' Julian's eyes lit up.

'No. Unfortunately that's only her daughter's idea.'

'Still, it's not a bad idea,' the Major said, surprising me.

'One reason Mrs Drake is holding back may be that she can't prove the De Dion is one of the original two competitors.'

'Did she say that?' the Mad Major barked out. He was on the edge of his seat, and in what my mother would have called a 'paddy'.

'No. She gave no reasons for her decision.'

'Then let her explain it to us face to face.'

I tried logic. 'If she won't tell her own daughter and grandson, she isn't likely to tell us, is she?'

Julian stared at me like King Midas seeing his hoard of

gold vanishing before his eyes. 'If this De Dion of hers is the real McCoy I'm going for it. What are the chances as to her being able to prove its identity?'

'I've never been a betting man,' I said wearily. 'You must know as well as I do that both the De Dions that took part in the original race have vanished, perhaps because they were scrapped or passed on to owners who left no record of what jewels they had possessed. The last mention of either of them as far as I can trace is that one of them was shown at the London Olympia Motor Show in 1907. It was mentioned in *The Times* report and also in the show catalogue on the De Dion Company London office's advertisement. It's possible that the other De Dion might have been exhibited at the Paris Motor Show the same year, because it was held at virtually the same time as Olympia. But this is only my speculation.'

The Mad Major was glaring at me impatiently as though any fool should know that Victoria Drake's car was the real one, but how could it possibly be identifiable without good provenance? Julian was looking equally annoyed with me and Helen looked warily contrite – if such a complex expression would be correctly interpreted. It might have been wishful thinking on my part.

As was the De Dion's on Julian's. 'We've got to move *now*, Jack,' he urged.

'Ring the woman up right now, Julian,' the Major demanded. 'What's the number, Colby?'

I could see this plan going down like a ton of bricks with Victoria Drake. 'Not a good idea,' I said firmly. 'I've met the lady and I can guarantee that you won't see the De Dion for love or money if you follow that approach. Leave it to me. I'll ring her daughter, Patricia Morris, in the hope that she can arrange for us *all* to go over, and I'll dangle the carrot of Nick Morris driving it. Then you can put your own case.'

They looked at each other. The Major was still for immediate (if disastrous) action, but Julian and Helen decided in my favour. I rang Patricia right away, wondering what I would do if she refused. She did at first, but a hurried conversation with her hand over the mouthpiece, presumably to converse with Tom or Nick, settled the matter. They would approach Victoria, provided we guaranteed Nick's role as driver.

'Why don't we just go over there and see the woman?' the Major muttered.

'Because she might be out,' I explained patiently. 'And three strangers and a man she's already turned down arriving unannounced are not going to be conducive to diplomatic negotiation.'

'He's right, Stanley,' Julian agreed, though I could see it was with reluctance.

Helen came out to the car with me to see me off – I hoped not just because she wanted to be sure I was off the premises. 'I'm sorry, Jack,' she said. 'I really thought you and that journalist had something going between you.'

'Not much of a compliment to me.'

She giggled. 'I thought she might have a gentler side.'

'Don't bank on it. What you can bank on is that she and I don't have anything between us but history and most of it bad.'

'Anyone else around in your life?' she asked, taking our relationship a quantum leap forward.

'Not now. And you?'

'Not now. One divorce. A couple of false starts.'

'Me too in all respects. Par for the course, I suppose.'

'A rocky one.' She hesitated. 'Can I take up the dinner offer?'

'Tonight?'

She grinned. 'I really have got something on. Julian's cooking for the three of us after the meeting.'

We fixed on Thursday evening. 'It will be more relaxed,' she said.

Only two days to wait.

The day was certainly coming up roses now, late though it was and despite the fact that I had a nagging feeling I was missing a trick somewhere. Furthermore, with all the emphasis on the De Dion I seemed to be getting too far away from Alf's death. The next morning, however, the roses continued. I had a call from Patricia to say that Victoria was willing – or rather, had agreed – to meet the trustees (and even me) on the Thursday morning if that was acceptable. A few phone calls and the deal was done. One drawback, however. Not to my surprise, Patricia made it clear that she and Tom would be present – and so would grandson Nick. It seemed to me that where money was concerned the Morrises had their engines racing. Not that I could blame them for that. I know what money pressures are like, and Tom, being redundant at his age, must be facing an uncertain future.

The meeting looked promising, and the Major had insisted on making the visit in style. Having demanded to know where the lady lived, he informed us that he would bring Julian and Helen over in his Bentley and pick me up at Frogs Hill en route for Lamberhurst. That suited me, although I was puzzled that he was surpassing even Julian's eagerness.

The speed at which the Mad Major drove made me realize how he might have got his nickname. I had joined Helen in the rear seat, and just to sense her so close greatly pleased me. I wanted to hug her, she looked so delicious. Business trip, I reminded myself, but nevertheless when the Major took a hairpin too fast and Helen was thrown against me despite the seat belt, she didn't rush to right herself and the proximity and the fragrance of her hair were intoxicating. I began to ache with pleasure at the thought of our dinner later that day. A cunning plan popped into my head whereby on our return to Frogs Hill the Major could just leave her at the farmhouse and I would offer to drive her home later (or not as the occasion presented itself). I decided not to do anything so crass, however, and told the plan to get lost.

I was so full of thoughts about Helen that I nearly forgot to navigate the Major to Shoulder Mutton Green. I remembered just in time and the Major hunched over the wheel as though he was making for the finishing line at Brands Hatch. As he made a swift turn into the gateway of Victoria's home, I began to say something but he had parked and leapt out of the car before I'd even undone my seat belt. Without waiting to see if Helen, Julian and I were with him or not (we were close behind) he simply marched straight up to the front door. This not only had an electric bell but a handbell dangling on a rope and it was the latter that the Major decided fitted his purpose. We heard its defiant clang echoing through the house as we stood behind him.

The door opened and there was Victoria. She didn't so much as glance at the rest of us. Her eyes were fixed on the Mad Major. And then she delivered her punch line:

'Good morning, Stanley.'

SIX

*G**ood morning, Stanley?*
Not only did Victoria Drake know the Major, but she wasn't surprised to see him. I knew now what had caused the niggle in my mind. The Major had known the owner was a woman before I had mentioned her name.

Julian and Helen looked as flabbergasted as I must have done. We were left like first-class chumps standing on the doorstep of a woman in control of a situation we didn't know existed. How, when and why did I let the matter reach this point without realizing that the Major himself was an unknown quantity?

Time for further reflection later. Right now – action.

Victoria had stepped to one side to allow the Major to enter since he was nearest to her. Helen made to follow him but Victoria had blocked her way before she could do so. Entry was barred.

'Not you,' she said to Helen, impassively. 'Nor you—' Victoria gave a cursory glance at Julian and me. 'Go to Brenda's house. She's expecting you.'

And with that the door was shut in our faces.

A memory of the Pied Piper of Hamlyn story came crazily into my mind. The mountain door slammed shut before the poor village boy could limp through it, but everyone else was safely inside. Victoria was less generous. One had been allowed in, the rest shut out. Forget Pied Pipers, think today, I told myself, as we retreated to lick our wounds. We reached the gateway before Julian stopped, white with anger.

'Just what is going on here? Have you any idea, Jack?' There was an accusing note in his voice as if I'd deliberately set up this situation.

'Not a clue. You, Helen?' I was trying to make sense of it. Was it coincidence that Victoria hadn't looked surprised to see him? Had she merely heard about him or did it mean the Mad

Major had been in collusion with her all along? If so, why commission me to find the De Dion and its owner?

Helen shook her head, and I could see she was too shaken to speak. I was in little better shape than she was. I could feel myself trembling and it takes a lot for that to happen. It just goes to show that the unexpected is a powerful weapon, be it a sniper's shot or a slammed door.

I needed to be clear where I stood – apart from at a gateway in severe need of paint. 'Did either of you have the slightest idea that Major Hopchurch *knew* Victoria Drake?' I asked.

'No,' Helen said. 'Did you, Julian?'

'I did not, and believe me I'm going to find out why. You told us the woman's name on Tuesday, Jack. Has he jumped the gun and been over here already?'

'He didn't know her address.'

'He could have discovered it. You did.'

I admitted that was true – indeed I hoped it was. If it wasn't, then there were deeper, perhaps darker, implications.

'So where does this leave us, Helen?' Julian continued.

'At the moment,' she said practically, 'gasping for coffee. Let's go to find dear Brenda, shall we? She might shed light on the situation. You know which house is hers, Jack?'

'Right next door to this one. Let's go.'

Patricia and Tom Morris had set up this meeting, so were they in Elmtree House with dear Stanley Hopchurch and Victoria, or had they too been consigned to Brenda's care? My guess was the latter and that whatever was happening between Victoria and Stanley was very private indeed.

I was proved right when we reached Brenda's door. She opened it, looking upset, to say the least. I wondered whether she had hatched up this scheme with Victoria or whether it was a surprise thrust upon her by Victoria this morning. Brenda clearly liked being 'in' on everything – who doesn't? – but as she played no part in what we were meant to be discussing with Victoria, I plumped for the latter explanation.

'Come in,' she said, doing a good imitation of being bright and welcoming. I introduced Julian and Helen to her and she led us through to the living room where I saw Patricia and

Tom occupying exactly the same chairs as they had the last time I was here, although there was no sign of Nick. I knew they lived on the far side of Lamberhurst village, and so, I reasoned, this disastrous non-meeting could have taken place in their home as it was nearby. The fact that it was here implied that they were as much in the dark as we were. Tom wouldn't like that, I thought. He wasn't the sort to be outwitted by mothers-in-law. Both he and Patricia looked somewhat sheepish, as well they might, when we told them what our reception had been.

Brenda had no sooner disappeared to fetch 'refreshments' as she put it than the doorbell rang again. It was no reprieve from Victoria, unfortunately. It was Nick, who charged in to join his parents. He too must have been refused entry by his granny.

'What the hell is going on?' he demanded.

'It's no use blaming us, darling,' Patricia cried shrilly. 'We were as surprised as you were. She only allowed Major Hopchurch in. She seems to know him.'

'She bloody well knows us too,' Nick pointed out viciously. 'What's her game?'

Julian entered the arena. 'I gather you're Mrs Drake's daughter, Mrs Morris. Do you know Major Hopchurch too?' His smooth tone suggested he thought cooperation was the best line.

'No,' Patricia said shortly.

'Who is this Major chap?' Nick asked simultaneously.

'Helen's and my co-trustee for the car museum and rally.' Julian's tone suggested this would not be for much longer if it had anything to do with him. 'You three –' he appealed to the Morrises – 'must have some idea of what this is all about. Is there or is there not a De Dion Bouton around here or are we on a fool's errand?'

Tom took exception to this. 'Ask your Major. He seems to be the only one of us in favour with its owner.'

I wouldn't put much money on that being the case, knowing the Major. Moreover the Morrises' visit to me had suggested they had their own game to play.

'Brenda –' Patricia turned a distressed (but determined) face to her – '*you* must know what's happening. My mother merely rang to tell me the meeting was taking place here, and now we find out it's not. What do you know about this Major and Mother's car?'

I felt sorry for Brenda as she immediately became the target of everyone's wrath. Even mine, however upset she looked. After all, she seemed to be on more buddy terms with Victoria than Patricia herself, but she shrank away from confrontation.

'Nothing,' she said forlornly. 'Victoria just telephoned me this morning to ask if I could hold the meeting here. I didn't know she wasn't coming herself.'

'But what about this De Dion?' Tom hurled at her.

'Very little.' Brenda regained her dignity. 'Only what Victoria told us when you were last here. I presume the De Dion is in her garage.'

'It isn't,' Nick threw at her. 'I checked it.'

'What one might call a spoke in our De Dion wheels,' Helen said, perhaps intending to lighten the mood but unsuccessfully.

'Do none of you have any thoughts on where the car might be?' I asked, reckoning that Victoria Drake had forfeited any claim to any consideration.

There was a general shaking of heads. Julian sighed. 'Are we all agreed that we want to know more about her De Dion, and if it claims to be one of the original 1907 rally cars, whether there is documentation. Also can Mrs Drake be persuaded to allow the car to be shown at the rally?'

A general nodding of heads this time.

'*Driven* at the rally,' Nick amended.

'It's only fair that such an important car should be seen and admired,' Patricia said piously. 'It's doing no good locked up in storage.'

Julian was clearly pent-up with frustration. I could see his problem. The De Dion might not only need registration and perhaps more restoration to get it ready for the rally but also its presence had to be prearranged for maximum publicity. The cash raised for Treasure Island would be multiplied if the event were thus catapulted into a different class. On the other hand, too much publicity might drive its price up to a point where it would ruin him financially even if Victoria agreed to sell it to him. His best chance lay in persuading her to sell it to him *before* the rally – but looking at the Morrises, it was obvious that the chances of that would be nil. Collectors have single-track minds, however, and Julian might not see it that way. Thanks to the Mad Major, his chances of buying it now would seem to be rapidly evaporating. As, it occurred to me, were the chances of my getting paid for my work. That was a side issue at the moment, but it would become painfully central shortly.

'Shall I ring Victoria?' Brenda asked, not very enthusiastically 'She might be ready to see you all now.'

'*I'll* ring.' Patricia strode purposefully to the telephone, but I had little hope that she would be successful. 'Voicemail,' she announced in tones of doom. 'I'm going round there to put an end to this pantomime.'

It was indeed a pantomime, and one in which I felt wolves might be running around in sheep's clothing. Someone in this room must know what was going on, but for the life of me I couldn't decide who, although I noticed that Patricia made no signs of leaving us.

'Look behind you,' Helen cried out of the blue, in true pantomime style. She was the only one of us to be facing the window which gave a view of the road.

The urgency in her voice made us all swing round and I was just in time to see a familiar car flash past – with two passengers, not one. Victoria and Stanley were on their way out in his Bentley, on which we were relying to transport us back to Frogs Hill and Harford Lee.

We gave it well over an hour to see if they would return. We adjourned to Brenda's garden, while she fussed over us, pressing more coffee and biscuits upon us and lamenting that she didn't understand what was happening. Join the club, I thought. All speculation about what Stanley's role might be ground to a halt for want of answers until eventually, with no Bentley in sight, I said wearily:

'Taxi anyone?'

*   *   *

I offered Julian and Helen a belated lunch at the local inn in Piper's Green if they wanted to break their journey. Neither accepted. Helen with regret as it was a working day and Julian without it. He was a man with a mission, a man who made it clear that whatever Stanley's game was, it was he and not Julian who would be responsible for paying my fees. I decided I would not be joining Julian's fan club. Collectors are usually the most affable of people, but occasionally something goes wrong and then they are capable – although fortunately they don't often pursue it – of becoming single-minded dictators to whom the whole world has to make way while they storm their path to the desired object, be it classic car, woman or the Third Reich.

Helen managed to indicate privately, however – and much to my pleasure – that she would be meeting me that evening for our date. The taxi dropped me at the pub before it continued to Harford Lee and after a quick sandwich I walked back to Frogs Hill which helped clear my mind. It's a couple of miles (not as the crow flies) because of the winding lanes and it's possible out there on the slopes of the Greensand Ridge to feel so far away from the cares of the world that problems float away and turn into wispy clouds which frisk in the blue sky and sunshine as though there wasn't a care left in the world, not even mine.

Today it didn't quite manage that, even though I fixed my thoughts on the evening ahead of me. The reason was a new niggle that I was not in control of the Stanley situation. I'd been outmanoeuvred by the Mad Major but hadn't a clue why. That had to change, not only for my sake but for Doris's. Until I proved that Alf's death was nothing other than an accident and that the De Dion Bouton was not connected to it, I was going to assume it was and that Doris had to see justice done.

My back straightened, my pace quickened and my brow lightened. I merely needed a plan of attack. Stanley would be the first line to tackle, and the second would be Dean Warren.

I'm usually in my car when I approach Frogs Hill and so my arrival is heralded by the crunchy gravel. Today it wasn't. My footsteps crunched but not loudly enough to disturb what was going on in the Pits. I stopped in disbelief, arrested by the racket. It was Len doing the shouting, but a Len I'd never known before, not the taciturn, easy-going mechanic who was a part of my life. Crusty he might be, but not out of control as he was now.

'Eynsford?' I heard. 'Your job's here, my girl. You can't just stroll in and say you've been helping at that nancy-boy's—'

There followed a cry of indignation, then a concentrated response from Zoe. I couldn't distinguish the words but in any case it was disregarded. Then came another tirade from Len.

'Leaving?' he said in a relatively normal voice. Then an explosion: '*Leaving?* Who said you could *leave*? There's that Porsche coming in, and a Delage after that. And you want to *leave*! What do you think you are? A fully-grown frog? A toad? You're a tadpole, that's what you are. You don't know a thing yet. You were shaping up, true enough, but you think you know it all. Well, you don't. You won't know it all until you're sixty. And *then* you can f— *leave*.' There were other words too that I'd never heard from Len's lips before.

I could make out Zoe's next response. It was in the form of those well-known words: 'He needs me more than you do.'

He being Dean, I presumed. She must be shaken to fall back on that line. I saw her as she marched out, two angry red spots for cheeks. She stopped when she saw me.

'I'm going, Jack. Right now.'

Take care, I warned myself. 'You can't do that,' I said mildly. 'You signed a contract that says I'm due a month's notice. You could at least fix the Porsche before you leave.'

A glare was all I got for my pain. 'I'm going now. I'll pay you a month's wages.'

'OK,' I said, meaning it to sound as if it was no great thing.

She looked taken aback, hesitated, then marched in high dudgeon to her Fiesta, got in, slammed the door and started it up – or rather tried to. The second attempt didn't work either. The third time it did, but it spoiled the dramatic exit. She drove off without a backward glance.

I groaned, and went straight into the Pits where Len was pretending to polish the bonnet of a Triumph. I noticed his hands were trembling. 'Sorry, Jack,' he mumbled. 'Got to me. Alf and all that. Not helping.'

'Len,' I said. 'I'd have done the same in your shoes and if I had your guts. She's got to learn. She's only a kid.' I could imagine what Zoe would have said if she'd heard this. She's in her mid-twenties. I had to get Len back on his emotional feet, however, both for his sake and for mine.

'Yup.' He cheered up a little. 'What next, boss? Advertise?'

'You're joking.'

He nodded. There would be no replacing Zoe easily, if at all. 'What then?'

'Len,' I said, 'we've got to get her back and there's only one way.'

'What's that?'

'Rob Lane.'

Rob and I have never seen eye to eye. I see him as a time-waster, he sees me as a hysterical car buff who prefers not to have him lumbering around my priceless classics – and preferably not around Zoe either. But, due to his upper-class connections, he can on occasion prove useful, and on this occasion could be vital.

Before I could sort out that problem, however, news awaited me at the farmhouse. A missed call from one of my contacts. No message left, which was a good sign. It meant he had something important to tell me and didn't want me ringing back at an awkward time.

So I rang him. He didn't sound too pleased, but I knew this was a second line that he kept for such purposes. He operates in south London and he'd like to keep it that way, so low profiles are mandatory.

'Toerag,' he greeted me less than cordially, as he read my number.

'Sorry, wrong number.' I paused, ready to hang up if he didn't respond.

'OK. That car you're thinking of buying . . .'

'News of one?'

'You'll have to get your skates on. The bidding's hotting up. International interest. Chris Mord is definitely in the picture.'

That was a no-brainer. Chris Mord would equal Connor Meyton. 'In or only sniffing?' I asked.

'Has some kind of stake in it. Like a vampire. A laugh a minute is Mr Lord.'

I wasn't laughing. Judging by Bob Orton's information, he might not be working alone. 'Michael Smart too?' I asked, keeping rigidly to his code.

A pause. 'Really wouldn't go there. Think babbling brooks, Jack.'

'Thanks. I'll do that.' So I would if I could work out what he meant. Was I to babble? Was his source babbling? Was Connor Meyton babbling? Mick Smith? International? No way could I keep out of it, however. Even if the Major's money had a question mark over it, I had to go on because of Dave's commission. Anyway, I could handle Connor Meyton. Couldn't I?

When Helen arrived for dinner I decided to play by the gentlemen's rule book and arranged to meet her at the Dering Arms in Pluckley. It's a handsome 1840s hunting lodge, set some way from the village centre and next to the railway station. I hadn't the heart to spoil such an occasion with work but I reasoned that as we both had it on our minds, it didn't make sense to ignore it. Even so on a summer's evening with birds twittering away, not computers, and good food and drink before us, work talk was somewhat delayed.

Then it began. 'Did Stanley turn up at Treasure Island?' I asked her. 'Did he ring you or Julian?'

'Not to my knowledge. I saw no sign of him and if he came to see Julian he's keeping very quiet about it. I don't think he did though. Julian's bent on a showdown tomorrow. He's seriously outraged. He wants me there, so it's official stuff.'

'Can I officially know about this meeting?' I meant, as she must have realized, did Julian know where she was this evening?

She smiled and the world was a happier place. 'I keep work and private life apart.'

'And I'm the latter? That's a compliment.'

She put out a hand which I took in the spirit it was probably meant, a 'we'll see' gesture.

'I think you should be present tomorrow, Jack, if you can

make it. There's something going on and I don't understand what it is. It must affect the rally, and if there's the slightest chance this is tied up with Alf's death you should be there. Stanley can't back out of attending, but unless he has a reasonable explanation for this morning's caper it could be we'll be chucking him out as a trustee.'

'Julian and the Major do realize I'm working for the police? That can sometimes put a barrier on plain speaking.'

'They do, but there won't be any barriers while I'm around. I need to know the truth, and your presence will be a plus.'

I hoped for her sake that was true, but we resumed more personal chat. Dusk was beginning to fall and the last of the commuters were scurrying or driving by from the railway station. It was a peaceful scene and a glorious evening.

'That was a wonderful meal,' she said at last.

Even more enjoyable for me was the walk we took afterwards along the lane and across the fields on the Greensand Way link route. I put my arm round her and it felt good.

'I'd like to see Frogs Hill,' she said. 'I only glimpsed it this morning.'

'Now?' I tried not to sound too hopeful.

'Yes, if you're willing, but . . .'

'Then you'll drive home,' I finished for her.

'Thanks for making it easy for me, Jack.'

'Another rain check?'

'Yes. Shall I still come to Frogs Hill?'

'I do a good line in coffee for the road.'

'Done.'

I served her the coffee, I showed her round the farmhouse and as much as could be seen of the garden in the dark. She looked at the old books on my bookshelves and the chipped Staffordshire figures with which I'd grown up. She liked Frogs Hill and it liked her. She looked at home there and for a while Louise tiptoed out of my life.

'Didn't you mention something called the Glory Boot?' she asked.

'I'll save that.'

'For next time?'

*   *   *

I drove over to Harford Lee the next day trying hard to be optimistic. Very hard. After all, the Major had been concealing something from us all, and so could hardly be relied on to put us in the picture now. On the other hand, yesterday's fiasco might not carry sinister implications. Something quite simple could have caused it, such as . . . I could think of nothing. At the very least we had been the victims of – in the words of the Sheriff in *Cool Hand Luke* – a failure to communicate.

I thought at first the Major was going to be a no-show. We were sitting in Julian's Cobba House study fidgeting, none of us liking to voice fears that he might not arrive. I'd thought Julian might object to my presence, but he seemed to be regarding it as useful ammunition.

The Major did arrive, albeit fifteen minutes late and looking truculent rather than abashed.

'What's this all about?' Truculence gave way to wariness as he took in my presence. 'What are *you* doing here?'

There was little to be gained in reminding him he'd commissioned me to find a De Dion Bouton. 'Neutral observer,' I replied.

That seemed to shut him up, surprisingly. He didn't even enquire what I thought I was observing. Julian came straight to the point. 'What the hell were you playing at yesterday, Stanley?'

The Major had had time to prepare his defence, of course. 'Easy enough to explain. Victoria felt intimidated by seeing so many of you and preferred to talk only to me. Quite understandable.'

'In preference to speaking to her own daughter?' Helen said caustically. 'Not so understandable.'

The Major exercised his option, if not his right, to remain silent. The best plan, probably. The Victoria Drake I had met wouldn't be intimidated if she met a roaring tiger.

Julian immediately launched a second salvo. 'You knew each other. That was quite clear. Have you been stealing a march on us by ferreting her out as soon as you knew where to find her? Have you already put in a bid? If you've scuppered my chances of buying that car . . .'

The Major did a good job of appearing shocked. 'Good

grief, no, Julian. I wouldn't do that. I met Victoria once or
twice way back in Paris. Name rang a bell when Jack mentioned
it. Nineteen sixty-eight it was, year of the student riots. Haven't
been back since. Victoria must have remembered me. Just had
a chat about it with her, that's all.'

'Was she one of the rioters?' Julian asked drily.

'No idea.' The Major glared. 'Quite a shock hearing her
name after all this time. Thought to myself, wonder if that's
the woman I met.'

'I doubt if it could have been,' I pointed out. 'Drake was
the name of her second husband.'

He turned purple. 'I know that, you fool. I put two and two
together. Name Victoria coupled with De Dion rang the bell.
I was just making it simple for you.'

I don't think any of us believed him, but there would be no
budging him.

'What did she want to chat to you about yesterday, apart
from old times?' Julian demanded. 'Does she or does she not
possess a De Dion Bouton and could it be the one we're
looking for?' A sudden thought must have struck him because
his face became a picture of horror. 'You went out with her
yesterday. Where? To see the car?'

'No.'

His face was flushed and he wasn't looking us in the eye.
Julian didn't believe him and nor did I. '*No?* Where then?'
he asked.

'To a pub for lunch. She wanted to get away so that we
could have a quiet talk.'

'She had the whole house to herself for a quiet talk,' Julian
snapped. 'She'd just thrown the rest of us out, if you remember.'

The Major collapsed. 'It's no use,' he blurted out. 'I did my
best for us. I pleaded with her to at least show us the car even
if she won't loan it to us.'

'But she didn't agree?' Helen said.

'Not show, not lend. I took her to lunch to soften her up,
but she wouldn't be softened.'

A stupefied silence while we all assimilated this, although
I don't know why this should have shaken Julian and Helen
so hard when this had been Victoria's position all along. I

suppose we took it for granted that the Major had softened her heart.

'Are you *sure* she won't loan it to us if her own grandson drives it?' Helen asked.

'She won't.' The Major's voice grew very clipped.

'But what *is* the story behind the car? Does she have any documentation for the provenance? Where did the family get it from and when?' she persisted. 'Could we talk to that journalist? That might put pressure on her.' She sounded distraught and I realized how much they had all banked on this bonus for the rally.

'She told me nothing more than we know already,' the Major shouted. 'Fact is . . .' He paused.

What the fact was we weren't privileged to hear because when Helen pressed him to continue he merely finished, 'I don't think she has anything in the way of proof.'

'I can't believe that,' Julian said. 'There'd be family photos of it at least. I'll ask that daughter of hers. Or have you done that, Stanley?' he demanded.

'No.' A very definite negative from the Major. He must have seen the look on our faces because he added, 'Wanted to. Victoria wouldn't let me.'

'So that's that,' Helen said.

'I'll resign,' the Major continued glumly. 'You won't want me after this.'

Julian said nothing, though the muscles in his cheek spoke volumes. Helen glanced at him and took charge. 'No, Stanley. I'm sure Julian would agree that we need you for the rally. Victoria Drake might even change her mind if you try gentle persuasion.'

'Offer her money,' Julian said tersely.

'Tried,' the Major said. 'Told her I had a buyer for it.'

Julian became very still. 'And what was her response?'

'Not for sale.'

I was sure on only two counts. Firstly that the Major's story might represent the truth, but it most certainly was not the whole truth. The second was that desperate measures were needed. Then a third reason occurred to me. The fact that the Major knew that in 1968 Victoria was married to her first husband suggested that he believed *her* family owned the De Dion Bouton and not Robert Fairhill.

So why didn't he tell me that when commissioning me to follow up the rumours of its existence in Kent?

I had a sinking feeling that I'd been taken for a gentle ride – and not in a De Dion Bouton. Could it be that the Mad Major had started those famous rumours himself?

SEVEN

Frogs Hill was a homestead at odds with itself. In the last week it had been transformed from providing a happy working environment for a team to a somewhat dilapidated farmhouse and outbuildings, inhabited by a grumpy elderly mechanic and a frustrated sleuth. The atmosphere was depressing. It kept reminding me that I had not yet managed to contact Rob Lane. I'd left several messages but they had been ignored. So had my emails. I'd even called at his flat without success. I guessed the reason. The Mighty Rob likes suppliants to approach on bended knee and messages to call me did not qualify in his book.

I know where his parents live, however, so I tried them. This was more successful. At least I knew that His Majesty was sailing in the Med. Of course. Where else? When would he be back? I asked. Next week, after the bank holiday. Should I text him, I wondered? No. I didn't want to forewarn him. Next week it should be. Meanwhile Len soldiered (and soldered) on alone in the Pits, with some help from me – or hindrance as he would have it.

I was stuck. I was getting nowhere on the Alf King case. I'd been to police HQ to read the statements which included Dean Warren's, that of the poor chap who had found the body and various people who had spotted other people. All cleared, save for a van or two delivering goods. What we were looking for was someone who had expert knowledge of car lifts, and no one fitted – except Dean himself. He claimed he'd been in Tunbridge Wells but there was no proof of that. Motive? With Meyton in the background as a partner, Dean had one. Proof of either of them being involved? Nil. Chance of tracking down delivery vans? Nil. Dean had no knowledge of any due to call that afternoon.

Then Helen called to tell me the latest. 'Bad news on the De Dion Bouton,' she told me.

'What's new about that?' My initial glow at hearing her voice was promptly extinguished.

'Julian went storming off on his own bat to see Mrs Drake.'

The worst. 'She refused to let him in?'

'She *did* let him in. The result seems to have been this: he blustered, she dug her heels in. He threatened her. She called the police. He exited in a hurry.'

'*Threatened* her?' I didn't like the sound of that.

'He said he'd take measures to see everyone knew where the car was, so she might as well give in now and discuss terms.'

'Subtle move,' I said in a hollow voice. 'So that's that. He didn't physically attack her, I hope?'

'No, or he says not,' she amended. 'He then toddled off to see dear old Brenda again, who was more sympathetic. Said she'd done her best but would continue to try to persuade Victoria to at least loan the car to us. I'm getting desperate, Jack. I can't hold the publicity schedule up much longer. Next week we'll be into June and so that's my deadline.'

'Given the situation, there isn't a damn thing we can do, except hope Nick Morris or his mother can talk her round.' I realized I continually said 'we' and not 'you'. I was taking the De Dion hunt personally and not only because it was my main line for Alf King.

'That's doubtful. It looks as if I'll have to forge ahead with the rally publicity without the De Dion. Julian won't be too pleased and nor will Stanley but between them they've dug their own pit. All three of us agree we don't want to cancel the rally, which means attacking the publicity from another angle. I'm working on it.'

'Does Pen Roxton enter your plans?'

A laugh. 'She's not too bad when you talk sense to her.'

'No,' I agreed. 'Not too bad at all. She'll wait a while before eating you wholesale the first time you turn your back.'

'Jack, you're prejudiced.'

'Helen, you don't know her.'

'So what were *you* thinking?'

'That I'd like to see you again. Halfway?'

'Halfway sounds fine,' she said gravely.

*   *   *

Thus heartened I had a last shot at the De Dion problem. There were unanswered questions about Alf's death, and some of them centred on that car. If Victoria Drake stood in the way of my seeing it, there was nothing to stop me from having an independent shot at finding it.

Would it tell me anything about Alf's death? It might, but Alf had last seen it in 2006. I felt I was staring at a jigsaw puzzle with more than half the pieces missing. None of the pieces I held gave that satisfactory feeling that comes when one piece slides into another with an effortless click. Or had one just done so? Suppose Alf *had* been in touch with Victoria and the De Dion much more recently . . .

Click. Alf knew where the car was.

That jigsaw piece had safely locked itself home and now everything began to click satisfactorily.

Click. That's why Victoria was at the funeral. She was still privately in touch with Alf over the De Dion, even if Doris had not been aware of the fact. Victoria's husband had been a regular customer and then she herself had brought a car to him. It followed that Alf could well have known where the De Dion was.

Click. That might be somewhere near Alf's workshop.

Click. Time for a trip to see Dean Warren and Doris – separately.

I decided on Dean first, even though this meant facing Zoe, whom I presumed was already working there. I was right. When I drew up, I could see her working on a Riley. I was delighted to note that she didn't look happy, either because of the Riley or because of Dean, of whom there was no sign.

'Hi, Zoe,' I called casually, as I climbed out of the Alfa to her complete disregard. 'Boss around?' I needed to make it clear I was not crawling here on bended knee on her account.

'Somewhere.' She opened the Riley's bonnet and peered at the engine with great care.

Fortunately the boss strolled out of the office looking less than pleased to see me. The Greek god looked like Zeus the Thunderer today. 'Just a quick word,' I greeted him mildly.

'What about?'

'Nothing ominous,' I assured him. 'You were in Tunbridge Wells the afternoon Alf died, so you're in the clear,' I told him mendaciously. 'I'm here about a different case.'

He seemed to relax slightly although the body language between him and Zoe suggested there was trouble in the air as well as petrol fumes. 'I've been told to check remote farm buildings that might be used as temporary storage for nicked cars. There's been a surge round this area. Do you or did Alf have any garages or workshops anywhere that you aren't currently using?'

'There's a storeroom at the farm up the lane,' he told me unwillingly.

'You've checked it. Know what's in it?'

'Yes.' The Greek god looked wary.

'Where is it? I'd like to see it.'

'Not without a warrant.'

'Something to hide?' I asked amiably. 'Did Connor Meyton ask to see it?'

'He's history but yes.'

Zoe looked up. 'He's still around. In a nice set of wheels too. An old E-type. Can't remember where it was,' she told me offhandedly.

'Perhaps you should give a formal statement to the Kent Car Crime Unit. Pop into Charing tomorrow. I'll tell Dave you're coming.'

She held my gaze. 'If I have to.' Then she relented. 'Down in the valley, Shoreham way.'

'There's a pub there he likes.' Dean decided to join the cooperation party. 'Took me there when we were mates.'

It was possible that Meyton might have other reasons for driving round here. 'Do you have all Alf's keys?' I asked.

Wary again. 'Yes, but you're on to a loser with that store-room. Have a look if you like. It's full of old files and bits and pieces. Went through it for Doris's solicitors.'

He was right. I followed him about a hundred yards up the track to the far end of the complex. Perhaps there was a gem I missed, but to me it was full of unsorted automobilia and not old De Dions. 'Was Meyton interested in this lot?'

'Don't think so. He was going to buy the joint, that's all.'

'Not hankering after finding a complete De Dion Bouton?'

'No way,' he whipped back a mite too quickly.

'And Alf had no other storerooms?'

Dean had tired of cooperation. 'No,' he yelled and stalked off back to the garage.

I was inclined to believe him and was also inclined to think that Connor Meyton had had no intention of buying Alf's business. He'd merely wanted a passport to nose around and probably pinched those records. For the De Dion? If so, he might hold pieces of the jigsaw that I lacked.

'Zoe,' I began, but she too turned away.

I'd only been going to say she'd put the Riley's bonnet catch on the wrong way.

Time to go. Zoe couldn't possibly be happy working here, I thought as I drove away, unless she was so besotted with Dean's prowess in their private lives that she was blinded to the fact that he was no Len Vickers. I could see that nothing on earth was going to shake her resolution, however, unless Rob Lane re-entered the scene. And even that wasn't a cast-iron certainty.

Back to Doris and the De Dion. I felt uneasy about her now that I knew Meyton was still around here, and so might the car be, not to mention the Morrises and Julian with their keen interest in the De Dion. They weren't going to remain cowed for long by two indomitable old ladies, one of whom was Doris. I might be seeing bogeymen where none existed but even so a warning to her might not come amiss.

I found her weeding in the garden and although I'd called out of the blue she didn't seem surprised to see me – probably because Alf still occupied her waking thoughts.

'Do you have any news, Jack?' she asked hopefully once more.

'Same answer, I'm afraid. Not yet, but I'm still working on it.'

'I thought you must be,' she said surprisingly. 'Mrs Carlyle rang me a day or two ago. Remember her from the funeral, do you?'

The bogeymen moved a little closer. What was all this about?

'She said she was ringing on Tom and Patricia Morris's behalf,' Doris continued. 'Pat's Victoria's daughter, you know. They told Mrs Carlyle they were trying to persuade Mrs Drake to cooperate in this rally that dear Helen's organizing and had asked her to ring me as they didn't know me. Apparently it could be very beneficial for Mrs Drake, but she, Mrs Drake that is, wasn't very sure where this old car was. Her memory's going, poor thing, so they said. Mrs Carlyle thought that Alf might have stored the car for her.'

I thought through the ramifications of this little surprise very fast indeed – and I didn't like them. Especially not the bit about Victoria's memory going. 'What did you tell her, Doris?'

'I don't know whether Alf did or not. It was work, you see. I didn't like to tell Mrs Carlyle anything without Mrs Drake's permission. She *is* the owner, after all.' Doris's lips set together primly.

And thereby, I realized, Doris would unwittingly have given Brenda the impression that she knew all too well where Alf had stored the car. I didn't like the idea of Brenda acting as a tool for the Morrises. The sooner the whereabouts of that car were established the better.

'I think Alf did look after it,' I said gently. 'And so it must be near here. It could have something to do with his death, Doris.'

That did it. Her eyes shot wide open. 'There was an old shed Alf used to work out of years back, before he had his present place. Nothing big or fancy. Then later he used it to store his dad's old car. I never went there, but Alf did every once in a while.'

I felt excitement grip me like a cramp. His father's old car might well be a cover for the De Dion. 'Does Dean have a key to it?'

'I don't think so. He has all Alf's business keys, but this wasn't one of them. He kept it with his house keys. He may have had one cut for Dean separately but why would Dean need it?' She paused. 'Do you think Mrs Drake's car might be there?'

'I do. Would you let me have the key, Doris?'

She looked at me uncertainly. 'You *are* the police, Jack, aren't you?'

This time I showed her my ID and she relaxed. 'I'll give you the key then.' Still she hesitated. 'Will you be asking Mrs Drake first?'

'I will tell her, but in case there's any risk I need to check it out immediately – just to ensure it's safe.'

'Risk?' she queried.

I had to ask her, even though it might worry her. 'Did you tell Mrs Carlyle where this shed of Alf's was?'

'Yes, I did. There seemed no harm. I mean, she's Mrs Drake's neighbour.' She looked at me piteously.

'Of course,' I reassured her, 'but don't talk to anyone else, will you? Except me of course,' I joked. 'Can you tell me where it is?'

She did, and I leapt into the Alfa. Shoreham is the next village to Eynsford, but the shed was not in the village itself; it was buried in the countryside just before one reaches it. I drove there immediately, and even though I had been given full directions and had a large-scale map it was hard to find. I only hoped that Connor Meyton had missed it on his cruise around the area. Or had he had precise knowledge of its whereabouts? Not a happy thought.

Doris had told me to look for a track with a granite marker stone, but I had several false starts before I found the correct one. I drove along it, as it looked as though no one had been up here since the Romans colonized us. Fields, a few sheep, woodland, and a farm, then a stone building that could have been a cottage once, but was now a ruin. The building adjoining it, however, looked in better shape.

From the track I could see only a solid wall facing me, so I left the Alfa and found a door on the far side. It was large enough to take a car, and it had a strong padlock on it. To my relief there was no sign that anyone had driven a car in or out recently or that the door had been forced.

With only a meditating cow watching me, I took a deep breath and opened the door. As it creaked, I looked inside and the magic began.

The De Dion Bouton, grey, polished, sublime. I felt a gulp

in my throat, even moist eyes, as I gazed at it. It was a privilege to do so.

Ridiculous. Grown men don't cry. Not often anyway, but when faced with a sight as truly glorious as this, it was allowed.

Despite the years that had passed, how could I doubt that this was one of the two cars that had driven from Peking through the wilds of Asia and through Europe to Paris in 1907 on one of the greatest motoring adventures of all time? I could see no number plates, but I didn't need them to convince me. I forced myself to a rational appreciation, but it felt almost an impertinence to inspect this princess's finer parts, grey artillery wheels, the adjustable jet carburettor, the remarkable De Dion suspension, the drip-feed lubrication system. I checked them almost in a dream and then stood back again to look at her.

Magic.

I'd seen her and somehow I had to force myself to close the doors on her beauty. I wasn't here just to admire her, but to rejoice that she was still here. Doris had asked me to keep the key so that she could tell anyone who asked after it that she had no key, but that the police did. Sensible lady. I was still reeling from the privilege of having seen the De Dion, but I had to grapple with the unpleasant thought that Connor Meyton might know where she was and be making plans to elope with her.

I reassured myself that there would be no point because without documentation of provenance the value would fall dramatically. Ransom? Again no point, because Victoria didn't seem exactly devoted to the car. Perhaps Meyton simply wanted to be convinced, as I did, that the car actually existed and where it was. I doubted this, however.

So what next for Jack Colby? The car was apparently safe, so my job for the Mad Major appeared to be concluded, even though I wasn't going to tell him where the car was. However, my job for Dave still had question marks galore. I needed a consultation with him but events forestalled me. Dave was on voicemail, so I left a message asking him to ring, although with the weekend ahead, I didn't know when that would be. Then Zoe called my mobile.

'I'm only ringing because you ought to know,' she whipped at me before I had a chance to welcome her back into the fold.

It appeared that wasn't on the cards, however. 'Of course,' I said. 'Know what?'

'Connor Meyton came round here an hour or two ago and he and Dean went off somewhere in the car.'

Sounded ominous. 'The best of pals?'

'I wouldn't say that,' Zoe said speedily, probably in case it reflected badly on Dean. Before I could ask her more the phone was put down.

At least it wasn't earth-shattering news. Or was it? It must have taken Zoe a lot to ring me, so she must have been more worried than she let me assume. It was probably nothing to do with the De Dion but was it just coincidence that it happened so soon after my visit?

The question mark hung over me, overshadowing my evening with Helen – typical. We met at the Dering Arms again, but the more I tried to forget De Dions the more sinister the implications that crowded into my thoughts. Finally Helen gave up all attempts to have a normal conversation.

'What's bugging you, Jack? Something good on TV you regret missing?'

I tried my best to reply in kind, but visions of that De Dion all alone in the countryside kept flashing through my head.

I used the time-honoured words: 'Just work.'

'Police or Stanley Hopchurch work?'

'Colby work.'

'So it's the De Dion. What about it?'

'I know where it is. I can't tell you, but I saw it today. I'm worried that it's not safe.'

She was very still. 'Why?'

'There's no reason that it should not be safe and yet I don't think it is.'

'That sounds more to do with Alf than Stanley, and remember that I'm a friend of Doris's. Does that help clear your conscience about putting me in the picture?'

I thought about the possible threat to Doris and decided

Helen was right. 'I believe it is connected to Alf's death but I can't see how. He had been storing the car for Victoria Drake. It's safe but in a place miles from anywhere with little security and a lot of people interested in it. True, only Victoria Drake and I currently have keys, but the locks look pretty flimsy. My key is Doris's, which makes me feel responsible.'

'Will it help you if you check on it again tonight?'

I looked at this wondrous Solomon come to sort me out. I remembered Dean and Connor Meyton's car trip. 'Yes.'

'Then let's go. Take a camera,' Solomon suggested. 'Then you'll have some identification if the car goes AWOL. Victoria Drake might not have any tangible proof that it's there, now that Alf is dead.'

'There's one in the car.' I wavered, thinking how much I would like to stay here with her and then return to Frogs Hill with all its comforts and— No, I would not think of beds. 'I could go tomorrow morning,' I nevertheless said.

'Tonight,' she pronounced. 'How far is it?'

'Under an hour's drive.'

'Then let's go right away. We could still be eating somewhere by eight thirty or so.'

Perhaps it was because it was dark as we drove along the motorway but with Helen at my side I was full of foreboding, as if the ghost of Hamlet's father were striding towards us along the hard shoulder.

'We seem to be heading to Eynsford,' Helen remarked as we turned off the motorway.

'Shoreham.'

'Good pubs there.'

'And great cars to be seen not far away.'

'Not an impostor then?'

'No way. That car is the real thing.'

A sigh of relief from Helen. I couldn't believe it was going to be plain sailing from now on, but I tried to, for her sake. Connor Meyton was hanging around like an evil smell and yet there was nothing I could pin down about him. Irrational though it seemed as I hardly knew the man, I was convinced that something was going on. Dave had told me Meyton had first come to the attention of the Met working in a car gang in the south London area – with Mick Smith, I presumed. He wasn't running it, but the Met reckoned he was aiming to do so. He was a fast learner, carving out his territory with four-by-fours, although not restricted to that. Classics to order were his ambition. He had disappeared from the Met's eagle eyes however and landed up in Dave's neck of the police woods when an Aston Martin had disappeared from the Meopham area.

I reasoned that if Doris stood in the way of this upwardly mobile classic gentleman, he was not going to let an old lady prevent him from getting to the car of his choice. In vain I reminded myself once again that no one, not Meyton nor the Morrises, would have anything to gain from kidnapping the car without proof of its provenance. The uneasy thought of Julian crossed my mind but I dismissed it as heebie-jeebies.

The evening sun looked gorgeous as for the second time that day I turned my car into that elusive track. There was a silence between Helen and me. I was bent on reaching the De Dion as soon as possible and Helen – what was she thinking? No doubt that she could think of better ways to spend a summer evening than driving on wild-goose chases with a car sleuth.

'This is a crazy way to spend an evening,' I muttered.

'I told you I like impossible challenges, so I like doing crazy. Are you sorry I came?'

'No.'

No doubt about that. Unless of course we ran into trouble, but there was no sign of anyone around. Only ourselves and the sinking sun. As we turned the last bend my tension level shot up. There were no visiting cars to be seen, thank heavens, and I slumped back in my seat, unable to believe how stupid I had been. I'm not used to making bears out of bushes and I'd made a prize fool of myself.

And I still was. A lurch of my stomach told me that the doors could be wide open for all I knew, as they were on the far side.

Fighting panic, I told Helen, 'Prepare for one quick look at this beauty, and then we'll go.'

Relief again. When we reached the door, it was padlocked just as I'd left it. Full of joy, I unlocked it, and pulled the creaky door open so that Helen could get her first view of the De Dion Bouton. I was looking at her so that I could share her delight, and was unprepared for her stifled gasp.

The shed was empty.

Doris. The name pounded in my ears. Had she been attacked? This was my fault, no doubt about it. I must have been white with shock and worry because Helen had to calm me down. She put her arms round me and hugged me to her.

'You said you had Doris's key and that there are only two,' she reminded me.

'Yes.'

'The padlock's intact. It didn't look as if it had been forced.'

I looked at her. 'Helen,' I said, relief pouring out of me. 'I'm going to kiss you. Any objection?'

'None at all,' she said politely.

It was a poor apology of a kiss, thanks to these circumstances. 'All the same, I'll check on Doris.'

Her phone rang for what seemed like forever. What the hell was I going to say? Did it matter? Just answer, *answer.*

And eventually she did.

'Hello?' She was a phone screecher, but today she could screech all she liked.

'Are you OK, Doris? No odd visitors?'

'No. Of course I'm all right. Why shouldn't I be?'

'Because someone other than me got into the garage today.'

'That would be Mrs Drake,' Doris replied happily.

'Are you *sure*?' My brain didn't seem to be functioning at full speed.

'I had to ring her,' Doris explained in surprise, 'to tell her the police had my key. It was only right.'

'But the car's missing.'

'She said she'd arranged for it to be picked up.'

I switched off, weak with relief, and feeling more than a little stupid as I told Helen what had happened.

'Good,' she said. 'Can we eat now?'

'Let's go,' I said.

But even as I drove, my brain was churning round. Who picked it up? Not Victoria. It wasn't licensed – no plates. Drivable? A garage would do it. A garage such as King's Restorations? Or Connor Meyton's chums?

The questions were back.

EIGHT

We parted in virtual silence that night, Helen and I. We both felt too flat to take matters any further – either on the De Dion front or privately. In the aftermath of anticlimax we had nothing to celebrate by dining in Shoreham so we headed for home. We had a nondescript meal in a nondescript pub en route, and then I drove her to where she had left her car. If 'friendship' was trembling on the brink of love neither of us was up to pushing it over – yet.

'Stupid to feel so low,' she remarked. 'After all, the De Dion's in the safe hands of its rightful owner, so what's to worry about?'

Quite a lot, I thought, but I told her I agreed with her, partly because I didn't want to face the truth. We were back at Square One as regards the De Dion and the rally. The De Dion was 'found' but I still had a stake in its story because of Alf's 'accident'. A phone call to Victoria Drake first thing in the morning was therefore essential. I needed to know from her own lips that her car was safe – and come to that, Victoria herself was safe.

When I did ring her it went straight to voicemail. It was going to be one of those days. Through the farmhouse window I saw Len arrive and stomp off into the Pits and knew I ought to be giving him moral and physical back-up. It was Saturday on a bank holiday weekend but Zoe's absence meant he had to work overtime. I needed back-up myself, however, so today was not the time. Leave a message for Victoria? No, that would give her a chance to back away. Ring Pat? No. Ring Brenda? No, again. Victoria owned this car and I couldn't spread the word that it had moved from its former home to anywhere else before I'd spoken to her. The one exception was Dave, and as it was Saturday, I was pleasantly surprised that he was available, at least on the phone.

Dave is wonderfully laconic in the face of potential night-mares. 'What's the old bird done with it, then?'

'Unlikely to be on a jaunt to the seaside.'

'What's biting you? Think she's about to flog it?'

Trust Dave to stick the knife in where it hurts. 'Maybe. Should I carry on?'

The pause was too long for my liking and the word 'mort-gage' writ itself on my horizon. 'Still think it's linked to Alf King?' he asked at last.

'Yes.'

'Carry on then. But keep in touch. The Serious Crime boys and girls are getting interested now.'

The possibility of DCI Brandon breathing down my neck was all I needed. Luckily Helen rang and the day cheered up, even though she only wanted to know if I'd spoken to Victoria.

'Voicemail,' I told her. 'Fancy a trip to Lamberhurst?'

'Why not?' she replied, to my surprise. I'd assumed she had plans for the weekend.

An hour later her Fiat 500 arrived with a scrunch of the gravel. 'My place or yours?' she asked gravely, unfortunately with only the cars in mind. I had the Gordon-Keeble ready for take-off – a treat, for me at least.

Len spotted our imminent departure and came out to see us off. A rare honour, but not without purpose. 'Seen Zoe, have you, Jack?'

'Yes,' I admitted. 'She's lacking your care, Len. There's a Riley over there missing your expertise.'

'She'll be back,' he muttered darkly.

I wished I had his confidence. Zoe's stubbornness is only matched by Len's. I comforted myself that Rob would be back in a few days. Then I came to my senses. Since when was Rob Lane a *comfort*?

Helen broke the silence, but not until we were driving through Sissinghurst on the way to Shoulder Mutton Green. 'Why aren't we happier about Victoria moving the car, Jack?'

I couldn't pin this down. 'Because it doesn't feel right?'

'Go on.'

I struggled. 'Victoria doesn't appear to give a damn about the De Dion – but suddenly it has to be moved immediately.'

'That's surely understandable. We've been harassing her, Doris was worried about it.' She changed tack. 'Not enough, is it?'

'Not quite. It's possible the Morrises have been pestering her so much that she's given in and brought the kiddies' inheritance nearer home. It could be good news, Helen.' Theoretically perhaps, but in practice Victoria wouldn't give way to an angry Rottweiler if it didn't suit her.

'What shall we do if she slams the door in our faces again?'

'I'll try making it an official visit.' This line hadn't worked before, but it was worth a go.

'Official or not, she won't be pleased that you borrowed Doris's key.'

'Tough. Legitimate police business because I had reason to suspect foul play.'

All looked peaceful in Shoulder Mutton Green when we arrived. Nothing more sinister than families out with toddlers and pushchairs, a dog or two, a postman collecting from the box, traffic gearing up for weekend jaunts. I decided to park by the roadside where I had before, rather than in the Elmtree House drive. Helen and I then strolled back to the house trying to pretend this was a normal social call. It didn't feel that way. The house appeared forbidding, with that empty look as though it were wondering when its owner would be back. Victoria's car was on the driveway, however, which was a good sign. At least, I thought so, but it seemed not to be. The doorbell clanged in the house but there was no answer. We waited a few minutes and tried again. Same result.

'Childe Roland to the dark tower came,' Helen remarked. 'Do you know that Browning poem?'

I didn't. 'What did Childe Roland find in this dark tower?'

'There was no reply when he blew his horn.'

'What was he there for?'

'That's the mystery. No one knows. Just like now.'

'Thanks, Helen,' I said ruefully. 'I can depress myself though. I don't need Browning to do it for me.'

'In the ballad on which he based the poem, his sister had been abducted by fairies.'

'Even worse.' I rang once again but there was still no sound within.

It seemed to me the hunt for the De Dion Bouton was getting to be a farce, peopled by avaricious relatives, avid collectors, obstinate owners and mad majors. Then I remembered Alf. Nothing farcical about his death.

'She could be at the shops or at Brenda's,' Helen said hopefully, 'or even in the garden.'

'Or walking the dog,' I added, 'or arranging a local garage for the De Dion. Perhaps it's inside her garage, which is why the Polo is outside.' I was talking to thin air. Helen was already peering through the garage window, and then she disappeared through a gateway to the garden, while I waited hopefully. She quickly reappeared.

'No sign of her or the De Dion.'

'Right. Let's see if Brenda's in.'

I put my arm round Helen's shoulders, and it felt comfortable. So comfortable that I wasn't prepared for a sharp jerk back to the real world as we walked back down the driveway to the road and saw mud on the grass.

Or what I thought was mud. It wasn't. It was dark red.

The colour of congealed blood.

'Stay there,' I told Helen sharply.

I forced myself to investigate, and she didn't stay anywhere. She was right beside me as I skirted the bushes and saw what was lying on their far side. I could see the iron lug wrench that had battered the life out of Victoria Drake, and the blood-covered gloves that the assassin must have worn. Her legs stuck out grotesquely, as if she'd fallen flat on her face just as she walked. Her light jacket and fancy black skirt looked as though she had been dolled up for some special occasion – before they were covered in her blood from the now all but unrecognizable head.

I've seen quite a few corpses over the years, but even so I had to look away. I pressed Helen's shaking body to me and led her back to the path, held her close for a moment, then suggested she waited in the Gordon-Keeble. I felt rather

than saw her shake her head, and she was right not to do so.
Who would want to remain alone after such a dreadful sight?
She needed the reassurance of a living, moving human being.
I rang the emergency services first and then tried Dave, by
now on voicemail. Of course. The whole bloody world lived
on voicemail.

I had to remain where I was, but Helen did agree to drive
the Gordon-Keeble nearer to the house, although not into the
drive, of course. The move was unnecessary, but it gave her
something to do and provided communication between us
while we still could not cope with the reality. It was beginning
to spit with rain and I was glad when Helen returned, bringing
my large umbrella from the car. She didn't seem surprised
when I held it over the corpse.

'Crime scene,' I managed to say jerkily, and she nodded.

There was more to it than that. It seemed a last attempt to
give Victoria Drake the dignity of being a human being. I knew
I should be looking critically at the crime scene myself but I
couldn't. I could only cope by distancing myself mentally and,
as far as I could, physically. I work for the police. I know the
routine of crime scenes: the first police to arrive would assess
the scene – and me. That happened. Then came the radio calls
and the resulting team converging from all directions on Elmtree
House. The tent over the corpse, the crime-scene suits and
shoes, the barrier tapes . . . It was out of my hands and thank
heaven for that. I could wait to be interrogated and join Helen
while I did so.

The crime-scene manager was not Brandon, but a woman,
a DCI Fielding, whom I hadn't run into before. She was one
of these efficient types, blonde, fortyish and cool. She gave
me the once-over, as I briefly explained my presence and my
role in the De Dion Bouton. The latter failed to make much
impression on her – and faced with this brutal murder I could
understand why.

Without my even noticing, local residents had begun to
gather, attracted by the police sirens and cars, and the incident
vans now parked outside. Helen and I were banished to the
narrow stretch of grass on the far side of the drive, and I realized I must be on automatic pilot because it was only belatedly

that I recognized Brenda and Tom standing across the road. Shortly afterwards I saw Patricia join them, so with the gateway roped off, I walked down to the fence so that they could come over to me if they wished. A white-faced and visibly shaking Brenda did.

'I'm taking Patricia and Tom home with me,' she began, not even questioning what Helen and I were doing here. Her voice faltered and she gave up the attempt to be practical. 'Did she suffer much?' She looked at me with hope in her eyes.

'No,' I said, lying because I had to. How could I know, how could *anyone* know the answer to that?

'Do join us . . .' she managed to say.

I thanked her, but explained that Helen and I had to wait until the DCI gave us permission to leave the crime scene. How long that would be, I had no idea. At least Fielding allowed us to sit in the Gordon-Keeble until summoned again, albeit I could see a PC keeping a close eye on us.

At last DCI Fielding and her sergeant – both of whom turned out to be quite human – came to take our initial statements. We made a cosy foursome sitting in the Gordon-Keeble, but at least we were away from the horror of Elmtree House and its terrible garden scene. I made another stab at explaining why we were here and gave her Dave Jennings' number to check me out. I also covered Alf's death, and she began to be mildly interested in the De Dion at last.

'The victim collected this car yesterday?' she asked.

'I was told she had,' I emphasized. 'I saw it in its storage shed in the afternoon and returned to find it empty in the evening.'

Not surprisingly she seemed to think this strange, until Helen explained it had been at her urging and why. Fielding still looked doubtful, however, even though I gave her Dave's direct number.

'Where is this car now?' she asked.

'I don't know. That's what we came to find out. From what we could see it wasn't in the garage.'

'That's empty, except for an old mower and garden junk. No sign of any old cars. You say it's valuable?'

'Very. And in a month or two's time it might be much more

valuable. If the car was the reason for this murder, it's odd timing. Any sensible thief would bide his time until the market value shot up. He'd also want to pinch any papers relating to its history. Was the house broken into?'

'No signs so far, so it looks as if the car couldn't have been the reason she was killed. She's been dead some time so it could have been a random attack last night.'

'With a handy lug wrench? More likely to have been someone she was with. There's a lot we don't know about the De Dion Bouton story.'

Her reply was dismissive. 'When you know it and *if* it's relevant, I'll take it on board.'

I couldn't leave it there, delicate ground or not. 'There's one angle you might want to consider. If this car is potentially as valuable as I think, the killer might be close at hand, family even.'

A cool look but not an unfriendly one. 'I'll bear that in mind.'

She asked us to call in at HQ to make formal statements but otherwise we were free to go, while her team crawled over every inch of garden and house for forensic evidence. Ours would only count as 'hearsay' but I was sure that in this case 'hearsay' would be a vital constituent.

Helen and I discussed joining Brenda and the Morrises. I had no option, but I suggested she might want to give it a miss. She didn't, but as outsiders we agreed not to stay long.

'Could a woman have killed her?' Helen asked as we walked along to Brenda's home. Her voice wobbled.

I'd been wondering that myself. 'Non-professional opinion, but caught unawares and in the right position, it's not impossible. It would take a strong-minded woman to batter away like that, though.'

She did not comment, and I didn't take it further. I was summoning my energy for what was to come. Brenda looked almost glad to see us – either to find out what was happening or because she needed help with Patricia and Tom. There was no sign of Nick. Patricia looked shrunken with shock and I began to think that Helen and I should not be here, but they accepted our arrival without comment. I was surprised that any of them were up to asking us questions but they seemed eager to do so. Tom asked most, but Patricia listened with great attention as Brenda fussed ineffectively with coffee cups and biscuits. In the end Helen went to carry the tray in while Brenda sank down in an armchair at last.

'When did it happen?' Tom asked me. One of those questions that even the questioner knows can't be answered but they fulfil the need for communication.

'Probably last night – she was dressed for the evening rather than the morning.'

'I was out,' Brenda moaned. 'When I came back, I saw there were no lights on in Victoria's house. Well, I didn't think anything of it, why should I? But all the time she might have been lying there. Dead. Oh I can't bear it, I really can't.'

Patricia said nothing; but her coffee cup remained undisturbed. I began to realize that what I'd taken for 'listening' could be silent shock.

And then it came. 'Did Victoria say anything about the De Dion to you?' Tom shot at me. 'Brenda's story is that Victoria was going to arrange to bring it down here.'

'That's what Victoria told me,' Brenda confirmed. 'Doris King didn't have her telephone number, so I had to give it to her. Victoria said she would arrange to get it here right away. I don't know why.'

'There's no sign of it at the house,' I pointed out, glad that the subject was at least on the table.

'Then where the hell is it?' Tom shot at me.

'In her garage, I suppose.' Brenda was rocking to and fro in agitation.

'It's not,' I told them.

'*Not*?' Patricia roused herself, while Tom and Brenda stared at me as though I were in league with the devil, for which I had no current plans.

'What the hell are you doing here anyway?' Tom belatedly shouted at me. 'You've got the car yourself, haven't you?'

The gloves, it seemed, were coming off with a vengeance, but the fact that they were wrangling over this now left me stuck for words.

'No,' Helen replied for me. 'He hasn't.'

'Then *they've* got it,' Tom swept on. 'By God, I'll see—'

'Tom, stop!' Patricia cried.

'Who are *they*?' I asked with interest. Connor Meyton for instance?

'That Hopchurch fellow and the crazy collector chap who came over to badger us all. Couldn't get her to part with it by legitimate means, so they did it this way.'

Helen flared up. 'Are you accusing Julian and Stanley of murder?'

'When a million or more is at stake, you have to think that way,' Tom snarled. 'That car's our inheritance, so where is it? The old woman hadn't a penny other than that falling-down barn of a house. So where the blazes is it?'

Once the word inheritance is on the table all sorts of maggots can crawl out of the woodwork, so I kept quiet. Unfortunately the maggots weren't given a chance.

'I suggest,' Brenda said with dignity, 'that you postpone this discussion for a more suitable time. Poor Patricia needs our consideration.'

Helen was still trembling when we reached the Gordon-Keeble, whether with shock or anger I could not tell. All I knew was that we needed to be out of this place, away from crime scenes, incident vans and police cars. From murder to car valuations was too big a jump for both of us.

'How can he talk that way?' Helen said. 'As if Victoria wasn't a person at all. She was his *mother-in-law*.'

I tried to be charitable. 'Unexpected death can have odd effects, especially when it's murder – people can't take in that it's for real.'

'Apparently they can when it means money for them,' Helen said bitterly. 'And accusing Julian and Stanley is way out of line.'

'I'm afraid,' I warned her, 'that the police might well be asking just the same questions.'

I did not get back to Frogs Hill until late that afternoon, as both Helen and I elected to make our formal statements right away. That done, Helen returned to Harford Lee and I came back home. She was spending the rest of the bank holiday weekend with her parents, and I didn't persuade her to change that plan. Distance can help shock.

Frogs Hill felt good as the Gordon-Keeble made its stately way over the gravel to its home next to the Lagonda. A platform for me to breathe again. Helen departed in her Fiat, and I strolled into the Pits, trying to feel 'normal'. To my pleasure Len was still there. He looked up and grunted as I came in.

'Give us a hand, Jack.'

So I did. We worked for an hour or so on the Porsche with great care, and that too felt good. I was under Len's supervision of course – he doesn't think I can tell a nut from a bolt. One drawback to this interlude: I'd never thought of describing our restoration workshop as lacking a woman's touch, but it did. Not any woman's touch, of course, but Zoe's. The horrors of the morning began to recede at least momentarily until just as Len was leaving he thought fit to mention that Dave had left a message for me to ring as soon as I came in. There was, I saw guiltily, the same message on my mobile. The news of Victoria Drake's murder must already have percolated to him, I realized. The message was to ask me to meet him for lunch on the morrow at the usual place. This is the Markham Arms, a pub that Dave favours because he fondly imagines that it gives him a low profile. The fact that he's kept to the same pub for years, however, means that every villain in Kent plus their networks had come to know who he is and by association anyone he meets there. Such as me.

It must be urgent if Dave wanted to meet me on a Sunday. That's usually sacrosanct as a family day. The Markham Arms is a sixteenth-century building and not too much has been done to it since, thank goodness. It's still possible to walk in and see the present-day conglomeration of local workers and other residents dissolve into a scene of their medieval counterparts.

It was the first time I'd been here on a Sunday, and the clientele was different, especially as its reputation for good food brought families here for lunch. The pub was packed when I arrived, but I could see Dave sitting in his usual place at a table in the window, a tomato juice before him and *The*

Times newspaper folded at the Sudoku puzzle lying beside it. It proved to be Friday's Super Fiendish one, which is suitable for Dave, who looks and acts benign and slow and is the very opposite. Many a villain has more than met his match by underestimating Dave. I never did, or do, make that mistake, which is probably why we get on.

'Morning, Jack,' he greeted me as I arrived with a half of bitter in my hand. 'This De Dion—'

'I take it that's now reached your official missing list.'

'Not missing.'

I blinked. 'That was quick.'

'Certainly was. On the list yesterday afternoon. Off it thirty minutes later. Had a call put through from a place on the A21 near Tunbridge Wells. Chap rented a solo garage out two days ago, car installed the same evening by elderly lady by name of Mrs Drake. He heard the news on the grapevine, checked the garage and was mighty surprised to find something out of a museum there. Car seems safe enough. Now tell me all you can about this Mrs Drake, Jack.'

I filled him in as fully as I could, and he listened carefully.

'Any luck with Connor Meyton?' he picked up.

'Yes. He's around, but no proof.'

'Not surprised. He's a slippery customer. We tried Dean Warren ourselves, but he's still saying he's no longer in contact. Former number doesn't work.'

'I've got one contact might help. Bob Orton. Only drawback is that he's tied in with Pen Roxton.'

'That *Graphic* woman? Careful as you go, Jack.'

'I hear you, believe me, but it's worth the risk.'

'You seem to have taken Meyton to heart,' Dave observed mildly. 'Why?'

I considered this. 'Because he's *there* like a raspberry pip stuck in your teeth.'

'Like that chap who's always hanging around Frogs Hill?'

'Who's that?' I asked, thrown.

'Fellow at the bar over there.'

I swivelled round – and lo and behold, the one and only Rob Lane was lounging there in his inimitable way.

He nodded casually as he saw me looking at him. I excused myself from Dave, saying I'd be back. He commented I should do just that or I couldn't charge him for the session. The word budget was mentioned.

Rob seldom moves towards you; you move to him if one requires an audience with His Majesty. And today I did so move – purposefully.

I forced myself to act cheerily and we relocated to a less crowded part of the pub. 'What are you drinking, Rob?' And, that settled, I added, 'Good cruise?'

'Rocky in the Med, but not bad,' he drawled. 'Cannes was much as usual.'

Of course. Just a dreary old round of high-society parties, celeb spotting, beach parties, restaurants and moonlight serenading interspersed with the occasional splash in the pool or stroll into one of the casinos.

'I need your help, Rob.'

Rob looked wary. It isn't often that I say that to him. It might need action on his part and that he dislikes.

'Zoe,' I began.

Even more wary.

'She's left Frogs Hill,' I told him. Rob thought this highly amusing – until I added: 'For a chap called Dean Warren at Alf King's old place.'

Less amused now. 'Working for him?'

'And whatever . . .'

Rob put his drink down on the bar, looking almost sinister.

'Who knows with Zoe?' I added hastily.

'*I* do,' he said grimly. 'Leave it to me.'

I longed to ask him how the 'dumb floozie' was, but decided to hold my peace. If Rob Lane's presence in my life was the price we had to pay for Zoe's return, it was worth it.

Having concluded my talk with Dave and agreed to contact Bob Orton I spent the rest of the day at Frogs Hill reading in a deckchair in the garden. Taking time off? No way. I was studying all the books on the Peking to Paris rally that I could find. It seemed a profitable way to spend a Helenless day. I'd told her I would come over on the Tuesday to see the

Mad Major as well as her, but he was nagging in my mind so much I had rung him to see if I could go straight over. No reply, but he did ring back eventually and we fixed a date for the morrow, Bank Holiday Monday. Well, spending a day racing cars at a model Brooklands track wouldn't be a bad way of unwinding from the horrors of yesterday.

I found his home easily enough. It was in Old Lilleys, a small village on the far side of Canterbury. Not many homes have a large stone Bentley in the middle of the lawn, nor, I imagined, a Brooklands race track in their rear gardens. I rang the bell but did a double take when he opened the door. He looked ill. Gone was the smart former army officer gear. He was unshaven, and in old cords and baggy sweater, and seemed to have forgotten I was coming. He ushered me in, and needless to say the place, as befitted a former army officer, was tidy, but devoid of family touches. Helen had told me his wife had died about six years earlier, and the house reflected it.

'You found her, I'm told,' he said abruptly. 'Victoria.'

'I'm sorry – even sorrier that Helen was with me. Her murder must have been a shock to you and Julian.'

He stared at me. 'A shock?'

Something odd here, but I persevered. 'Because you knew her in the Sixties, didn't you?' A love affair? It seemed likely.

'You should have seen her, Jack. Got a photo somewhere.' He rummaged in a desk drawer and brought out a framed picture of a woman standing by one of the bookseller stalls by the River Seine in Paris.

It was a young Victoria – still a woman of purpose, judging by the strong face, but smiling happily at the photographer, probably the Major himself. 'Was she married then? Or were you courting her?' I asked, not so much for information as to keep the conversation going.

A nod was his only response, but to which question? Or both, of course.

No help for it. I'd have to plunge in. 'You knew about the car then, didn't you?'

'Car?' He looked bemused.

'The De Dion Bouton. She told you she owned one, or that her husband did.'

He came alive at that. 'Good grief, no. That cad Fairhill? It was hers.'

Right. Something established. 'She told you the story behind the car?'

'Yes.'

'The *full* story? Not just that it belonged to her family?'

'I knew it.'

I let this oddity pass. 'Did Mrs Drake say whether she had any documentation relating to the car, anything that might prove its origins?'

'I have it.'

I couldn't pass this one. Even accounting for shock, something wasn't gelling. 'Have what?'

'She stole it,' he said flatly.

'*Victoria* pinched the provenance documents?'

'The car,' he said impatiently. 'Florence. It belonged to my grandfather, Pascal Merrault.'

So that was why he started the rumours about the car earlier this year. I seemed to have hit the jackpot without even pressing any buttons.

NINE

Tell me this is a joke, I pleaded silently, but Major Stanley Hopchurch merely stared at me defiantly. It must have taken willpower on his part not to burst out with a defence or apology – or even, heaven forfend, an explanation. Never had his nickname seemed more applicable.

'You'll get your money,' were his first words. That was a relief but believe it or not it wasn't top of my agenda at that moment.

'Do you mind telling me why you got *me* involved in this wild-goose chase?'

'Because you found the goose.' The Major seemed to think this was adequate as an explanation.

'True, but why not tell me in the first place that you had a stake in this car?'

His eyes went out to the racetrack in the garden, clearly visible through the windows, as though only that could provide salvation from this confrontation.

'Not an answer,' I said briefly. 'You knew the car existed, you'd met Victoria Drake, albeit some time ago, and you knew she thought she owned the car. You had a private talk with her last . . .'

I stopped right there, as the truth belatedly dawned. At last, at last, I could see a pattern in this crazy story. Talk about 'in the clouds'. This one was in an alternative world all its own. 'It wasn't the car you wanted to find, was it? It was the *woman*. You wanted to find Victoria Drake herself.'

The Major found his tongue. 'Nonsense!' he roared.

His expression told me I'd hit pay dirt. This whole charade had been a mere cover for finding a lost sweetheart – or, it occurred to me, lost enemy. Whichever it was, it was no problem of mine. I rose to my feet. 'I'll send in my invoice to date.'

The Major gave no reaction, so soft soap leeway was over;

it was time for the hard facts. 'You realize I'll have to report this to the police, as there could be a connection between her death and the De Dion Bouton. You're going to have to be ready to talk some time, so why not tell me now?'

From bully boy to punctured balloon in one swoop. The Major became putty in my hands, although he did summon up enough energy for a weak attempt at control.

'Sit down,' he mumbled. 'Shaken me up a bit, this news of Victoria's murder.'

As an apology it wasn't much, but it would have to do. I sat down.

'Suppose I'll have to tell you,' he said grumpily.

'You suppose correctly.'

'Know anything about France and 1968?' he began.

I did know quite a bit but I shook my head.

'I was twenty-two,' he continued. 'Sent to Paris for six months – army liaison duties. Been there in the fifties on a school trip, but by sixty-eight everything had changed practically overnight. Students protesting and all that. And not just the students. Everyone shouting the odds. French police out in force. Champs de Mars choc à bloc.'

'Protesting against what?'

'Who knows? French johnnies like a good rebellion once every so often. Old regime. Time for new things, Sergeant Pepper and the Beatles, that sort of thing. Victoria Fairhill was one of them. Met her in a café. My word, she was a sight to be seen. Sparkling, funny, and a stunner to look at. When it got rough, I tried to get her out of there. She wouldn't come at first, but I more or less dragged her out before she got herself arrested. She was furious at first but finally gave up and laughed at me. "What's your name?" I asked her. "Victoria," she said. "Where shall we have dinner?"

'My mouth dropped open, I can tell you,' he continued gruffly. 'I wasn't used to that sort of thing. A chap did the asking in those days. "We'll go for a walk first," she told me. We walked along the Champs Élysées and passed the Renault showroom-cum-museum. "Let's go in," she said. "I like old cars." I did too, so there we were. Spotted a De Dion Bouton. "Got one of those," she said. "Old family car. Took part in the Peking to Paris rally." That floored me. Thought I hadn't heard right. "Your name isn't Florence, is it?" I asked – cautiously, mind. "No, but I had a grandmother called Florence." "Florence Manning?" I asked. Well, she looked surprised at that, and said yes. So I told her all about it. "I'm supposed to shoot you on sight," I joked. "My grandfather Pascal Merrault owned that car but it was stolen from him by an ex girlfriend called Florence. My father's got all the paperwork." "So have I," she said simply. "Here?" I asked, unable to believe this. "My mother has it in Scotland," she told me.

'I said next time I was on leave I'd get in touch with her and we could check to see which of us had the legitimate papers for provenance.' Another harrumph of embarrassment from the Major. 'When I tried, I found she'd given me a false address. I don't mind telling you I was damned annoyed. After my wife died, I started thinking things over, and when the idea of this rally popped up I thought I'd spread the word about that there was a De Dion that took part in the 1907 rally still around in Britain somewhere. Thought it might turn up something. It hadn't, and I was pretty desperate, since I knew it existed. That's when I called you in.' He eyed me hopefully to see how I was taking this.

Reasonably OK so far. 'One hitch,' I said. 'You spread the rumour that the car was around in Kent.'

He looked me straight in the eye. 'Had a hunch. Went back and looked at the records my grandfather had left me. This Florence lived in Kent, so it was worth a try. Maybe her granddaughter did too.'

I tried again. 'But it was Victoria you wanted to find, not just the car?'

His face went blank. 'The car,' he maintained. 'The car, man, the *car*. Dammit, with Julian wittering on about it I'd no option. The rally and that De Dion Bouton – all fitted like a glove.'

I was not totally convinced, but I let him have his way. 'OK,' I said. 'So tell me what you know about the car, and how it got to the UK.'

His eyes lit up then settled into that fixed faraway look of the true car buff. 'The Peking to Paris rally,' he breathed almost reverentially. 'You probably know all about that.'

'A little. Fill me in though.' It would be interesting to hear him talk about it.

He needed no urging. His eyes lit up. 'You probably know the limelight focused on the Itala, driven by that Italian johnny, Prince Scipione Borghese, and the Spyker, which had a madcap former jockey at the wheel, Charles Godard. They lassoed the headlines all the way. Borghese because he was dead set on winning, and Godard because he was forever having to be bailed out of trouble one way or another. The two De Dions, though, chugged their way across deserts and mountains, the lot. *And* they played the game helping the other out – occasionally,' he added fairly. 'One of the De Dions was driven by Georges Cormier, who tended to be the boss, and the other one by Victor Collignon – both of them regular drivers used by the De Dion Bouton firm from time to time.'

'Wasn't there a fifth car, a tricar, involved?'

'Yes. The Contal driven by Auguste Pons, but that was a bit of a dud. He got lost in the Gobi Desert, had to abandon the car and come back by train. Prince Borghese had the sense to take a journalist as passenger and announced he was going to arrive in Paris on the tenth of August, exactly two months after he left Peking, and so he did. He and his forty h.p. no-expense-spared Itala. Those two De Dions were only ten h.p. but, by Jove, they survived the whole route. They got to Paris on the thirtieth of August, twenty days after the Itala, and the Spyker came in even later after a bit of hanky-panky. Understandable enough. They'd all been through a pretty tough time.'

'The publicity seems to have gone on for a while,' I observed. 'Appearances at car shows and so forth. That included the De Dions, given that one of them was at Olympia in 1907. Given that, tell me the missing link. How does your documentation tie in with your grandfather?'

The Major looked hunted. 'Pascal married a count's daughter, Françoise, a year or two after he split up with Florence. They had one daughter, Marie, who married General Basil Hopchurch and came to England to live. Here I am.

Grandfather Pascal died in the First World War. Neither of my parents was keen on cars, but they noticed I liked playing around with them so my mother turned over to me in due course the papers about the De Dion.'

'Proving its provenance as one of the two original cars?'

'The whole caboodle, Colby, including a letter to my mother explaining that before he married Françoise he had been engaged to an Englishwoman who had run off with the car itself, but he still had the papers to do with it, and here they were.'

'Run from where to where?' I asked patiently. 'You – and I – need to know the full story.'

He glared at me. 'Come and look at the stuff if you like.'

If? Try and stop me. The Major led me – still reluctantly – to an antique desk that suggested it might double as a drinks cupboard although if so that compartment remained firmly closed. He swept various piles of papers off the surface of the desk, and heaved a suitcase on to it. The suitcase was an ancient one which needed a leather strap around it, probably because of the flimsy clasp. There was a generally battered look to it that Lady Bracknell would have dismissed in an instant. The Major made a great parade of opening it, more for effect than with good reason, I suspected. I stood at his side almost panting with anticipation.

On the top was an old photograph album to which my hand went immediately as he gestured to me to help myself. No urging needed. It was a treasure trove, I could see that. On the first page was a picture of a De Dion – whether *the* De Dion or not was impossible to tell. At its side stood, I presumed, Pascal, who looked every bit an early-twentieth-century version of a Dumas musketeer. His arm was around a full-skirted damsel, who simpered out at the viewer with blushing pride at her choice of beau (or car). Then followed photos from the 1907 rally whose provenance was unclear and I had seen them or very similar ones before, such as one of Collignon at the De Dion's wheel in Warsaw, and a photo of both cars trying to cross the bridge over the Cha Ho River. There followed several more photos of Pascal and Florence, all with the car, including one captioned 'Dunkirk docks'.

'What's the rest of the story?' I asked.

'Read it for yourself.' He irritably gestured at the papers lying underneath the album.

I only wished I had several days to study it – a wish I was unlikely to be granted. From what I could see, there were work sheets for a garage in Dunkirk and a report on the De Dion's condition dated November and December 1907 respectively. There was a bill of sale dated early January 1908 and a letter headed by the De Dion Bouton company, and goodness knows what else.

'Can you precis it for me?' I asked the Major.

He heaved a great sigh. 'Florence was going to take the car back to England after he bought it, because he had nowhere to store it. He was a young man just setting out on a journalist's career.'

'So what was Victoria Drake's claim to it?' I asked. I didn't like the way this story was heading.

Drawn back to the present day, I thought the Major was going to break down, but he didn't. 'Victoria and I had a laugh about it,' he said. 'She was the daughter of Muriel, Florence's only child – she'd married in 1912. From what we worked out, Florence had proof that she, not Pascal, had bought the car, as he was skint at the time. She intended to make it a wedding present for him, so she kept it here and waited for Pascal to come over and marry her. Which he didn't, so she kept the car.'

'That doesn't add up,' I pointed out. 'Here's a bill of sale made out to Pascal.'

'Unfortunately,' he admitted, 'Victoria told me she'd seen an identical bill of sale in her box, made out to Florence. That's why I did nothing more about it at the time. Forgot all about my own claim.'

If true – and I was by no means convinced by this odd tale – it was not good news. The existence of two bills was going to throw a doubt over the whole ownership issue. One vast practical joke? I wondered. The car existed, however. I'd seen it. I looked carefully at the car in the photo at the front of the album. I could see a number plate that looked French, but couldn't read it. How to tie it down to the 1907 rally car? The

De Dion Bouton company had ceased to exist decades ago, so no hope of tracing anything there.

Which bill was the fake one? None of the answers would necessarily prove the car was not one of the original Peking to Paris survivors. If it had 'disappeared' on the way back either from Dunkirk or the Paris motor show to the De Dion works, however, it would need a bill of sale in order to resell it or prove its provenance.

And here I was dumped in my own heffalump pit again. If it had been nicked, it couldn't have been sold as the rally car without attracting attention from the De Dion Bouton company, which existed up until nearly the end of the 1920s.

'Your solicitors are going to have to see this,' I told the Major gently, 'and perhaps the police too.'

'Why?' Another glare.

'Because it might have something to do with Victoria's murder,' I told him bluntly.

I'd caught him off guard, and there was a split-second silence before he replied. 'My dear chap, her murder . . .' His voice quivered. '. . . can have nothing to do with the car. That's mine and I shall consider claiming it.'

'Is this question of ownership what you and Mrs Drake talked about the other day?'

'Yes, she showed me her documents on it. Not as good as mine.' He seemed to find difficulty looking me in the eye.

I said nothing.

'No doubt about it,' the Major added more confidently. 'The car's mine. Of course I'm consulting my solicitor. What I want you to do now is find that car and bring it over here.'

I reeled at his cheek. 'Not in my remit,' I said firmly. I could see myself buried in my own Gobi Desert of legal complications.

His eyes bulged in annoyance. 'I'm paying you, aren't I? The rally—'

'Major Hopchurch,' I said patiently. 'The Police's Serious Crime Directorate will be in touch with you if there's the slightest chance that this De Dion Bouton was the motivation for Mrs Drake's murder. No way could I touch that car in the meantime, even if I knew where it was. So far as the Morrises are concerned, it's hers. In any case, it has to be her murder that takes priority now, not the rally.'

'Do you think I don't know that?' The Major deflated quicker than a burst balloon. 'I just want to talk to them about it – the family . . .'

Talk to them? I sighed. 'Were you in love with Victoria Drake in 1968?'

He fired up again. 'She was a married woman.'

'That doesn't necessarily rule love out,' I said drily.

'Get out, Colby.'

I went, but that didn't stop me thinking.

Next on the list was contacting Orton about Meyton as Connor seemed to specialize in being anonymous. His own number was, as I'd been told, permanently on voicemail, so I had no option but to play into Pen Roxton's hands by ringing her stooge.

The stooge sounded alarmed on my behalf. 'Contacting Meyton? Sure that's a good idea, Jack?'

'No, but I have to do it.'

'On your head be it, but I hope it's not.' Chuckle. It wasn't a joke I shared. 'This one might reach him. I ferreted it out – I was told it's the one Mick Smith uses when he wants to contact him. Did it for Pen. Cost her, but worth it, I reckon.'

I tried it on the Wednesday morning, and, glory be, it worked. 'Thought I'd keep in touch, Connor,' I said more cheerfully than I felt.

'So glad you did.'

'You heard about Victoria Drake's murder?'

'I did. You found the body. Why ring me?'

That struck a false note. 'I had a glimpse of the De Dion. The real thing, Connor.'

'A coincidence. So did I.'

'Did you move it for her?'

'It's in a garage on the A21.'

'Let's hope it stays there.'

'You'll be the first to know if it doesn't.' He rang off.

Had I accomplished anything by making contact? I thought I had. If Connor Meyton had designs on the car Victoria's death could have featured in them. I didn't flatter myself that he would be put off by the fact that I was on his case, but just a whiff of police interest never does any harm.

It was beginning to worry me that I had not heard from Helen nor had she returned my calls. I couldn't think of any reason she would be lying low so I put it down to her associating me with the shock she had received on Saturday. The bank holiday was now past and, remembering that Wednesday was one of her Treasure Island days, I decided to drive over to see if anything was amiss.

Someone was there, but her Fiat was not. Nevertheless the door was wide open and in the office I found Julian. Not exactly a substitute for Helen, and I expected to be given a brush-off. He seemed embarrassed rather than angry at my arrival, however.

'I'm expecting someone,' he muttered.

'I'll pop a donation in the box and make myself scarce then. Is Helen around?'

'She took the afternoon off.' He hesitated, as a familiar Volvo saloon drew up. 'That's Tom Morris and his son arriving.'

It was clear that they couldn't be coming for a spot of sightseeing, but with Victoria's murder less than a week earlier it must be important.

'I suggested they needed to see the potential for the De Dion by appreciating what the rally is all about and what it supports,' Julian added.

And maybe you could put in a bid for the De Dion while they're here, I thought meanly. It also seemed very quick for the Morrises to be making plans for the De Dion. I wondered if Patricia knew they were here. 'We're up to nearly fifty entries so far,' Julian added.

'That's good,' I murmured. Indeed it was. There was a limit to the number of cars that could take part in a rally on the British roads and that seemed perilously close to it.

'Terrible thing, this murder,' he put in hastily, perhaps interpreting my expression correctly, 'but the rally preparations have to go on. That's why Tom decided he and Nick should come over now. Patricia didn't feel up to it although she'll be the official owner of the De Dion.'

Not if the Major has anything to do with it, I thought, wondering how much if anything Julian knew about his co-trustee's involvement in the De Dion story. I could not probe further because Tom and Nick were approaching and Julian wanted me out quicker than one can say Gordon-Keeble. At least I thought so. In fact it was he who rushed outside to greet the visitors first, so I merely strolled after him and hung around.

'Have you seen the car yet?' Julian was wasting no time with trivialities.

'Can't rush things. I'm an executor and that gives me responsibilities to observe,' Tom announced.

'After the funeral we'll get things moving with the solicitors,' Nick put in. 'It's all been police, police, police so far.'

Julian managed a polite 'of course'.

I wondered if they realized that the funeral could be much delayed given the circumstances of Victoria's death.

'Will you still be bringing the car over here?' Julian enquired, taking me by surprise to say the least. What was all this about?

'As soon as my co-executor gives his OK,' Tom answered. 'Your garage is secure, is it?'

'As the Bank of England,' Julian assured him – a not too happy comparison I thought in today's economic times.

It was clear that having failed to persuade Victoria to take part in the rally or sell him the car, Julian thought he stood a better chance with the Morrises. He was probably right, but how far had he gone to achieve this? I baulked at the word 'murder' but it was right there on the cards.

I drove back to Frogs Hill, feeling that there was a V8 engine running away without my being in the driving seat. Tom's mother-in-law is murdered and in a few days Tom is busy counting his banknotes from the sale of the car. Did Helen know about it, or had her fellow trustee 'forgotten' to clue her in? And where was the secure lock-up around Cobba House, and how did that affect matters if the car wasn't yet his? Julian had shot off immediately the Morrises had left, possibly to avoid these very questions.

The rally, I reminded myself, was not my affair, but then I changed my mind. Anything to do with that De Dion was my affair. Not only was there Alf's death to bear in mind, but now Victoria Drake's.

When I reached Frogs Hill, I found a pot of gold at the end of my non-rainbow day. Helen's afternoon off *had* included me. Her Fiat 500 was parked in the forecourt and I could see her in the Pits where Len seemed to be showing her around. Maybe he saw her as a replacement for Zoe, or, possibly, Helen was thinking in terms of our doing the restoration on the piles of dusty jewels in Pompeii and Herculaneum. That would be Len's idea of heaven – save that he would need several lifetimes to finish it all.

Helen came straight out when she saw me. I put my arms round her and hugged her, to Len's disapproval. He thinks romance might get in the way of the serious things of life, such as cars.

'What's up?' I asked her.

Something was troubling her and it wasn't the fact that she hadn't seen me for four days. I took her into my garden where we could be alone in the sunshine, and produced a Pimms for her to induce her to stay for a while.

'Now tell me,' I suggested.

'Something's wrong, Jack. I don't know what, but when I came back yesterday Julian and Stanley seemed to be acting very out of character. It must be Victoria's death and the De Dion. Should I tackle them about it or just see what happens? Or do you know what's up? They've been closeted together since I told them about her murder, but they clam up if I enter.'

I told her I had seen them both and that I too found it odd. I could not tell her about the Major's claim to own the car, unfortunately. Not until the police knew about it anyway. And that would not be long now, once I rang either Dave or DCI Fielding.

'I think they're acting on their own accounts, not the trust's,' I told her.

'Over the De Dion and the rally?'

'Yes. Having the car in his own garage would be a good step forward for Julian.'

'Is he doing that?' Helen looked dismayed. 'I didn't know.'

Damn. I'd gone too far. Time to put the brakes on.

'Probably because this is a private arrangement of his, not the trust's.'

She dismissed this impatiently. 'It's too close for me *not* to know. It affects the rally. Jack, are you backing out of this mess now?'

'I never reverse if I can go forward. Don't like the bleeps going off.'

'Good.'

We decided we'd take a walk, so we strolled down to the track running along the Greensand Ridge and walked towards Elvey Farm through the fields. Out here we felt miles away from the world of murder and intrigue and even cars were left behind. I entertained her with funny stories from my oil days – there were some – and that made her laugh.

Finally she sighed as we turned for home. 'That's better, Jack.'

'Good. Would a drink and dinner at Frogs Hill make it better still?'

'They would.'

'And?'

'I don't eat much breakfast.'

I took her in my arms. 'I do a particularly fine line in porridge.'

'With a single red rose stuck in a vase at its side?'

'Two if you like.'

The evening past and then the night . . . A night with Helen. I woke up once in the small hours and saw her hair spread on the pillow. I put out my hand and stroked it, but she woke up and smiled.

'I'm reading my Browning now,' I said. 'Pippa passes.'

'I'm right here.'

'Then all's right with the world.' I reached out for her and indeed it was.

Full of renewed joy of life, I went out to the garden and plucked the rose. I would say I enjoyed the dabbling in the dew but the rose was a happier reminder. There was no red rose in flower but there was an orangey-yellow one almost the colour of her hair, and if I heard Louise sigh as I presented it to Helen it was only for a fleeting moment. Here wrapped in my towelling robe, handing her the marmalade at the breakfast table, life felt good. Not a word was spoken about murder or rallies or even cars. Instead we talked both of nothing and of us. Until the phone rang.

Not about a classic car restoration. Not a call from Dave Jennings. It was DCI Fielding.

'Does the name Connor Meyton mean anything to you?' she began without so much as a comment about the weather.

'Yes.' Caution needed. 'Also to Dave Jennings,' I added. 'He's a four-by-four nicker and seems to be dabbling in the classic car field. Territory formerly south London, now thought to be heading this way. He hasn't yet demonstrated his true colours to us though.'

'Wrong. Let me show them to you. Dave's already here.'

'The De Dion?' I asked in dread. 'Gone already?'

'Nothing to do with the De Dion – as far as I know. But it could be to do with Alf King. It's his garage at Eynsford. You should come.'

Zoe was my instant fear. 'What's wrong?' I asked sharply.

But the DCI had been called away judging by the cracklings on the phone and the line went dead. Len saw me leave, but I didn't stop to fill him in on this. It only takes one to panic. I explained my fear to Helen, leapt into the Alfa and drove straightaway to King's Restorations. As I turned the corner into Lea Lane, something seemed to have happened to the pit of my stomach. I couldn't see the garage. I saw fire engines, I saw smoke in the air and smelt the heavy scent of burnt-out wreckage. Zoe was all I could think about, though. Where was she? When had the fire broken out? Had she been here? Were others here?

I parked where I was in the lane and hotfooted it along to the fire scene, sick at the thought of what I might find. And then, blessed relief, I spotted Zoe, huddled in a blanket sitting by Dave's car, and I rushed up to her.

'Are you all right?' I asked fatuously. Of course she wasn't all right. She was no more all right than Helen and I had been when we found Victoria Drake's body.

Zoe valiantly nodded.

'Dean?' I asked

'He's not here, so he's OK too . . .' Her voice trailed off and I didn't want to press her. I kissed her cheek and went over to Dave who had already spotted my arrival.

Where the office and workshop had been was just a flattened area of dark burnt twisted shapes. Even Dr Who would have baulked at facing these nightmarish sights. Almost worse was the knowledge that this fire couldn't have been accidental as Dave and the DCI were both here. It must be suspected arson.

'Hi,' Dave said. 'Good old mess, isn't it? Scenario: arson. Fire seat there.' He pointed to where Alf's office had been. 'Then it spread to the workshop, paints and so forth, then everywhere else. Nero himself couldn't have done a better job. Roads closed all around, only just opened up when you arrived.'

'When did it happen?' I asked, surveying the remains of Alf's pride and joy.

'Four, five o'clock this morning probably.'

'So no one hurt.' It seemed to me there were a lot of police around for 'no one hurt'.

Dave grimaced. 'I wouldn't say that. Come and have a look. We can't move him until we get clearance from the fire chief.'

Him? Dean? Perhaps Zoe had been wrong about his not being here.

Heat seemed to hit me from all directions as I scrambled into a scene suit. Dave cleared me at the cordon and we picked our way over to the rubble – some of it nearby was still smouldering – where the office would have been. Everything in it would be amongst these charred fragments now. Lying to one side was something worse, however. A blackened shape that could only be a corpse.

'Who is it?' I managed to ask. Then I remembered DCI Fielding's phone call. 'Not Connor Meyton, is it?'

'Not yet known. Possible, but whoever torched the place thoughtfully provided a name for the poor guy lying there. The labs have to do their stuff first, but it might be Mick Smith, erstwhile of the south London car crime scene.'

'And Meyton's one-time partner in crime, I'm told.'

Dave grunted. 'According to our chums in the Met he ran

foul of Meyton. He was maybe shot elsewhere and his body dumped here for disposal.'

'Can the lab tell that?'

'Probably, but there's not much left of him. And before you ask *how* we knew who he might be, there was a call to the Met telling them where to find him.'

'Got the number the call came from?'

I recognized it as soon as Dave passed it over. I'd been ringing it. It was Meyton's.

'So Meyton's involved somehow,' Dave said, when I told him. 'With the Drake murder too?'

'I don't know – yet.' I had a foreboding about this. 'Why bring the body to Eynsford if he was killed elsewhere?'

'Probably as a warning. A "you're next".'

'Me?' A fatuous reply from me. Now I thought more about this. Connor Meyton couldn't be that fond of me.

'Not yet,' Dave said comfortingly. 'More likely Dean Warren. But don't go out on a dark night without a tin hat.'

TEN

Zoe was in no state to drive and in any case her Fiesta, which had been on the forecourt, looked as if it might be permanently out of commission. That was one tiny silver lining in this ghastly affair, I supposed. She was very shaky and I took her to a pub after the police had finished questioning her. She ate virtually nothing of the pasta she ordered, but I think she felt a little better afterwards. I didn't think she should be left alone in her flat when we arrived at Pluckley but she was insistent that she was fine.

'What about Dean?' I suggested cautiously. 'Should I call him?' He had not appeared at the fire scene and I knew the police had gone to his home. Whether he was there or not, I had no idea. I had driven over with police permission to break the news to Doris. As I expected, she had taken the news on the chin, but nevertheless I arranged for a neighbour to stay with her.

'No. He's disappeared.' For a moment I thought I saw a glimpse of something resembling a tear in Zoe's eye but if I did it was hastily despatched in favour of a good attempt at not caring. I was not sure what she meant by 'disappeared'. Was the arsonist after him too? Was he dead? Had he scarpered? I couldn't question her too hard however.

'Any idea what this is all about, Zoe?' I asked her gently. 'Or do you want to leave it awhile?'

'Leave it,' she said promptly. 'Just go, Jack. *Go.*'

I probably wouldn't have obeyed except that the cavalry belatedly blundered in. Through the window I had seen a familiar Porsche. (A Boxster, naturally. Rob would have nothing less.) Zoe had seen him too, and reluctantly went to open the door. I followed her, ensuring I was out of the visitor's sight line.

'Hi,' Rob greeted her, with his best 'I know you're thrilled to see me' grin on. 'Fancy a night out on the town?'

A split-second silence, as I materialized on the scene. 'Not tonight, thanks, Rob,' I told him graciously. 'I'll be off, but Zoe has had a nasty shock. She'll explain what's happened. Look after her, will you?'

'I don't need—' the lady began to yell, but Rob, recovering from his own shock at this unexpectedly welcoming Jack Colby, marched right in and flung a possessive manly arm around her shoulders.

'Sure, Jack.'

I felt somewhat guilty at abandoning her, but better the devil you know, I thought as I started up the Alfa. At least Zoe would have company – of a sort.

And so it seemed would I. No sooner had I collapsed into an armchair at home than my mobile rang. Pen Roxton. Of course I might have known she would be hot on the trail.

'Heard about the fire at Alf King's old place?' she asked.

'Yes. I'm just back from there.'

'Good. We're coming over,' Pen blithely announced with the air of one doing me an enormous favour.

'When, where and who's we?'

'Now. Frogs Hill and Bob Orton. I'm a mile or so away.'

The line went dead, and I groaned with self-pity. I could have done without this, even though it was good news in a way. Bob Orton had access to the crowd who knew Connor Meyton's background and that of Mick Smith. Somehow they tied up with the fire at Alf's garage and possibly therefore his death.

It wasn't hard to see that this was Pen's line too. I almost pitied Meyton with Pen on his trail, and I certainly pitied Orton in his glorious role as her stooge. I had little doubt that she was busy tying all this in with Victoria Drake – and how could I blame her? So was I. Pen could hardly not have known about her murder or that she was the owner of the De Dion, nor would the fact that I found Victoria's body have escaped her. This had all appeared in the press reports. I wondered whom Pen had in her sights for her death. Me perhaps?

She and Bob turned up ten minutes later in Pen's Toyota, which hadn't seen a car wash for many a long year. Bob climbed out with all the swagger of one who thinks he was born to something rather better.

'Nice place,' he said appreciatively, having surveyed the Frogs Hill estate. Surprisingly I think he meant it. I'd put him down as a townie but now I wasn't so sure. 'Sorry to land on you like this, but you know Pen. I've heard about your Dad's Glory Boot.'

'Under restoration,' I said firmly. Pen doesn't know Frogs Hill well enough to know whether the Glory Boot is inside or out, so this was an easy put off. I don't want her poking her nose into it. She'd be bashing out an article on the Giovanni paintings as soon as she laid eyes on them and I'd be figuring in it as the Scrooge who won't let the great British public see their rightful heritage – regardless of the fact that Giovanni is Italian and still alive and kicking. Instead I seated them in the living room, where Pen promptly marched round inspecting every photo she could. She was probably looking for one of Louise, but if so, she was disappointed. I'd hidden it the first time I brought Helen here.

Pen then produced from her battered rucksack every gadget known to technology including a voice-memo recorder. 'So tell me, Jack,' she began briskly. 'How does this fire tie up with Victoria Drake's murder?' She shot the voice-memo under my nose. It got up it quicker than Pen herself.

'I wanted to ask you that. *Does* it tie up?'

'No games, Jack. It must do. And *you* somehow forgot to tell me about her death *and* the De Dion. So is Connor Meyton involved with murder and fire? Bob thinks so.'

Bob grinned nervously, clearly taking his lead from Pen. Mistake, usually. 'Not that I knew the victim,' he said virtuously, as though that ruled him out of any conspiracy theories in the making. 'I know about the De Dion of course; Pen here said Mrs Drake was the owner, and I've heard how Meyton works.'

I can do virtuous too. 'I'll suggest DCI Fielding calls you.'

'Great,' he said. 'I'll enjoy being police flavour of the month.'

The guy had charm, I thought, and maybe Pen was smitten with him. If so, work came first for her. 'Bit of a coincidence

you finding the Drake woman's body, Jack, *which* you overlooked reporting to me.'

'Too busy reporting to the police, Pen.'

'Then you'll know if Meyton's a murder suspect.'

'Steady, Pen,' I said. 'He's no more under suspicion than
I am.'

'*Are* you under suspicion, Jack?' Dulcet tones from Pen.

I sighed. 'Let's stop fencing, Pen. What's in this for you?'

Pen chuckled. 'A story. A great one. Heard there was a body
found at the fire. Went round to see Dean Warren.'

Breathtaking. 'Before or after the police?'

'Just after,' she said complacently. 'I followed them.'

Dave had told me Dean hadn't come to the fire scene because
he claimed he was ill. Zoe had come though. My brave Zoe.
I forced myself to crawl to Pen, mentally that is. Full marks
for her persistence. 'What did he think caused the fire?'

'Late-night revellers dropping a match.'

'Sure,' I said. 'Did he put a name to these late-night
revellers?'

'Oddly enough, no.'

Which might mean Dean was taking the fire as a serious
warning.

'Whose body is it, Jack?' Pen persisted doggedly.

'Is it likely I would tell you if I knew?'

'No, but—'

'Could be Mick Smith's,' Bob announced, knocking to
smithereens any hope I might have had of keeping confidential
information to myself. 'Could go like this: Meyton falls out
with Mick and moves south. Meyton sees a good opportunity
in getting Alf King's garage cheap as a front for his less than
legal activities, including getting hold of this De Dion, but has
to rid himself of Alf who won't sell. Mick finds out, blackmails
him – Connor gets rid of him.'

'Flaw,' I pointed out. 'Why burn the place down if he wanted
to buy it?'

'Easy,' Pen said dismissively. 'Dean Warren is causing trouble,
so Meyton changes plans and gives him a warning by showing
what happens to sneaks who get in the way of his trading
arrangements. Being close to the Channel, Kent's a good place.'

'Many poets have felt the same,' I murmured.

'Matthew Arnold's Dover Beach,' Bob picked up in a show of erudition. 'Oscar Wilde too. He liked it too. And that other chap, Gough. Some sweet Kentish hill. Know him?'

I blinked. 'No.'

'Victorian. Good stuff.'

Pen was goggling too, but not about poetry. 'Mick Smith,' she said firmly.

'Certainly, Pen.' Bob mock saluted her. 'Pen wanted me to ask around about the gent, Jack, but he seems to have gone off the scene.'

'So has Meyton. No harm in telling them that. There was talk before the fire about his plans to buy Alf King's garage but then he softly and silently vanished away.'

'Lewis Carroll,' Bob said, pleased. 'That's said to be a danger sign with Meyton – vanishing. Buying a garage was way out of line for him. His usual game is to find cars to order, then charge one heck of a high commission.'

'Nothing illegal about that,' I said, 'unless the cars are hot.'

'You got it, Jack. Except when things go wrong as they did with Mick Smith. Meyton's a guy not to tangle with. Liable to land up as food for the fishes.'

'Dean reckons it was only the records Meyton wanted to see,' Pen said. 'Then you came along, Jack. Not only are you snooping around about possible murder but, as Meyton must see it, you've put your own nark in there.'

Zoe. That was scary. I hadn't thought of that angle. 'Have you had any luck on contacting Meyton, Bob?' I asked. I like to sleep at nights and I wanted Zoe to do so as well. 'The police are going to be asking you.'

'No. Perpetual voicemail on all of them. I'll give you another one though.'

Pen was getting restless. 'So you confirm there's a link, Jack, between this Meyton and the Drake murder. The Old Bill must think so too. They're not daft.'

'Generous of you to admit it,' I murmured.

'They just don't have the resources that I do.'

'They have me.'

Pen smiled sweetly. 'That's why we're going to work together more closely, Jack.'

'Like hell we are,' I said without malice.

Beware the Greeks bearing gifts, I thought, watching Pen and Bob drive off. I wasn't entirely clear as to why she'd come. It could mean she was storing up brownie points for some plan of her own; or it could mean that she herself was haring off in a completely different direction and wanted me off the track by roping Bob Orton in. I hadn't forgotten that little trip she made to Treasure Island.

Accordingly, I made a plan of my own for the next morning. After dropping in to see how Zoe was, I drove over to Harford Lee, not least because there was a message from Helen asking me to come as soon as possible. She had sounded fairly frantic. Something was brewing, she said, and I should get there before boiling point. It seemed to me that given the Major's temperament and Julian's collecting zeal, that boiling point was always close, although I granted there was currently more at stake. I seemed to be in the middle of a triangle, the three points being Treasure Island, the Morrises and as always Connor Meyton. The question was which way to turn first. I'd like to think I was pulling the strings but at present it seemed more like a game of blind man's buff in which I was reaching out to anything that might give me a clue where I was. Driving blindfold into any of these three situations would be dangerous, as Victoria Drake and Alf King had found to their cost.

Helen had told me to come straight to Burnt Barn Bottom, but as I drove past Cobba House I saw two cars parked outside, Helen's Fiat and the Bentley. Treasure Island was locked up, so I walked back until I heard raised voices in the garden. In fact raised was understating the case. Julian and the Major were in fine form.

'It's my car, isn't it? Do what I damn well like with it and that's that.'

'We had an agreement.' Julian was more controlled but definitely in high-pitch mode.

To my dismay, Helen too was taking an active role. When I opened the gate to join the party I could see Julian and the

Major sitting at a table on the terrace, with Helen pacing around in agitation. She had not yet seen me and was shouting, 'What agreement? And why don't I know about it?'

It was clear that the pot had boiled and there was trouble afoot. When they noticed me, Helen came straight over. I'd never seen her really angry before, and a detached part of my mind registered that it suited her. She looked aflame with beauty. The rest of my mind tried to focus on the De Dion.

'What's happened?' I asked, when I reached the terrace.

'No damn business of yours,' the Major promptly yelled at me.

'That, Major Hopchurch,' I said cordially, 'is where you are wrong. If this argument is about the De Dion Bouton then it is a part of an ongoing case for the Serious Crime Directorate. Very much ongoing now that Alfred King's garage has been burnt down.'

That stopped them all. Helen looked horrified. 'When?' she cried. 'Is Zoe all right? And Doris? I should ring her.'

She didn't add, 'You should have told me,' but there was no need. Her reproachful eyes told me that. With so much going on and my preoccupation with Zoe, I had not thought to do so. Stupid, *stupid*. 'They're both OK,' I told her, 'but it would be good—'

'My De Dion is a private matter,' the Major interrupted, impatient at this diversion.

'Nothing's private in a murder case, where it might have relevance to the victim.' I felt a first-class prig but I was beginning to get extremely bored with these two jokers.

'The car's found and your job for us is over, Colby.'

'Certainly—' I began, but Helen intervened.

'No way, Stanley. I too need to know what's going on here.'

Julian and the Major looked at each other, and Julian climbed down. 'It's a matter of ownership, Helen. In fact Stanley believes he is the rightful owner of the car. The matter is being referred to his solicitors in Canterbury.'

Helen turned another reproachful eye on me and then the Major. 'And Stanley didn't seem to think I needed to know about it, either.'

'Couldn't tell you,' the Major said gruffly. 'Victoria Drake had the same documents as I did, but showing her as owner.' Helen's eyes grew rounder and rounder, and he added hastily, 'It's all nonsense of course. No woman in Edwardian times would go around pinching automobiles. If anyone did the pinching it was my grandfather.'

By Edwardian women he must have a pretty picture of ladies in long motoring coats, hats and veils in mind rather than militant suffragettes, I thought, but I nodded encouragingly, as Helen seemed incoherent at the Major's unhelpful explanation. 'She might be capable of hanging on to a car that wasn't hers though,' I suggested, 'if she thought her love had been spurned.'

'True,' Julian grudgingly agreed, 'but in this case Stanley has the valid claim. His solicitor agrees.'

'Has he or she seen Mrs Drake's provenance documents yet?' I asked.

Silence. 'No,' the Major finally admitted.

Neither seemed inclined to tell me more about the argument in progress, so I kicked off on my own track. 'Is that why, Julian,' I asked gently, 'this disagreement broke out, because you expected to be able to buy the car before or after the rally from Mrs Drake or the Morrises?'

'Or now from Stanley,' Julian added stiffly.

'Nothing wrong with that,' I said, 'if the Major does own it.'

'You're not feeble minded, are you?' the Major threw at me. 'I've shown you enough to convince a jackass. You're no lawyer.'

'No,' I agreed, 'but I'm associated with the law.'

'Then you'll know I can damn well do what I like with my own property.'

'Not in this case, Stanley,' Julian said. 'We've an agreement.'

The wheel seemed to have come full circle.

'*What is the problem?*' I said, emphasizing each word in a crescendo. Volume seemed to be winning the day with this pair.

Helen answered for her two suddenly silent co-trustees. 'Stanley has agreed with Patricia Morris that she and he will jointly own the car no matter who has the better claim.'

I was taken aback. The last thing I would have expected. It didn't seem Major-like behaviour. 'That sounds reasonable,' I said cautiously. 'The trust could negotiate with both parties which would be difficult but surely possible.'

'Unfortunately,' Julian retorted, 'Tom Morris is insisting that Patricia pursues her case for complete ownership.'

'And does Patricia want to do that?'

'In that household, of course. She's gone back on her word with Stanley. And I,' Julian added vengefully, 'have been led up the garden path both by you, Stanley, and by Nick Morris.'

'In what way?' I asked.

'I was sponsoring that dreadful young man to drive the De Dion in the rally, provided I was first in line to buy the car.'

'Julian has omitted the vital phrase beginning with *if*,' the Major declared with awful clarity. '*If* the decision of owner- ship went against me. He has been negotiating behind my back and undermining my claim.'

I still couldn't see it. 'Where do you go from here?' I asked firmly.

Helen looked weary. 'Tell him, Stanley.'

The Major cleared his throat. 'Patricia has agreed the De Dion can appear in the rally, but only, it seems, if I withdraw my claim to the car.'

'Have you agreed to that?' I could see the problem now. Tom Morris was pulling the strings with a vengeance.

'I'm thinking of doing so,' the Major muttered.

'You're a fool, Stanley,' Julian said, cold with anger.

'And you, Julian, are a nincompoop.' The Major's eyes blazed with fury. 'I wouldn't sell you my car if—'

I intervened for Helen's sake. '*Stop!*'

It was so sudden that both men did. All three turned to me, a Solomon come to judgement. I couldn't live up to his standard, but I could make a stab at it. 'In the short term, you all want the same result. You want the rally to succeed and the De Dion to be in it. But you're about to sacrifice the first for the second? Surely you can squabble about ownership afterwards.'

Helen leapt in on cue. 'I'll go over to see the Morrises,' she said, 'to try to sort the situation out. Jack's right. Let's concentrate on making the rally a success.'

There were reluctant nods from her fellow trustees.

'I'll go with her,' I said, to even less enthusiasm. This was no mere desire on my part to be alone with Helen. Great though that would be, the meeting with the Morrises would be hard work. Even so I wanted to go, as somewhere I sniffed there was a factor I was missing, and it could lie with the Morrises.

By agreement, I took the lead and fixed the meeting (with some reluctance on the part of the Morrises) for the following Monday, and then returned to Frogs Hill, while Helen took up what she described as 'normal' Treasure Island duties. It seemed to me, however, that this morning's pandemonium was getting to be 'normal', and I was looking forward to a peaceful lull in my own 'normal' duties.

I caught up with some paperwork, then had some lunch, and then strolled out from the farmhouse, coffee mug in hand, to enjoy the sight of the sun, which was beaming down on the Pits. Within, I could spot Len and Zoe happily—

Zoe?

I plonked the mug down on the gravel and rushed inside. There they were – my trusty team of two working harmoniously on the – yes – Zoe's Fiesta. I was almost glad to see it. Zoe was clad in her usual overalls and seemingly engrossed in her work. Len was busily pretending he hadn't seen me.

'Hi,' I said weakly.

Zoe glanced up. 'Hi,' she said and went back to work.

Normal life resumed – and thank heaven for it. No more would be spoken of Alf and his garage or of Dean Warren.

Or would it? Could Zoe have anything valuable to add to that story? It was possible, but I knew from experience I wouldn't get anything out of Zoe until the dust had settled. There was one further blessing. There was no sign of Rob. True it was early days, but if he was permanently back in the Zoe picture I wouldn't count on that being the case for long.

*   *   *

The atmosphere at Lamberhurst was frosty, to say the least. Helen and I were the warmest things around. The Major had been anxious to come with us, but fortunately Julian had taken our side. Helen had come over on Sunday, and we had spent a happy day (and night) together. The Morrises' home was a modern house on the far side of the village from Shoulder Mutton Green, and looked as opulently plush as I would have expected. Keeping up with Joneses was evident in everything from the stylish Tree of Life door knocker to the designer dog who feebly woofed as we went inside. Even he looked downcast.

Tom led us through to the garden, which was as designer conscious as the house, with neat weedless lawns, and bedding plants that obediently kept to strict rules by not sprawling around. Patricia was hunched in a chair between the two important members of the family – as they no doubt saw it. Helen and I were allotted two upright garden chairs facing the enemy battalions. Perhaps I exaggerated the importance of this factor, but somehow I didn't think so.

Helen and I had agreed that she should lead the discussion, so that I could play silent sleuth and take over if the conversation seemed to be going awry. Officially we were there to check the position of the De Dion for the rally, rather than whether it had bearing on Victoria's murder. Unofficially I had it very much in mind. I had had few clues as to the direction of the police investigation; all I knew for sure was that the inquest and burial had been adjourned.

'In the circumstances are you happy for the De Dion to take part in the rally, Mrs Morris?' Helen pointedly addressed her question to her.

'Of course,' Tom promptly answered for her. 'Provided Major Hopchurch gives up his claim to own half of it. I thought I had made that clear.'

'His claim is for all of it, I believe,' Helen said. 'Although I understand he has offered to go halves with you on the ownership, Mrs Morris, which is generous.'

'He seems a sweet old thing,' Patricia said uncertainly.

A sweet old thing? I wondered if we were talking about the same man.

Tom snorted. 'He's out to wheedle you out of your rights. That car's only taking part in the rally if he gives up this stupid claim.'

'He won't do that.' Patricia changed her tone. 'But I *am* sure the car belonged to my mother and now to me. The Major did suggest though that Nick and I drove in it in the rally.'

'Did he?' Tom's face darkened. 'We decide who drives in it. What's the old codger think he's up to?'

'*I'm* driving it,' Nick shouted.

'I take it it's all settled legally?' I hastily asked, seeing all the signs of a diversionary row breaking out.

'Not yet. Our solicitors, Benson & Hawkes, have all the papers to do with the car though,' Tom informed me. 'My poor mother-in-law must have given them to Benson after your sweet old thing, Pat, came over to bully her.'

'Is that how she worded it?' Helen asked.

'Yes,' Tom shot back at her, just as Pat answered:

'No.'

'The problem is this.' Helen took charge again. 'We need to know where we are for the rally before we can begin publicizing it, and there's only two months to go now. If ownership is still in dispute and the Major won't give up his claim, are you still telling us that you won't let the car take part in the rally?'

'Yes,' Tom said instantly.

'No,' Nick objected. 'I'm going to drive it, Dad.'

'It seems not,' Helen said coolly, 'if the Major has to give up his claim before your parents will allow the car to appear in the rally. He won't do it.'

Father and son glowered at each other.

'Mum—' Nick began.

'*No!*' Tom thundered.

Helen sighed. 'I take it therefore that we can't have the De Dion in the rally.'

'Not until that madman gives up his claim.'

'Isn't that for the solicitors to decide?' Nick persevered. 'Possession being nine tenths of the law, we own it anyway. So the De Dion will be there. *And* me, Helen darling.'

Helen darling didn't move an inch. 'Not unless Mrs Morris agrees.'

Patricia hesitated, looking in appeal at her husband.

'I think you'll find Julian Carter will dole out a fair sum to buy the car,' Nick said casually. 'He's after Mum to sell it to him.'

So we hadn't quite heard the full story from Julian. There was a look in Helen's eye that said he would be hearing from her.

'You didn't tell me that, Pat,' Tom said grimly.

'Why should I?' Pat said with a show of spirit. 'It's my car. In fact I think it's a very good offer.'

'I told you to leave this business to me,' Tom yelled at her. 'And that goes for you, too, Nick.'

'It's my car,' Patricia said with flushed face.

'We *all*—'

There was a gentle cough. The others had their backs to her, so I was the only person who had noticed that Brenda Carlyle was standing in the garden. She must have come through the side gate while the fury was raging.

'Actually no,' she said hesitantly, and instantly had everyone's full attention.

'No what?' Tom hurled at her.

'You don't own the De Dion. None of you does.'

'What the hell are you talking about, Brenda? Who owns it then?'

'According to Mr Benson, it seems I do.'

ELEVEN

I can only describe the stunned disbelief at Brenda's revelation as seeing someone you thought to be a car lover proceed to chuck a can of red paint over a Rolls-Royce. Such things do not happen, although one look at Brenda should have been proof enough. Her happy smile indicated she was under the impression that she was amongst friends who would rejoice at her good fortune.

The stunned period then ended. After a string of expletives that would make a trooper blush, Tom declared, 'I'm ringing that creep Benson *now*. He told us we get the lot except for a couple of bequests. Some bequest!'

Galvanized out of stupor, Nick rushed after Tom as he strode into the house. Patricia took one scared look at us and scuttled after them.

Helen drew a long breath. 'What now?' she said flatly.

I could see how shaken she was. Once again her plans for publicizing the rally were thrown into the melting pot and this pot had come out of the blue. Brenda was clearly shocked at the Morrises' reaction and hadn't yet foreseen the ramifications of her announcement. I had – all too clearly.

'Here,' I said to her, drawing up a chair. 'You should sit down. You're going to need that.' She would. Nevertheless I was watching her carefully. Her arrival seemed too good – or bad – not to be timed. Surely no one could be that innocent of the ways of the world?

Brenda did look genuinely bewildered, however, and took up my suggestion. 'They seem upset,' she ventured. 'It was Victoria's wish, however, and I would have thought she would have told them.'

'Perhaps you misunderstood what the solicitor said,' Helen said hopefully.

False step. 'I did not,' Brenda said with dignity. 'I'm quite clear on the subject, thank you.'

After that put-down, we sat there in silence while I tried to make sense of the situation. The silence went on for so long I thought the Morrises might have gone straight to the pub to drown their sorrows, but more probably they were drawing up hasty plans for attack. If so, would that imply Brenda's statement was true? If not, Tom would have been back in the garden with the news faster than a Ferrari.

After twenty-odd minutes the Morris family came storming back, this time presenting a united front. Needless to say, Tom was spokesman. 'That jackass Thomas confirmed your claim, Brenda. Now kindly explain to us, if you please, how this came about.'

'There's no point taking that tone with me,' Brenda said bravely. 'I don't see why I should tell you anything, except that it was obviously Victoria's decision.'

'It isn't in the will we hold,' Patricia said instantly.

'Benson said she made a new will a year or two ago,' Brenda said. 'Perhaps she didn't discuss it with you.'

'A new will?' Patricia snorted. 'I don't believe it – and if it's true who pushed her into that? Why leave it all to you and not her own daughter? It's just not fair.'

I might have felt sorry for her except that I'd noted the look of sheer hatred she shot at Brenda. It spoke not just of disappointment and anger, both of which would have been understandable in the circumstances, but of something more personal. It showed a tough side to Patricia Morris that I had not seen before.

'It's only the car she's left to me,' Brenda said quietly. 'And as for the suggestion that I influenced her, that's ridiculous. Although I demurred, Victoria insisted I should have it. She believed very strongly that the De Dion is part of France's heritage and should be displayed there. My French neighbour and I plan to marry and I shall live there permanently, so I shall ensure that Victoria's wish is honoured.'

'And what,' Tom sneered, 'if that old gargoyle Hopchurch claims it's his car?'

In the excitement I'd clean forgotten about the car's disputed provenance and from the expressions around me it seemed I wasn't alone in this. Would the Major extend his fifty-fifty offer to Brenda? I wondered.

'Mr Benson is looking into that matter,' Brenda said shortly. 'Until proven otherwise, however, the car is mine subject to probate.'

Tom eyed her. 'No way. You took advantage of an old lady and we'll fight it.'

Brenda dismissed this so quickly I knew the solicitor must have discussed it with her. 'You'll lose,' she said briefly.

'You old bat,' Nick said almost admiringly. 'You're going to flog the De Dion to the gargoyle, aren't you? Settle with him out of court.'

'You can't,' Patricia shouted, now fully geared up for the fight. 'If you're so bloody keen to do what my mother wanted, you'll have to bear in mind that she didn't want it shown at this crazy rally of theirs.'

I felt for poor Helen but wisely she seemed to be keeping a tight rein on her feelings. Not one word of protest did she utter. I also felt rather sorry for Nick, who was already in panic.

'But I'm driving it in the rally, Mum,' he cried. 'No doubt about that.'

'I'd say there was quite a lot of doubt.' For the first time a note of tartness entered Brenda's voice.

Helen's tight rein began to crack. 'Mrs Carlyle, perhaps I should telephone you at a more suitable time to talk this over.'

'We'll settle it now,' Nick said viciously. 'Don't forget I hold the only keys to the garage where my gran put it, Brenda.'

'Perhaps you do,' Brenda said primly. 'However my De Dion is now in the formal possession of Benson & Hawkes. It was moved early this morning.'

Nick lunged forward so quickly I was on my feet to stop him attacking her. Luckily, Nick must have realized he'd be doing himself no favours by throttling Brenda, and retreated.

'Keep your cool, Nick,' Tom barked at him. 'We'll have a word with this Major Hopchurch. He'll see this farce is ended. He's got a claim out against it, so he'll want it in the rally – and you can drive it.'

A quick turnabout, I thought admiringly.

'The Major,' Brenda said firmly, 'is in no position to promise you anything. Probate is not yet granted and until it is and the solicitors involved have looked into the question of his claim, Mr Benson is the sole executor and responsible for the car.'

Tom bristled, as this new challenge presented itself. 'I'm my mother-in-law's executor.'

'I'm afraid not. I understand from Mr Benson that the new will was the same as its predecessor save for the De Dion and an executor. Mr Benson remains one of the two, however.'

'Who's the other then? Patricia?' Tom asked.

'Alfred King.'

'We can still hold the rally,' Helen said desperately as we set off home. 'The De Dion isn't the be-all and end-all so far as that's concerned.'

I pulled my mind back from Brenda's bombshell to consider this. 'No, but its presence could double, even triple, the takings.'

'I was trying to be optimistic.' She pulled a face. 'Who's going to break the news to Stanley and Julian?'

I thought this through. There was no doubt about it that the number of those with reason to wish Victoria Drake out of the way had omitted one major player. Brenda Carlyle's role in this affair was increasingly mysterious. Nor did the fact that Patricia Morris didn't inherit the car as she had expected rule her out of suspicion, nor her husband or son. There were others too, amongst whom were the Mad Major and Julian Carter, both of whom had seemingly their own separate agendas where the De Dion and Victoria were concerned.

We agreed that Helen would break the news to the Major and I would talk to Julian. First I needed to talk to Dave and via him get this news to DCI Fielding – though it was possible she already knew through the solicitors. Helen occupied herself with a visit to my Lagonda.

Dave is usually fairly laconic on the phone but I had his full attention when I explained the rumpus. He had heard about the bequest because Solicitor Benson had rung him about moving the car.

'Wily old bird, isn't she?' was Dave's comment on Brenda.

'My jury's out,' I said. 'OK for me to talk to Benson direct? I'd like to know where the car is and how it's guarded.'

'Fire ahead. Talking of firing, about that arson case and Mick Smith . . .'

'The body wasn't his?'

'It was.'

It looked as if Pen and Bob's theory about Meyton was right, I thought, as I hung up. On the other hand, Meyton wasn't in the habit of leaving obvious clues, even given the fact that he was giving a warning to Dean Warren. That left me with another niggle and in the crime world niggles can be the difference between life and death.

Helen and I drove to Old Lilleys and Harford Lee respectively in our separate cars. Unfriendly, but sensible, she told me. She had enjoyed wandering around my 'estate' while I had been on the phone.

'Frogs Hill seems an enchanted place,' she said.

'I think so too. For me it has memories, of course. My parents, growing up, all the people who've come here over the years.'

'Was this your married home too?'

'No, for which my parents were duly grateful. Eva wasn't the calmest of daughters-in-law.' I told her a little more of my early brief marriage and daughter.

'Was your marriage spent in Kent?' she asked me.

'Yes, but luckily a reasonable distance from here. Canterbury. Then I scuttled back here to lick my wounds.'

'That's what's so enchanting about Frogs Hill.'

'Define?' I asked her.

'It's an away place. Over the hills and far away.'

'You make it sound like Harry Potter's Hogwarts.'

'Different kind of magic.'

'Helen – after the rally . . .'

'That's a different place too. Let's get the rally over first.'

I found Julian at Cobba House where he was working that day. He looked completely thrown at seeing me and even more at my news.

'Brenda Carlyle?' he asked blankly. 'It can't be true. The

woman who gave us coffee and biscuits that morning? Sure
you're right about this, Jack? Why on earth should the De
Dion be bequeathed to her? She doesn't look like a car lover
to me.'

'Maybe not, but that's the situation.'

He looked more cheerful. 'Good. If she's not a classic buff
herself, she'll sell it to me. I'll get on to that right away.'

'What about Stanley's claim?' I asked gently.

He was thrown only for a moment. 'We can use that as a
handle to buy her out, now that his crazy idea of a fifty-fifty
offer to Patricia Morris is off. I'll pay her the probate valua-
tion and more if I can have it right away. I'll talk to her
solicitor. She's an old woman. She won't care. She'll be happy
with a bit of cash.'

Sexist, ageist – I was beginning to dislike Julian. 'Somehow
I don't think so,' I warned him. 'Women are capable of infinite
variety. Victoria apparently wanted Brenda to take the car to
France and live happily ever after there.'

Julian's eyes took on a somewhat manic look. 'All right.
She can sell it to me and I'll take it to bloody France for her.
After the rally. Is it still in that garage on the A21? Benson
never got back to me on my offer to store it.'

So that was what Julian had had in mind. 'No,' I answered
him. 'Benson had it removed this morning. The Morrises have
the keys to that garage which might have influenced his decision. I doubt if even Brenda knows where it is now. There's
still Stanley's claim for him to sort out.'

At that moment I heard a car drive up – the true lover of
motor cars can identify an engine as easily as a dachshund's
bark from a Rottweiler's. The car engine I could hear was a
Bentley and it was sweeping to a grand halt in front of Julian's
house. Through the window I saw a red-faced and purposeful
Major emerging and, from the far side, Helen. Julian ushered
us all into his living room, as his office would have been too
cramped for full-scale histrionics from four people. Within
seconds we were plunged into battle again. Helen winked at
me, so I knew whatever had happened after she had broken
the news to Stanley it couldn't be too bad – at least for her.
Not for us, anyway.

The phone rang just as hostilities began, however, and Julian went out to answer it. It took ten minutes for him to return, during which time Helen tried to talk to Stanley on routine rally matters, while I waited impatiently for the next development. And development there certainly was. Julian returned, looking bemused.

'Bad news?' I asked.

'Far from it. It was from Benson.'

The Major went red with annoyance. 'That was for me. I told him I'd be here.'

'No, he wanted to speak to me, but he's holding on for a word with you, Stanley.'

'What did he want, Julian?' Helen asked, as the Major stomped off.

'He's sending the De Dion over this afternoon. To be kept in my secure garage,' he announced complacently.

Alice in Wonderland was back in town. Curiouser and curiouser. Julian was an interested party in this affair, so why on earth should Benson suggest the car come here? Then it was the Major's turn again. Hardly to my surprise, he returned looking annoyed.

'Benson rang me earlier to tell me Mrs Carlyle was concerned that we might be worried about the rally because of my claim and this news about her inheritance. So she has suggested – against that fool solicitor's advice – that the rally goes ahead with the De Dion either just displayed or driven in it as we wish, Julian. We could sort out ownership questions, if not before, then afterwards.'

So why was he looking annoyed? I wondered. This seemed good news to me.

Because of course there was a catch. While we were still reeling from this shock, the Major added, 'Just one thing though.' A cough. 'I told her I wanted Nick Morris to drive the De Dion in the rally. Only fair for the Morrises.' Benson was ringing back to tell me the answer. 'Mrs Carlyle doesn't agree.'

'Then I'll drive it,' Julian announced, agony writ large on his face as he saw the prize so nearly slipping from his grasp.

'Afraid not, Julian. She's happy to be passenger, but she's got someone else in mind to drive it.'

'Lewis Hamilton maybe?' Julian said angrily. 'Stirling Moss?'

Another cough from the Major, then: 'No. I don't like it, but I've agreed. She wants you to drive it, Jack.'

Helen travelled back with the Major to collect her car, and I returned to Frogs Hill, still juggling the events of the day and hoping to make sense of them. He had reluctantly cheered up, perhaps in the hope that I would persuade Brenda that Nick not I should drive. Fat chance of that. There was a warm glow in my stomach every time I thought of driving that glorious De Dion. It was the only piece of this crazy jigsaw that I could grasp. I'd driven an early Panhard and an even earlier Daimler, but never a De Dion or indeed any car with such a pedigree as this one. Why me? I couldn't help but wonder. I had no special chemistry with Brenda Carlyle. I quite liked her, but I had gained no impression from her that I was flavour of the month in any respect.

I decided to sleep on it before I rang Brenda with my thanks – even then I would not take it for granted that this was a firm date. A lot of water might flow under the bridge before the rally. Julian could step in with an offer, or Tom Morris contest the will on Patricia's behalf. Nick Morris might twist Brenda round to favour him as driver, or the Major decide he wanted to drive it himself. To crown it all, there was always the possibility of Connor Meyton waiting in the wings, although I hoped he was a ghostly spectre rather than a physical threat. His interest in the De Dion might have waned. Somehow I couldn't believe that.

Just as I closed the farmhouse door the bell rang. Zoe stood belligerently on the doorstep, her body language telling me she didn't want to be here, but she had no choice.

'Come in,' I suggested wearily, not sure I was up to this. She duly followed me to the living room.

'I've got to tell you this, Jack.' She plonked herself on the sofa. 'But only because of that police job of yours. I don't *want* to.'

'That's obvious. Is it Rob?' I asked, almost hoping it was.

'Dean.'

'Have you seen or heard from him since the fire?'

'No.' She didn't seem inclined to continue, so I pushed further. This sounded ominous. 'Think anything has happened to him?'

'Don't know. Probably not. Not yet anyway. He might just be lying low. Has Dave Jennings talked about him?'

'Not to me.'

'Dean's running scared, Jack.'

'That figures. Of Meyton?'

'Yes.' She was retreating inside herself again, trembling. It was clear she was not yet over her ordeal.

'Let me make it easy for you, Zoe,' I tried. 'Is Dean mixed up with Alf King's death? Did he do Meyton's dirty work and loosen that nut?'

'He says not, and I believe him. He says he was fond of Alf.'

'Would he have done it if he'd been forced to?'

The pause was long enough to make me realize that's what she had been fearing. 'I don't think so,' she said uncertainly. 'He isn't the sort to take direct action himself or for anyone to entrust him with a mission like that. He'd chicken out and run away. Thing is . . .'

'Go on,' I said gently when she ground to a halt.

'I think he knows who did do it. He made a few remarks that were odd and he can't keep his mouth shut, can Dean. That didn't seem too bad when I met him at the funeral, but it got worse.'

'Because of the fire?'

'Yes, but it wasn't just that. Dean was upset over those records vanishing. He says he took them to Meyton.' She glared at me. 'Now you're going to say I should have told you.'

'No, but you should have done so.'

'Well, I didn't,' she yelled at me. 'Do you want to hear the rest of this or not?'

'Yes, please,' I said placatingly. 'I already guessed about

the records, if that's any comfort. It's Meyton I'm interested in. Did he do the dirty work himself as regards Alf?'

'I don't know. Dean thinks it's more likely he ordered one of his mates to do it.'

'Don't tell me – Mick Smith?'

'That's my guess.'

'Is this all theory, Zoe? Or pillow talk?'

'Jack!' She flushed. 'Too far.'

'Zoe, I have to know.'

We exchanged glares (although I like to think of mine as an implacable gaze) and she capitulated. 'Not pillow talk. Garage or pub and phone talk. I did have a call from Dean. That's why the fire was a warning to him and why the body was there.'

'Why would Meyton kill Mick just as a warning to Dean? Tough on Mick, isn't it?'

'Dean said Meyton was annoyed now the police were interested in Alf's death.'

'Even so, for Meyton to kill Mick makes it clearer that Alf didn't die through an accident. Not a good move.' Something odd here, I thought. 'Unless of course Mick was blackmailing him.'

Zoe looked alarmed. 'Dean's a loose cannon, Jack. If he even hinted to Meyton that he had seen Mick Smith around the garage at the time of Alf's death, Meyton might think he had got rid of one blackmailer only to find another.' She paused. 'Am I seeing bogeys where there are only bushes and not many of those either?'

'No, I don't think you are, but take care if you're in touch with Dean again. And even if you're not.' I prayed that Zoe wouldn't realize she herself might be in the firing line if Meyton decided I'd planted her at Dean's garage as my informant or that Dean could very well have confided any information about Mick Smith to her.

'*Not.*' A pause. 'Rob and I are giving it another whirl. His floozie's history.'

'Good.' Rob Lane being back was *good*? This was the sharpest U-turn of my life.

What Zoe had told me about Meyton didn't affect the De

Dion – yet. It would be child's play for him to have found out where Victoria Drake had secreted the car that night, although I reasoned that if he had discovered that, why not pinch the car? Had he killed her? Had Mick Smith killed her? Or had Meyton himself done so? If so, I hoped Julian's security on his garage was as good as he claimed. To me it was now quite likely that Connor Meyton was still in the De Dion picture. What he was planning to do there, however, was another matter.

On Wednesday morning, I returned from a trip to Charing Police HQ to find a note pinned to the door. In typical style it read: 'In the pub, Pen and Bob.' As invitations go this wasn't warm, but Pen's like that.

I debated whether to give it a miss and decided I could not take the risk. Whatever Pen wanted, I knew it would be in her interests not mine, but sometimes, just sometimes, that worked. And Bob, I reminded myself, was still my only line of contacting Meyton. He claimed to be out of touch, and indeed the new number he had given me was now dead, but I had my hopes. With Pen breathing down his neck, he might well be carving himself out some leeway.

Our local pub in Piper's Green was busy, even though it was a weekday lunchtime. That's because its sandwiches are an art form in themselves and partly because there's nowhere else to go to eat – except Liz Potter's garden centre. Liz, the lady in my life a few years back and now a chum, does a good line in snack lunches but garden centres aren't on Pen's radar and Bob might faint without strong liquor.

I found them both at the bar, and we moved to a table where we could all three sit without looking like the three wise monkeys all in a row.

'We've got a story, Jack,' Pen began, when I'd joined them with my modest half pint.

'Will I like it?'

She chuckled. 'Doubt it. Bob wants to warn you, though, and that's OK with me.'

'How good of you both,' I said warmly.

'We're serious,' Bob said reprovingly. 'Thought you might want to be in on it.'

'Pull the other one.'

'Seen today's press, Jack?' Bob fished in a bag and produced the *Graphic*.

Something went *clang* inside me, like the snap of a clutch cable. Wednesday was publication day. There was someone I recognized on the front page and it wasn't a grinning blonde. It was Nick Morris looking mournful under a heading 'My Vow'. There I read that in the tragic aftermath of the tragic death of his grandmother, Nick Morris vowed he would still be driving the De Dion Bouton in the August rally mock-up of the Peking to Paris race. It was apparently his grandmother's dearest wish to see him do so. Now legal considerations and red tape were putting obstacles in his way, but owing to factors he was unable to reveal he was convinced that when the rally came he would be driving that car.

'Great,' I said. 'I like the bit about being "unable to reveal" etc. Where do I come in, Pen? You seem to have it wrapped up.'

'Not quite,' Bob answered for her. 'It's the follow-up. Got some grapevine news for you. That's where you come in, Jack.'

'Wrong. This is where I *go*,' I told them. A minefield loomed ahead if I mentioned I was being asked to drive the De Dion myself. 'There's nothing the police can do,' I continued on behalf of Dave Jennings.

'But you can,' Pen sweetly insisted. 'You know all about this rally and I reckon you know where the car is. I think, and Bob agrees, that our Nick is in touch with Meyton. That's the factor he says he can't reveal.'

'It's a possible theory,' I agreed. *More* than possible, I thought, but it doesn't do to give Pen too much encouragement. 'But you're wrong. I haven't seen the car since Victoria died.' True enough.

'Wherever it is it won't stay there long with Meyton on the case,' Bob said.

'You betcha,' Pen agreed.

'Even so, the ownership of the car and who drives it is not up to me. The car's in the hands of the solicitors now, both legally and physically.'

Bob brushed this aside. 'Meyton knows where it is. It's in Julian Carter's garage. It was one of Meyton's chaps did the moving job.'

TWELVE

All appeared well, or so I tried to tell myself as the clock ticked and days passed, bringing the rally ever closer. After all, the De Dion seemed to be off my responsibility list, and there was no sign of Meyton. Julian's vested interest in the car still made me somewhat uneasy about his guardianship, bearing in mind there had been two murders, both (or neither) of which might relate to it. In vain I told myself that if either was connected, the point at which the assailants would most likely show their bloodstained hands would either be at the rally, due to take place on the third weekend in August, or during final preparations for it.

Helen was frantically busy collecting placards and posters from their printers in Canterbury, dashing around the Kent and Sussex countryside and cheering on the numerous troops involved in turning villages and towns into their Chinese, Mongolian, Russian and other European counterparts. I gathered they were all supposed to be in charge of their own temporary name and culture changes for the day on which the rally would pass through them, but some places were more on the ball than others; others needed jollying along and helping with the organizational spadework. I went with her once or twice and began to appreciate at first hand the work involved. Police had to be included in the discussions over roads and closures to other traffic. A whole army of volunteers had to be ready to display temporary signposts to Mongolia or Warsaw or wherever, all costumed more or less appropriately. Local caterers and craftsmen would be displaying appropriate wares – under Helen's overseeing eye – rally route maps had to be provided for participants and arrangements coordinated with hotels.

It was hard to remember that I was a participant myself, and I was caught on the hop when Helen first handed me a route map. I stared bemusedly at it: Urga, Kiakhta, Omsk . . .

Fortunately there was an English equivalent printed on the reverse side.

Sometimes she stayed overnight with me at Frogs Hill, but the rally and its timetable often demanded early-morning starts. On one of my lucky days, I woke up to find her still asleep. When her blue eyes eventually opened, she murmured, 'I was having a nightmare about the Khyber Pass.'

'Kalgan,' I corrected her. 'Khyber is Afghanistan. Off-route, thank heavens.'

'So it is.' She smiled at me. 'So we might make Paris after all.'

'We'll head there ourselves when this is over,' I promised her.

'How about now?' she said grimly. A rhetorical question alas and we both knew it.

My private nightmare, the De Dion's safety, also resurrected itself from time to time as summer wore on. However much I reasoned that Meyton would gain little by stealing the car at this stage, the niggle remained. Julian himself was unperturbed when I discussed the possible threat to it. His security system was unbreakable, he told me. Having inspected it, I agreed it was remarkable. It had more lights, bells and whistles than a Broadway musical. Nevertheless the word 'unbreakable' had an unfortunate resonance with the *Titanic*'s 'unsinkable'.

I'd telephoned Brenda and thanked her for suggesting I drove the car, but privately I wondered how practical this was – although not because of my skills or lack of them. Far from it. A car that has not been seriously driven for over a hundred years, however, was likely not only to be fragile, but showing every sign of resentment, especially if asked to carry two stalwart persons. Two, as Brenda had disclosed that she would be my passenger.

In addition I had not forgotten Pen and Bob's theory that Meyton might have teamed up with Nick Morris. On the whole I now thought this unlikely. Meyton would have his own game and be playing for high stakes, which Nick would be unlikely to bankroll. Nevertheless, I reasoned, he could be playing a role as Meyton's stooge. The road to the rally still looked murky, although Julian was behaving as though the car already belonged to him. He was talking in terms of 'our' car and what 'we' would do with it, and I sensed that the 'we' did not include Jack Colby or even the Mad Major. It was more likely to be Julian and the ghost of his grandfather. Who was I to knock that? Did I or Dad own the Glory Boot at Frogs Hill? No contest.

With the De Dion there *was* a contest. The Mad Major had a stake in it, so did Brenda, and so did Tom and Nick Morris. Stanley was taking a suspiciously back seat at the moment – but as a De Dion doesn't have a back seat, he could reappear at any moment. Brenda too was all for a quiet life.

'I'm leaving the unpleasant matter of ownership until after this rally, Jack,' she told me on the telephone. 'And then we'll just see what happens.'

She took this attitude to surprising extremes. When I asked her in late July if she'd like to come over to Julian's house while I had a test run round the yard, she declined. The solicitors might not like it, she told me, and secondly she would rather not spoil the excitement of her first ride in it. This would be when the rally left Dover Castle, the starting point of the route. She had no objections to my trying it out, however, and even – after a pause – Julian and the Major.

'After all,' she said, 'I'm sure Mr Carter will see it remains in his garage. I don't want the Morrises driving it.'

No contest there either, although every so often the Major put in a quiet plea on Nick Morris's behalf. Julian ignored him. He was too busy consulting with Parr & Son on the De Dion about registrations, MOTs, insurance and the work that Alf had done in restoration.

When I arrived at Cobba House for the test drive, the car was already parked in the forecourt and Julian was fussing over it as if it were a babe in a pushchair. The Major was there too, admiring it, as was Helen, so I joined the sideshow.

Julian's dominance began to worry me. There was a factor here that I wasn't getting, especially as I still could not fathom why Benson & Hawkes had chosen his garage and not one on neutral ground. Then it occurred to me that they too might have their doubts about the Morrises and believed that Julian *was* neutral. His secure garage was hidden from view on the far side of the forecourt, tucked behind his usual garage and shielded by an eight-foot stone wall. Cobba House was sufficiently remote and far away to make an assault by the Morrises unlikely and Benson might be unaware of 'professional' threats from the likes of Meyton.

Although they had started the De Dion up during the last few weeks and driven it a short way, this was indeed the first major test of the De Dion. It was now registered and insured, so we could even take it on the road if we wished, but we agreed that was a step too far at present.

'Who's going to crank the lady up?' I asked chattily. The Major had told me they had pushed it from the garage to this point so the first cranking was going to be a significant moment.

Julian looked at me in amazement. 'You are. I'm taking the wheel.'

Of course, I thought, but even cranking this car was a privilege and I took the handle from Julian with due reverence.

At first there was no response to my cranking, except a cough or two. I felt my arms were being yanked out of their sockets, but then it happened. The most beautiful noise in the world, the sound of an engine that had fired and caught. I leapt out of the way and the De Dion *moved*.

We all lost our heads, united at last, at this wonderful sight. Julian drove round the forecourt and chugged down the path to Treasure Island at a stately eight mph or so, while the Major, Helen and I ran beside it, cheering, laughing and singing like kids. Doubt and danger were put aside. This was the same car that had driven all the way from Peking to Paris in 1907, up mountains, through rivers, over broken bridges, and across deserts. That was well over a hundred years ago, when cars themselves were in their infancy, when driving was an adventure and the joy of motoring at its peak.

I swung Helen off her feet and high into the air in sheer jubilation. I stopped short of doing the same for the Major, even though he was cheering as enthusiastically as we still were. We watched in exhilaration, as Julian turned into the tarmacked area in front of Treasure Island, drove past it and stopped in front of Pompeii ready for the return trip. The De Dion had moved roughly three hundred yards, but it had given me an idea that I stored away inside my head for later consideration.

Julian somewhat ungraciously allowed me to take the wheel for the return trip. He cranked and I was lord of all I surveyed from the De Dion driving seat. Sir Edmund Hillary on Mount Everest had nothing on me as regards views, as I drove her in majesty surrounded by my enthusiastic courtiers. The De Dion was now a 'she' not an 'it'. A bond had been forged between us. When at last I drove her back into her garage, however, I noticed the Major was looking doleful to say the least.

'What's the matter, Stanley?' I asked quietly, as I jumped down and came outside to join them.

'This car,' he said awkwardly. 'Victoria's. Doesn't seem fair somehow, our being here, her not.'

He was right of course. Victoria had been murdered and the likelihood was that this had been the reason for it. And, I couldn't help bearing in mind, two of those with motives for the crime were here beside me. I found that hard to believe – but that's always what neighbours say when criminals are carted off to meet their deserts.

I returned to Frogs Hill in sobered mood. How could I even have thought it was not my job to investigate Victoria's death? How does one define such a concept? It had been my job to hunt down the De Dion and my job to investigate Alf's death – which had brought me on to a collision course with her murder. No, it was my job all right and the rally was almost certainly part of it. Dave would not be paying me for that, but at least I could face Doris King and Patricia Morris with a clear conscience.

Len looked up as I walked into the Pits in the afternoon. 'Chap looking for you,' he grunted.

'Unless his name's Connor Meyton I haven't the time,' I told him.

'It is.'

Great. Just when I wasn't up to coping with him, here he was like a genie out of a lamp. 'Where is he?'

'Around.'

Not good. Planting a firebomb in the Glory Boot? I found his Jaguar tucked by the barn conveniently out of sight. Meyton wasn't in it, and I seethed, guessing where he'd be. And he was. Right *inside* the barn where I keep the Lagonda and the Gordon-Keeble. No professional technical skills required of him today, however. He was with Zoe. She was talking; Meyton was listening. He was good at that, I suspected. That would be the way he worked. Snake-like, waiting for the enemy to move first. Sizing up the terrain. I only hoped that Zoe was not his prey. Or, come to that, me. I suspected this was more a prospecting call, however.

'Good morning, Jack,' he greeted me.

'And to you, Connor,' I said. We shook hands like well-brought-up gents before we entered the ring. 'Coffee?'

'Why not?'

I could think of quite a few reasons, but I could play a waiting game too. It irked me to take him back to the farm-house but I'd little choice. It was beginning to spit with rain – or was it snake venom? Zoe opted to return to the Pits, to my relief. Meyton told me what a jewel I had in her; I agreed and escorted him to my living room. We chatted as I waited for him to play his hand, which took some time.

'Really looking forward to the rally, Jack.'

This sounded ominous. 'Spectator?' I asked cautiously.

'As if.' He grinned as though we were buddy-buddies. 'I'm a fully paid-up participant.'

'I didn't see your name on the list.'

He shrugged. 'Down as a passenger maybe. Haven't yet decided.'

I couldn't resist it. 'Taking a classic four-by-four?'

He looked shocked. 'Bad taste, Jack. A Sunbeam Alpine Tiger.'

'Sounds good.' I longed to add, 'Is it yours?' but decided to bite my tongue. Instead I asked: 'What can I do for you today then?'

'Not sure.' He frowned. 'This De Dion . . .'

On guard, folks. 'What about it?'

'Carter seems to be keeping a close eye on it.'

'Can you blame him?'

He considered this. 'No. Tell him to take care though. Such a shame if the car didn't make it to the rally.'

I stayed silent. If he expected to lure me into a description of the safety arrangements – although he must already know them – he'd be disappointed, and if he wanted to provoke me into discussion of any other issue the result would be the same. Let him make the running.

'That crazy fellow,' he continued, 'the Major. He's an oddball. Know this Brenda Carlyle, do you? And the Morrises?'

'Yes.'

'Interesting story about Nick wanting to drive the De Dion.'

I waited to see if he came forth with any indication that he knew I was now in that lucky position.

'Doubt if that will happen, Jack,' he continued.

'Why's that?'

He smiled. 'Solicitors and all that. Know Peter Benson, do you?'

Nice one, I thought. It was time to goad the snake into making his move.

'That why you signed up for the rally, Connor? Just to see the De Dion?'

'I'll see it before then, Jack.'

A gauntlet had been tossed down. 'Not a chance,' I said.

'I understood the De Dion is to lead the rally procession, Jack. It will be at Dover Castle before the festivities begin, surely.'

He'd caught me, but these were minor points. Time for gloves to be off, not just a gauntlet dropped. 'What's in this for you?' I asked. 'The car's value can't be worth all the effort you're putting into this.' If he wanted it on behalf of a 'client' then his commission would be peanuts to him, and yet I couldn't see him as a collector in the sense that Julian was.

The snake went very still and his reptilian eyes flickered. 'I don't like being double-crossed. Never have, never will. That's what's in it for me. Tell that to your mates, will you?' He rose to his feet. 'Oh, and thanks for the coffee. Not bad at all.'

*   *   *

The writing was on the wall unless Meyton was bluffing. Somehow I didn't think he was. What he had said rang true – though that word sat oddly in relation to him. Mick Smith was possibly blackmailing him, Dean Warren was scared out of his wits and Zoe could be next. What other 'mates' of mine could he have in mind? Nick, his father – mother even? Julian, the Major, Brenda? I ruled her out but then wrote her back in again. She had inherited the De Dion.

One 'mate' needed to be informed of Connor's 'interest' right away: Julian Carter. He remained unavailable by phone all day and it was not until the next morning, Friday, that I could get over to see him. I'd arranged to call at his home at ten, but when I arrived, I found I was too late. There was a police car parked outside Cobba House. Just one. My thoughts flew to the De Dion. For the life of me, however, I couldn't see how Connor could have spirited it away without half the police sirens in Kent blaring after him in minutes.

There was no one in the car, so I rang the doorbell. One of Dave's team, a Sergeant Blake, opened it and my fear escalated.

'What's on?' I asked.

'Car pinched.'

My stomach did a three-point-turn far too quickly. 'What car?'

'Four-by-four Range Rover.'

I remembered Connor's 'I don't like being double-crossed.' I remembered his 'warning' to Dean. I remembered his usual line in car theft. It seemed he had decided to 'tell' my 'mates' himself. Was the warning just to Julian, or did it include Helen and the Major as a threat to the rally?

'Any more cars gone?' I asked Blake.

'Not that I've heard.'

Fear subsided a notch, even though I didn't like this omen. Nor did Julian. He came out just as Sergeant Blake left.

'When did it go?' I asked him.

'During the night. Didn't hear a thing.'

'Was it in a garage?'

'No. Parked in front of the house. The security lights blinked on and off, but no engine noise, so I thought it was the cats setting off the lights.'

More likely to be snakes, in my opinion.

'This is a coincidence, Jack,' he continued. 'But no one could get at that De Dion.'

'I wouldn't be too sure,' I said. 'Time to take steps, Julian.'

I drove straight over to Old Lilleys. There was no answer to the doorbell so I went round to the garden and sure enough found him racing cars on the Brooklands track. From what I could see the Bentleys seemed to be losing. They were way behind at the Byfleet Banking.

The Major looked up irritably. 'Blast you; you've put Woolf Barnato off his stroke. What do you want, Jack? I've paid you your money.'

He had, and I'd been duly grateful. 'Where do you keep your Bentley, Major?'

'Garage.' He indicated a ramshackle Sixties affair, set well back from the house.

'Secure?'

He looked cornered. 'Reasonably.'

'Better notch up the security. You've heard about Julian's Range Rover?'

'I did. He seemed to think it was my fault,' he grumbled. 'He's convinced Nick is behind it.'

Julian hadn't mentioned that scenario to me, but from his point of view it was a reasonable one. Was I so set on Connor Meyton pulling the strings that I couldn't see the wood for the trees? That was conceivable, I acknowledged. Nick might have pinched it out of spite, although it seemed more likely he'd have a go at the De Dion itself rather than a Range Rover. What would he do with a stolen four-by-four? I played with the theory that Nick was indeed in league with Meyton. I pitied him if so, for he was no match for that snake.

'Why does Julian think that?' I asked him.

'Because he's convinced the Morrises are behind everything. They're not. They've got enough to contend with.'

'It's tough on them that Mrs Carlyle was left the car,' I agreed. 'But then you're claiming it too.'

'One half of it would go to me if the Carlyle woman hadn't poked her nose into the will,' the Major grumbled. He had one eye on Woolf Barnato who was speeding along the Sahara Straight.

'Have you offered the same deal to her?'

'No. She's not a bad old stick, but obviously she leaned on Victoria to leave it to her, and carefully forgot to tell the family. Legal johnnies are working on it, anyway. My claim's better than Victoria's. It was obviously Pascal's in the first place.'

'You both had a bill of sale for it.'

'Maybe there was a bit of hanky-panky about it,' he agreed fairly. 'Don't know. Anyway, it was his.'

'The bill of sale was from a legitimate firm though?'

'Vaugirard in the Rue Fort Louis, Dunkirk. Are you doubting me?' The lion was beginning to roar.

'Just checking. The solicitors will.'

'All Victoria had was a copy of the bill of sale.'

'But made out to Florence,' I pointed out.

'Of course it was.' Roar again. 'Just to get Florence through customs and get the car registered in England. But she just hung on to it. Pinched it.'

'Didn't Pascal ever get in touch to claim it?'

'The woman disappeared and Pascal was killed in the First World War, so who knows? But it was still his. *Now mine.*'

'A sad story,' I said. I meant it. I'd got a mental picture by this time of a happy-go-lucky Frenchman and his English girlfriend, enjoying a late Edwardian summer with the De Dion. And then love had flown out of the window – or, correction, driven off in the De Dion to an unknown destination.

'Pascal had married; he started a family,' the Major said fiercely. 'Couldn't go looking up his previous girlfriend. Anyway, the car wasn't worth much in those days. Excitement of the rally died down. De Dion Bouton firm busy designing new cars. Pascal did them a favour by taking the old wreck off their hands.'

It struck me how often such situations come about. I thought about incidents in my own life where I knew the truth but if I'd fallen under a bus no one else would have done. The De Dion was another such case. Two lots of documents, one adjusted for customs maybe, but both faked? Would Pascal and Florence have bothered to sit down to concoct evidence to prove this was the Peking to Paris De Dion car when they could hardly have foreseen its future value? The Peking to Paris rally was flavour of the month in 1907 but new rallies and adventures were taking place all the time. Its value would have decreased not increased. That argued well for the Major's explanation being true, and that this indeed was one of the two 1907 rally cars.

Nevertheless I still felt I was not getting the full story from the Mad Major. He had started off this whole merry chase by spreading rumours just because he wanted to find Victoria again. How important to him was the car? Did it matter much to him now? The car was safe and sound (we hoped), the rally would take place in less than a month, and the lawyers were dealing with the ownership issue. Nevertheless out there somewhere Connor Meyton could still be planning trouble.

When the phone rings in the middle of the night, it's hard to orientate oneself. Mine rang at three o'clock on Sunday morning. It was Helen and she was panicking. The only word I could distinguish at first since she must be speaking from her mobile was 'fire'.

'The car?' I yelled.

'Yes.'

I was already out of bed and dragging some clothes on. Then I rushed for the Alfa. Fire couldn't break through the solid walls of that garage – or could it? Was that the plan – to ruin the car out of revenge? Or was it to get it out of its secure cell intact and then nick it? Crazy scenarios flashed through my mind as I set off.

Driving late at night can be an exhilarating experience. With the cool air, the stars in a darkened sky and the roads almost to oneself, man seems in tune with nature. Tonight it didn't relax me though; it made me all the more apprehensive.

I could already smell smoke in the air as I drove through Harford Lee. As I bumped along the track to Cobba House I could see smoke above the trees, pluming into the air, hear the noise of engines. When I arrived at the forecourt, I could see two fire engines, plus security and police vans, presumably all that would be needed for what might seem to them a routine fire. But to Julian and Helen it must be the worst of nightmares: black shapes in the darkness, flames still flickering up and around the garage like some weird Bonfire Night brought forward to summer. I reversed and parked my car some way back, clear of the drive and forecourt, then ran back to join Helen and Julian who were standing in the porch of the house. I'd brought a torch but flames themselves were lighting the last part of my way. If I'd needed any proof that Meyton was still in the game, it was here. This was not just a warning, but was it the main operation or only the beginning?

'Are there any other fires or just here?' I asked Helen urgently.

She understood immediately and looked horrified. 'You mean Treasure Island? Not so far, but . . .'

Our eyes met. Could Meyton still be about? Was he out to destroy the museum too? Now I really was scared. 'Let's go,' I told her, and we ran. One of the firemen heard us and a police car picked him up and drove after us. I thought Julian had remained glued to the terrible sight before him until I glanced back and saw him running behind the car. The air seemed increasingly full of smoke and I feared it came from in front of us as well as behind, but with a sob of relief as we reached Treasure Island, Helen cried, 'It looks OK.'

We checked the museum and sheds for any obvious fuel accelerants – petrol rags or traces round windows and doors or any sign of other tampering with them that might indicate that Meyton's plans extended to include Treasure Island.

Finally we, the senior fire officer and the police were all satisfied. 'Back,' I said to Helen, catching her hand. I didn't want to give anyone who might be watching ideas for future attacks.

By the time we reached the forecourt again, it was clear the firemen had won. The smoke was worse, but the flames had been vanquished, so that it was easier to see the extent of the damage. The doors were burnt through, and the firemen were able to break down what was left of them so that we could see within.

I heard Helen catch her breath. Or was that me? Inside was a charred wreck where the flames had broken through. If Connor Meyton had hoped to drive the De Dion out he would have miscalculated on two counts. Firstly, there was no way the fire could have left the De Dion in anything like a drivable state. Secondly, what Helen and I were staring at was not the De Dion. It was one of the old wrecks from Pompeii.

It had been a long shot, but it had paid off. I was so weak at the knees that my forebodings had been justified that I was unable to bask in the glory that Julian was showering on me. The Major had at last arrived, looking much the worse for wear, but who wouldn't at four thirty in the morning? One glance at the wreck told him what had happened.

'Good work. Where's the De Dion?' he asked gruffly.

'In Treasure Island, disguising itself as a Darracq,' Julian said complacently. 'Jack's idea.'

The Major looked suitably impressed. 'Appreciate it, Jack.'

'But where,' Helen asked, very pale, 'do we put the car now?'

I leapt quickly into this awkward problem. I didn't want Julian producing his own suggestion, nor could we risk Meyton knowing where it was. 'I'll talk to the police and try to get hold of the solicitors later on,' I said firmly. 'They'll need to move it – but I doubt if they'll use the same delivery firm.'

THIRTEEN

With all the TV and press cameras that had squeezed on to the slip road by Dover Castle, as well as swamping the Castle's grassy slopes, it looked like a film set and I had to concentrate hard to remember that this was for real. It was Friday and August, and the rally was about to begin. I was a mixture of anticipation and dread. The dread was because not a word or whisper since the fire had emerged to indicate anything untoward would happen, and yet I could not believe that we had moved forward on the Alf King front, and nor had DCI Fielding made any apparent progress on Victoria's death. Plenty of DNA – but no matches. Except, it seemed, the kind that lit fires in the hope of destroying the De Dion Bouton in which I was now sitting.

I had travelled to Dover in Charlie's cabin with Len and Zoe – Charlie being the Frogs Hill name for our ancient but trusty low-loader. On its flatbed and well wrapped up against the drizzling rain, the De Dion had travelled in state to her date with destiny. Now I was sitting beside Brenda at the head of the procession shortly to leave the castle, with most of the other rally cars tucked behind us or still in the car park.

'Exciting, isn't it?' Brenda said.

It was hard not to agree. She was suitably togged up in a huge motoring hat, veil, goggles and dustcoat against the vagaries of the Gobi Desert. I doubted if the Romney Marsh would be so demanding, but she looked splendidly weird. I flattered myself that I didn't look so bad myself, in goggles, natty chauffeur's motoring hat, buttoned jacket and heavy gloves and leggings. I'd probably end up ditching some of this heavy gear as the day grew warmer, but it looked good for the start.

Already the scene looked like one of Giovanni's paintings from the Glory Boot. Bathed in the sunshine that had replaced the drizzle, and against this dramatic background, it was a petrol-head's dream come true. Veteran, vintage, Fifties, Sixties, it seemed to be a car show on its own, I thought admiringly, with classics now sorted into an agreed order of departure and ranging from Alvises to Wolseleys. Full marks to Helen for setting up this splendid start to the rally with the powers that be.

With the castle keep towering in the background and perched on cliffs high above the sea, it was easy to see oneself as part of history. The still standing Roman Pharos had lit the way for Roman ships in the Channel; the forerunner of the present Saxon church of St Mary in Castro had seen the Roman invaders, and if legend was fact also King Arthur. Then the Saxons had come marching in, followed by the Normans, each stamping their own mark on this fortress. The French had laid siege to it in vain, and a procession of Kings of England had galloped up to snatch at history to underline their own importance, albeit often adding contributions of their own. And that was just the buildings overground. A whole world of its own lies underground with passages tunnelled into chalk that had provided defence and protection in two world wars.

Today, however, Dover was standing in for Peking, another city that in 1907 was guarded by hills, forts and castles. The 1907 rally cars had passed a fortressed castle as their drivers sallied forth for the battle ahead of them. I too might have a battle to fight today. My problem was that I didn't know who I was fighting or what or why. What I did know was that passions were all too likely to come to the fore in this weekend jaunt. The Morrises had signed up for a start, which was a bad sign. Brenda was beside me and somewhere in the procession was probably Connor Meyton. Add to that Julian and the Mad Major and here were all the ingredients for trouble at this otherwise jolly event. Oh, and Pen must be around too.

'We might be moving soon,' Brenda said hopefully, and indeed there was an increased movement and noise level around. Time to think De Dion. I'd read the books on the original rally and talked to the De Dion Club and was all too well aware that one had to be ready to deal with the unexpected while driving such veterans. That's why Len and Zoe were bringing up the rear of the procession in Charlie. We had another plan too; because there had been comparatively little running time I couldn't be sure how the De Dion was going to take to the hills of Dover and Folkestone. The Mongolian mountain ranges they were not, but nevertheless they might prove formidable for an engine over a hundred years old.

Behind me Julian was driving the Iso Rivolta – but I wasted no time in envy. For two whole days I had the De Dion. Then came Helen with the Major in his 1930s Bentley drophead. Although I was sure that trouble lay behind me somewhere in this cavalcade, on this sunny day, and absorbed in the collective happy glow of classic car owners who know they have a treat in store for them, I was aware that it would be easy to let my fears recede. I could not afford to let them, however. Two, perhaps even three, people had died because of this car, yet here I was sitting next to the lady who owned it (or thought she did). She was proudly anticipating what might lie ahead. I doubt if it even entered her mind that it might not all be Chinese lanterns and spring rolls, as the decorations and food stalls around us suggested. Here be dragons, I knew, and not all of them red paper ones like those on the gateway arches ahead. Dragons spit fire

The first dragon to spit was Nick Morris who strolled up to us from his position towards the rear of the procession (I'd agreed that with Helen). Baulked of driving the De Dion, he had brought a Morris Minor, and he didn't look happy. He looked Brenda up and down. 'Making a statement, are we?' he sneered. 'Dolled up like a spring chicken.'

'Why shouldn't I be?' she replied with spirit. 'Everyone else is.'

That was true. Chinese robes and smocks with a variety of pointy hats were to be seen everywhere from the food stalls to the sightseers and even the occasional journalist had entered into the spirit of the thing. Drivers and passengers had also turned themselves into sporty Edwardian daredevils.

'Why?' Nick echoed mockingly. 'You're riding in my car, that's why.'

'Your grandmother's doing, not mine,' Brenda reminded him gently.

He reached up, grabbed her wrist and hissed, 'You're going to regret this, you old cow.'

'Drop it,' I yelled at him, jumping down from the car. 'Fight this out in court, not here, not today.' When he saw me coming for him, he instantly relaxed his grip.

'It's not going to be yours for long,' he hurled at her. 'Going to keep it at Shoulder Mutton Green, are you, Brenda dear?'

'No,' she replied coolly. 'I have plans for it.'

'And so, darling Brenda, do we.' Then he did move away, but it had been an unpleasant episode. And what were all these plans?

'Nick's not all bad,' Brenda said. 'He was a kind little boy and Victoria was devoted to him. But he always did like getting his own way.'

'Most people do,' I observed. 'It depends how they go about it, though.'

A much more welcome visitor was Helen who came to tell us that we were about to move. 'Two minutes, Jack, and the flag does down.' She was doing the event proud, clad in a long cream shiny satin coat with a cream hat to match and veil tied under her chin.

Brenda adjusted her own hat, and I prepared for my moment of glory by handing Len (who had insisted on this job) the crank.

One, two, *three*. That welcome sound of the engine catching. The flag was down, dropped by the Governor of the Cinque Ports, and there I was driving the De Dion through the 'Gate of Triumphant Virtue', the earlier rally's exit point from Peking. Here it was the Constable's Gateway dressed up with red silk flags over the arch, dragons, pagoda-like mock towers. On the far side I could see the press and sightseers lining the way down to the road that would take us on down the hill and through the town of Dover.

Somewhere Pen would be amongst them, and I was equally sure she would then leap into a car and follow the procession. I hoped there would be no other stories than the rally itself on which she could gorge herself.

Brenda had attached a small flag to our car as on the original De Dion driven by Georges Cormier, which had led the five contenders out of Peking, only to lose two of the procession immediately. Over a hundred years later, sixty cars were just as eager. Brenda's flag was fluttering in the breeze, and so was I. Half my fluttering was wondering where Meyton was, the other half was from the sheer exhilaration of driving the De Dion. Was there really a threat from Meyton? I asked myself. Surely he would not be so daft as to make an attempt on the car while it was moving? What would he gain by sabotaging it or stealing it? Any plan of his, I reasoned, would surely be at one of the stops or at the finale. Even then it was doubtful. It was true that he was bent on revenge but not to the extent that he would endanger himself. Revenge served cold, which seemed to be his preferred method of dealing with old scores, brings an objective eye to a situation. Somewhere, somehow, his plans must have gone wrong, and he had fixed the blame on someone whom he reckoned was the guilty party. I had a nasty feeling it might be the lady sitting next to me but I couldn't reason out any connection.

'My' De Dion's first major test was the hill down to Dover town. Len had double-checked the brakes and then checked again, and had declared himself satisfied with them. The car, by agreement with Brenda, with whom Julian seemed to be getting interestingly chummy, had been given a good last-minute check by Parr & Son. Len still wasn't altogether happy though, which is why he had announced he would be following the rally procession with Charlie. For good measure, Dave Jennings said he thought he'd do that too. No missing this chargeable bonus, I thought, perhaps unfairly.

The De Dion's steering seemed a little uncertain on the way down the hill, and I had a sudden nightmare at one point that we might fly into the police guard keeping the crowds back. For crowds there were along the road to 'Kalgan', otherwise known as Town Wall, Snargate Street and the A20 towards Folkestone. As we drove along, heading for the Western Heights, I rethought the situation. Not that the De Dion was giving any trouble now we were on the flat. On the contrary, judging by her purring, she was enjoying the trip as much as we were. Nevertheless I pulled over before we attempted the climb up to the higher road. I justified this by reminding myself that on the 1907 rally, drivers had run into trouble in varying degrees shortly after the start and through no fault of their own. It was the terrain.

The Dover to Folkestone road couldn't match the horrors of the bridges over the River Tsing-ho, but, alas, we had no willing bands of peasants arranged to pick up the cars to carry them over the mountains. I'd asked Len and Zoe if they'd be interested in taking part in this, but they weren't enthusiastic. Len pointed out that we had Charlie for that sort of caper. With Helen's permission and reluctantly the Mad Major's, Brenda and I had agreed that periodically the car would be safer on Charlie than attempting all three days without respite. It could do short stretches by itself, including the final drive up the Roman road from Westenhanger to Harford Lee.

The rest of the procession drove on while we loaded the De Dion, all the while being whooped and cheered by half of Dover, who were, I hoped, busily throwing donations into the buckets held by volunteers as well as contributing to the revenue of the food stalls selling rice cakes, spring rolls and noodle pots.

Our decision met the approval of the Morrises at least. 'Looking after our car for us, are you?' Tom yelled, as they passed in a Fifties Humber. It could have been theirs, but I suspected it had been borrowed for the occasion.

Brenda did not reply. Not to them anyway.

'It's very hurtful, Jack,' she said. 'I used to be such friends with Patricia. But the car *is* mine.'

'Or perhaps the Major's.' I had divided loyalties here, so it was best to play for safety.

'That remains to be seen,' she answered sharply, then rearranged her face in a smile for another group of photographers and journalists. This one included Pen. She was on her own and had stopped to see if there was a story waiting to be invented.

'This is it, eh?' Pen glanced at Brenda and winning charm took over. 'So you're the lucky new owner then,' she cooed woman to woman. I stood ready to intervene when the going got tough.

'I am, yes,' Brenda replied.

'I heard there was some dispute over ownership. That must be worrying for you coming on top of Mrs Drake's death.' Pen looked so sympathetic I almost believed she had no other object in mind.

Brenda hastily backed out of being bonded with Pen. 'A nuisance claim, that's all.'

'Poor you,' Pen said. 'But this rally now? There's no doubt that this is the car that drove in the original one?'

'We believe it is. It takes time to sort out the provenance, so one can't be definite about it yet.' Brenda was doing pretty well at Pen-fencing, I thought, although it might be a mistake to stop smiling.

Pen decided it was time to take a photograph – of Brenda, not me. I could see why. 'Owner looks on in distress as her beloved car has to be consigned to a low-loader in disgrace.'

The Major and Helen had driven on in the rally's vanguard, but Julian stopped to ensure his new buddy Brenda was looked after. 'Come on with me, Mrs Carlyle.'

That was good in one way because Charlie's cabin would definitely be overcrowded with four of us in it, but all the same I wasn't too sure about the wisdom of pairing Brenda and Julian. I told myself the worst he could do would be to persuade her to accept an offer for the car, which was none of my business, even if the Major did court martial me afterwards.

Another visitor pulled up as Charlie was ready to leave. 'Trouble?' Dave stuck his head out of his patrol car. 'Forgot to put petrol in, did you?' he jeered.

'Not at all. Merely a preventative measure,' I assured him.

'Against mechanical or man's assault?'

'Both. We won't take it round the lanes. We'll find alternative better roads.'

'Good plan. That'll fox the Meytons of this world.'

I doubted that, though it might help. 'Are you following us or the rally, Dave?' I enquired.

The route later today would take to the lanes of Romney Marsh and then Walland Marsh (temporarily known as the 'Gobi Desert'). On the far side of the desert was 'Orga', our first overnight stop, better known as Rye. The lanes might fit a more robust De Dion under her own steam as well as the rest of the rally cars, but weren't so brilliant for Charlie. Moreover although the main roads are used to hold-ups, they are not of the kind that might stem from the likes of Meyton or the Morrises. On the lanes, however, rally cars would undoubtedly get split up, thus offering more possibilities of trouble from human sources.

'You,' Dave answered. He seemed unenthusiastic about this choice however. That's the trouble with rallies. You get into the spirit of the thing all too easily.

Before the Gobi Desert, however, lay Folkestone, a few miles west of Dover, which had turned out in force to greet us. It had the honour of being designated 'Nankow', which in 1907 China was a mere village, but Folkestone was rather different. It too was fortified with not one, but three Martello Towers, built with the intention of keeping Napoleon Bonaparte from laying his hands on Britain. He never did of course, but mothers frightened their children with tales of Old Boney coming to get them for many a year thereafter.

Charlie was still following the rally procession at this point but I was glad we had decided to transport the De Dion on him, for the A20 road runs high along the cliffs here. Sorry, I mean of course the mountain ranges leading to Kalgan, which for us was Hythe, which we would reach shortly after Folkestone. In China these mountains are between Nankow and Kalgan, but our route had to use a little licence as the A20 has different ideas. Perhaps I had been somewhat over anxious though. However fragile the De Dion might look it had sturdily survived the vicissitudes of Peking to Paris, despite its mere ten h.p. against the Itala's forty h.p. The roads of south-east England should be a cinch.

From Folkestone to Hythe was easy going for all of us, however hard it had been from Nankow to Kalgan in 1907. Kalgan had been the first overnight stop. In theory the rally participants had agreed a mutual support pact before leaving Peking, but it didn't take long for that to break down and I wondered whether that was going to happen here too. In 1907 Kalgan was the intended end of a railway line that had not yet been built, but Hythe fares better. It has its own, claiming

to be the world's smallest public railway. It's a little short on
the pagodas and temples for which Kalgan was noted but
otherwise it did us proud. It has a canal – also part of the
defences against Napoleon – and this was standing in for
the river Hun Ho – even if the Hythe natives did seem a bit
reluctant to push our cars over it.

Hythe is a long stretched-out town, with the road running
along the seashore for part of it and hiding its centre. Our
progress was slower travelling through it, giving the good folk
of Hythe plenty of time to toss cash into buckets, cheer us on
and appreciate the spring rolls, Chinese lanterns, crafts and
decorations. There even seemed to be some Chinese wrestling
going on in one corner.

I regretted for a moment that I wasn't in the De Dion and
reflected that Brenda must be cross at missing the crowd's
adulation. The Major must be enjoying it, however, as he was
now leading the cavalcade. On a brief halt I saw him push
back the roof of his drophead and wave at the crowds. The
question of ownership of the De Dion didn't seem to be troubling him unduly. The Morrises had overtaken Julian and
Brenda which must have given them some satisfaction.

Our first scheduled coffee stop was at a large hotel on
'Kalgan's' seafront, but it was a brief one owing to the fact
that not everyone in the hotel was devoted to classic cars and
had other pursuits to follow. Even so, Charlie and his precious
load were surrounded by admirers and I found myself giving
autographs for no apparent reason. One little boy seemed to
think I had driven in the 1907 rally and kept asking me questions about Mongolia, which threw me somewhat. Luckily I
remembered my school history lessons about Genghis Khan
and gave the lad information a mere thousand years out of
date. At least, remembering Genghis's antics, I hoped it was.

I saw the Major and Brenda giving a joint press interview,
so perhaps Julian was no longer her best buddy and she had
reverted to Stanley. The hotel was decorated in true Chinese-
cum-Mongolian style, and tea with rather stalwart Chinese
costumed maidens was doing the rounds with rice biscuits. I
opted for the more interesting looking food stalls, and felt
very regal as I sampled little bits of preserved fruits, peeled

lychees, and strawberries. I could see the Morrises greedily eyeing the De Dion but then my gaze was distracted by Helen. I was about to join her, when reality struck in the form of Connor Meyton. He came gently, like the mythical breezes at the end of March, sipping tea and munching a prawn toast.

'Good morning, Jack. Should we bow to each other?'

'By all means,' I replied courteously. We did so. 'How's the Alpine going?' I asked in true rally style. I'd seen it in the procession, and a fine classic it was.

'A purring tiger. And the De Dion? I saw that it broke down.'

'No. It was a safety measure. All precautions taken.'

He looked at me thoughtfully. 'I had understood it would be driven the whole way.'

'So it will be, partly on the low-loader, though. Maybe on the same route, maybe not. Any problem with that? Run up against any plans you might have?'

'My only plan is to see Carter's museum does well out of this. Excellent cause,' he added approvingly. 'So good to see such a turnout of those interested in De Dions.'

'Even the police,' I agreed.

'I'm terrified.'

Enough backchat. 'Planning any more arson attacks?' I asked casually.

He pursed his lips. 'Just here to safeguard my interests, Jack.'

'One of which is the De Dion. Any others?'

'My interest lies in those who can't keep their avaricious paws away from it.'

He said this with such an agreeable smile that I thought it was a joke and that I could have been misjudging the snake. After all, I had no proof he had killed Alf, no proof he had killed Mick Smith (or arranged either of their deaths), nor any proof he had killed Victoria Drake. No proof either that he had set up the fire at Julian's home. And yet he was always *there* with an avowed mission, true or false. Against whom? I didn't know the answer. What was clear was that he still had some mission to fulfil and that the De Dion was involved.

One interested party strolled up to join us: the Mad Major, in colonial hat and hunting gear for some reason. He peered curiously at Meyton. 'Good to see you here,' he said patronizingly. 'What are you driving, or are you a sponsor? All in a good cause, eh?'

'Tiger, no, and yes,' Connor said briefly.

The Major was not deterred. 'Nice little Sunbeam, eh? Had one myself once. Not too good in the snow.'

'And you have a Bentley,' Connor replied to the Major's surprise. 'Do look after your charges, both of you. We're off to the Gobi Desert now, and I seem to remember a spot of trouble there in 1907. The Contal died, didn't it?'

Perhaps I was getting paranoid but that seemed to convey a message. If so, who was target number one? I began to feel up against a Great Wall of China myself. That was the next high point of the 1907 rally, the entry point to the plains and deserts of Mongolia. Unfortunately Kent couldn't provide a Great Wall, so we had to make do with the landmark of Saltwood Castle, the Martello tower and the Royal Military Canal in the way of protection. What lay ahead of us now was the network of lanes that would have confused Genghis Khan and given William the Conqueror cause to blink if they'd been there when he was choosing his landing place for invasion.

While the main rally route went through Romney and Walland Marshes, we in Charlie would be on the coast road, and then drive to 'Udde' (otherwise known as Lydd) where we would hope to rendezvous with as many of the rally cars as had not already lost their way. We would then give the De Dion another outing under her own steam (or rather her ten h.p. engine) driving along past Camber Sands and on to Rye. Even though we weren't in the lanes, this was wonderful countryside with the sea on one side of us and only sheep on the other.

We stopped on the seafront ready to unload our precious burden, and without much traffic passing were able to eat sandwiches on the dunes without worrying about the De Dion being spirited away. It was the holiday season and there were plenty of holidaymakers about but the dunes gave us an illusion of privacy. The calling seagulls and the miles of flat sands made this an eerie experience though, and I was glad to be with my staunch team. Reasonably staunch, anyway, given Zoe's recent defection. I remembered Meyton talking of the 1907 Contal whose driver Auguste Pons had to abandon it in the desert, along with his dreams of glory. Perhaps the tricar was still there. Who would know given that wild and remote place? Camber Sands was quite creepy enough for me but I had no intention of abandoning myself or the De Dion here.

'Connor Meyton,' Zoe said out of the blue, increasing my goose pimples. 'He asked me if I'd seen Dean.'

'What did you say?' I asked warily.

'The truth. That I hadn't. He just smiled and said that if I did, I should give him his regards.' She looked worried. 'Jack, you haven't seen Dean round here, have you?'

'Not so far. But if not, what's Meyton doing here?'

'Enjoying the rally?' Len muttered.

'He hasn't been following us, has he, Len?'

'No. Shook him off way back.'

Not exactly cheery news and this did not bode well. With the wind blowing sand in our faces this was beginning to feel uncomfortably like a real desert.

Rye, our stopping place for the night, was temporarily 'Urga', a holy city in Mongolia devoted to Lamas (the priests not the animals) and to quiet contemplation. Somehow I did not think Rye, lovely though it is, was going to prove like that tonight. Our hotel was on its outskirts, and I hoped offered somewhat better accommodation than that offered to the original competitors.

Not everyone on the rally was staying overnight, some preferring to return home, but forty or so, plus passengers, were present to grace the occasion. The afternoon was free for those who wanted to explore Rye. For those who preferred to admire the cars, there was a special team keeping an eye on them in the hotel car park. Rye is unique, a town perched on a hill, reeking of the past, part of which was its devotion to smuggling. Now it is so civilized I wondered what I was worrying about.

It continued civilized for a while. The Major and Julian were dinner jacketed, as were many of the other guests at the bar before dinner. Helen shimmered in a gold evening dress, and Brenda and the Morrises came to join us – albeit not together. It could have been any normal social gathering.

It didn't take long, however, before I was proved wrong. I was enjoying talking to Helen, until Connor made his suave entrance, like something out of a James Bond film only not so friendly. He looked round, saw me, nodded, turned away and bought himself a drink. I relaxed – but too soon.

He came straight up to me. 'Is that De Dion safe?' he asked.

'Of course,' I said dismissively. Brenda looked somewhat surprised, but I realized that to her Meyton was a stranger. I introduced them all, watching to see if Nick in particular betrayed any signs of recognition, but he merely looked bored and Meyton inscrutable.

'Hoping to keep it that way?' he then asked Brenda chattily.

I was about to gallop to the rescue, but it wasn't necessary. 'I'm not sure how it concerns you,' she informed him, 'but I am indeed. I shall be taking it into my own care after the rally finishes. I plan to take it to France. It will, I am sure, be far safer there.'

From the looks on everyone's faces, I could see this was as new to them as it was to me. The Major was first to recover, bristling with fury. 'Ownership still under discussion, Mrs Carlyle.'

'You have to prove ownership, Major,' Brenda said kindly, as to a child. 'I have the executor's consent to do it, and I shall.'

This was one purposeful lady, I thought, although I simply could not believe that Benson & Hawkes would allow such a thing before probate was granted on the bequest and with the ownership issue not settled.

Nor could Nick Morris. 'Make sure you bequeath it to Mum when you pop off,' he said sweetly.

'I shall leave it where I choose. To my husband probably.'

'He died ten years ago.' Nick thought this very funny.

'I am to remarry,' Brenda informed him, pink in the face, 'and if I don't—'

'She'll flog it,' Tom interrupted.

Patricia burst into tears. 'That's all you want it for, isn't it, Brenda? All this stuff about Mummy wanting it to go to France. Nonsense. You've already lined up a buyer, haven't you?'

'I shall not sell it,' Brenda shouted, goaded.

Connor nodded approvingly. 'A wise choice,' he said quietly. 'It won't be worth what you think. Either Mr King or Mrs Drake did explain to you that it couldn't be the original rally car, didn't they?'

FOURTEEN

I didn't take Connor seriously – at first. Then it dawned on me that he was taking himself *very* seriously. At the very least he was announcing he was a major player in this chess game. I noticed that he had materialized just after Dave had left for home, as though Connor was pointing out that I had no direct power in my police work. He had carefully timed this bombshell. Although the authenticity of the De Dion was not strictly relevant for me, it most certainly was for Julian, the Major, Brenda and the Morrises, and their faces reflected the shock Meyton's declaration had given them, especially as it had been so confidently delivered.

Brenda gathered her wits first. 'How on earth would you know – and who *are* you?'

A mistake to treat Meyton with scorn. He would be fully prepared.

He ignored the latter question. 'I base it on Mr King's records of his restoration of the car. There was a note that from the car's condition he could not agree that this was one of the two 1907 De Dion participants. Dean Warren would confirm to you that it is in Mr King's handwriting.'

'Where are these records?' I enquired politely.

'In my possession.'

There was no use in pointing out that they belonged to Doris. In any case Brenda spoke before I could. 'They are irrelevant – *whoever* you are. Benson & Hawkes and Major Hopchurch's solicitors have ample proof that Mr King was not correct.'

The Major galloped to her support. 'She's right, sir. I don't know what business it is of yours, but we can do without your damnfool interference.'

For once the Morrises, even Tom, looked out of their depth. The show had moved on so far and fast that all Nick could manage was: 'Of course it's the real car. Been in our family since the year dot.'

Then Brenda weighed in again. 'I should point out that if this story were to be spread the laws of defamation come into play.'

Connor was unmoved. 'A car cannot be defamed.'

'Its owners can,' she whipped back. 'We know it to be genuine and malicious statements do harm to reputations.'

'Truth is the ultimate defence,' he murmured.

I could see the Major at explosion point, so it was time I took over. I had to deal with the snake without its head shooting back to bite me. 'Did Alfred King specify what exactly he thought wrong with the car's condition? Or are you saving that for the press?'

'Certainly I'll tell you, Jack.'

I cursed myself. He'd been waiting for this opportunity to show how chummy he and I were. It's called splitting the opposition.

'Firstly,' he continued, 'there was no sign that a reserve tank had been carried – as the 1907 rally car had. Secondly, the French registration plate is missing. The car in question had been registered at some point from the evidence on the car, but Mr King could find no proof of what number that was. Odd, don't you think, if one wanted to claim that this was the genuine article?'

'Not so odd,' I whipped back at him. 'The car was taken to England, no doubt with a plan to register it here, and there was little thought for its future value. The French plate was removed, but for whatever reason it never did get registered here. Alternatively, the plate could have fallen off if the car remained off-road. Everything degenerates without care.'

'That is true,' Connor said sagely. 'Unfortunately there is more. Alf was a keen enthusiast about the Peking to Paris rally, and Mrs Drake must have brought him her documentation to study. Mr King refers to a report to the De Dion Company written by a Dunkirk garage mechanic stating that the car could not be repaired after severe damage at the docks; also a letter from De Dion authorizing the wreck's disposal. He also mentions a subsequent bill of sale to Miss Florence Manning from a car agency in Dunkirk.'

'What about it?' growled the Major.

'The car that Mr King examined, so he noted, showed no signs of the extensive damage the original car had suffered at the Dunkirk docks. The chassis in particular did not seem to have suffered greatly.'

A silence even from me. This had the ring of truth and I could have kicked myself for not looking more carefully at the Major's documentation. I had concentrated on those dratted bills of sale, of which one at least was undoubtedly faked.

'Are we supposed to take your word for this – based solely on the jottings of an elderly man?' Brenda said haughtily.

'Not at all. You're at liberty to refute it as I am to spread the story.'

Storm clouds ahead. 'Documents exaggerating damage,' I intervened, 'do not necessarily mean that the car isn't what it's claimed to be, merely that its origin has been concealed.'

'Jack, clutch at your beanstalk if you wish.' Connor beamed. 'But at the top you will find a giant called Reality.'

'You surely won't give the story to the press now?' Brenda's bravado vanished. 'Without proof?'

'I haven't yet decided,' Connor said. 'I do feel for the sake of truth that the press should be warned that the provenance of the De Dion you are so enthusiastically vaunting is not yet established.'

That unified everyone else present. Julian looked as though he was going to be sick, Helen was comforting him, Brenda seemed close to tears, the Major was comforting Patricia and Nick and Tom were rallying to lead the next round.

'If you do,' Tom yelled, 'my solicitor will be on to you with a writ!'

'He's conning us, Dad. Trying to get us to pay him off,' Nick contributed.

Connor cocked his head to one side as he considered his reply or pretended to. In fact he obviously knew all too well what he was going to say. 'I thought at the end of the rally might be a suitable time to speak to the press – at that museum of yours, Mr Carter. There'll be plenty of media people around then.' A pause. 'And perhaps others who are currently missing from this scene might appear.'

Missing? He didn't mean Dave; this was a hit against Dean

Warren. I was even more glad that Zoe had chosen to go into town with Len for an Indian supper.

'Do you think this is true, Jack?' Helen asked despondently after King Connor had made his exit. The gold of her dress shimmered but in this pantomime the demon king seemed to be making all the running, not the princess who deserved it. She had remained very silent during the fracas with Connor, and I was afraid that on top of all the organizational work Helen had to deal with, this would be too much for her. True, she showed few signs of it. She looked magnificent. If only we had been on our own and not caught in the middle of this spider's web, what an evening we might have had.

In the hotel restaurant the Morrises ostensibly settled themselves at a table of their own, no doubt plotting their next move. Brenda sat in solitary state, and at our table Helen and I had the honour of the company of Julian and the Major.

Before I could answer her question, the Major cleared his throat. 'Think that fellow's going to broadcast that story?'

'It's not looking good,' I admitted, 'but the evidence he thinks he has is hardly conclusive, save that Alf and Victoria seem to have believed it.'

'Perhaps,' Helen said gloomily, 'he's holding something back for the press.'

'That, I'm afraid,' I contributed, 'is all too possible where Meyton is concerned.'

The Major went red. 'Could be,' he mumbled. 'The fact is . . .'

I groaned. 'Don't tell me you've still been holding back on us.'

'Stanley?' Julian became glacial.

'Not too much,' the Major mumbled. 'Fact is it didn't reflect well on my grandfather – or,' he added, glancing across at the Morrises, 'on Victoria's grandmother.'

'Tell us the worst,' I ordered him.

'Patricia should hear it too.' The Major looked as if he wished he'd never opened his mouth but a sip of brandy obviously strengthened him.

I sighed and went over to ask her to join us. With her came

Tom and Nick, of course, but there was no help for it. They almost ran me down in their eagerness to move tables, and Brenda quickly followed suit.

'The De Dion,' the Major began unhappily. 'It's the real McCoy all right.'

The sighs of relief that greeted this announcement were quickly over.

'But our forebears didn't get hold of it very, shall we say—'

'Legally?' I finished for him.

'Perhaps,' the Major grunted. 'Who knows now? What it looks like to me is this: when the car was shipped back to the French company by their London branch after the Olympia Motor Show there was indeed an accident at Dunkirk docks, as that smooth-talking lounge lizard said. No fancy stuff then over handling cars. Craned on and off like any old merchandise, and they dropped the poor old thing. It was taken to a local garage and the damage assessed by the chief mechanic who signed the write-off report that the Lizard mentioned.'

'But that was a bit of fancy work from your grandfather?' I suggested.

'Looks like it.'

'Because it wasn't a write-off?' Nick asked.

'Can't have been. Pascal, my grandfather, was the son of Jean-Marie Merrault, the owner of the garage, and he saw his chance. Greased the mechanic's palm with silver, and bought the so-called wreck at a knock-down price without the car even leaving Dunkirk. They were rip-roaring days for cars. Business was booming and the Count de Dion and Monsieur Bouton had more to do than worry about one of their clapped-out cars. No one guessed then that the rally was going to go down in history. It was just one more crazy motoring adventure.'

'So,' I summoned up from this and from my memories of what I had briefly seen at the Major's house, 'there was a fake report of the car's condition for De Dion, presumably a letter from the company authorizing the sale, and two bills of sale, one for Florence and one for Pascal. All fake.'

'Good Lord, no,' the Major said indignantly. 'The bill of

sale was pukka. The car wasn't such a wreck, that was all. But it was legal.'

'If that's how it could be described,' I said, but he didn't pick up the irony.

'By Jove, yes.'

Patricia now entered the ring. 'If it was legal why were there *two* bills of sale, one to your grandfather and one to my great-grandmother?'

'Ah.' A cough of embarrassment from the Major. 'Looks odd, I know. I talked it over with Victoria when we met in Paris when we realized there were two sets of documents. Pascal thought he should lie low with the car for a while as he couldn't go flashing around Paris in it without registering it with a different number. Florence was going back to England so he gave the car to her to keep in trust for him plus a bill of sale in her name to get it registered there and copies of the other documents. That's why the French number plate would have gone. Just like Pascal, she couldn't flash around in the car with that on, not with the London branch of the De Dion company around. So Pascal faked Florence's bill of sale. His was genuine, though. See?'

He looked round the unresponsive faces. 'Damn it all, Pascal was a youngster. He and Florence both thought it a great lark. After all, the car was genuine enough. There was even a letter included from Georges Cormier, who drove the De Dion in the Peking to Paris 1907 rally, saying he's pleased to hear the car has another life.'

'Faked?' I enquired.

The Major turned bright red as he realized he'd scored an own goal. 'I don't know.'

'Copy for Florence?'

'No. She had one sent from Victor Collignon, the driver of the other De Dion.'

'Right,' Tom said heavily after we'd absorbed this little titbit, 'you've had your say. Firstly you overlook the fact that the car still belongs to Patricia's family unless you can *prove* otherwise. You can't. You've admitted that Pascal was a first-class crook.'

'A first-class *player*,' the Major roared. 'His bill of sale is genuine. Anyway, it was all a game.'

'A game that ended in a draw,' Helen observed.

'Shouldn't have done,' the Major rumbled. 'Poor show. Pascal married someone else, Florence took offence and wouldn't let him have the car back.'

'Seems reasonable to me,' Helen said drily.

The Major glared. 'Different times.'

I pointed out that different times were usually pretty much like our own times, as regards human feelings. 'You're claiming that this is the real car, Major, and that only some of the documents are false. Yet Alf and Victoria were both convinced that the car was not the original.'

Tom remembered his own interests. 'They were wrong. It *is* the real thing. We'll soon prove that.'

Brenda had been silent for so long I had almost forgotten her presence. She made it clear now though. 'There would be little point,' she said primly, pink in the face. 'Mr Benson is in full agreement that the car is no longer safe in this country. I shall be taking it to France – as Victoria wished.'

When I went to the hotel's secure garage the next morning I half expected the car to have disappeared already after Brenda's announcement. Gone was yesterday's exultation in the sheer wonder of driving the De Dion. The row that had broken out scotched that. Brenda swept away all arguments. The car, even by what the Major had told us, was the genuine article, it was hers and she was taking it as soon as she could. Any objections could be referred to Mr Benson. I was beginning to wonder whether she was eloping with him, such was the fervour with which she announced this. I was also increasingly uneasy. Just how quickly did she intend to move the car?

The De Dion looked as innocently splendid as yesterday, however, ready to lead the rally procession as far as 'Irkutsk', twenty miles or so, at which point she would be borne aloft by Charlie for the rest of the day. 'Irkutsk' was Battle, so called because the Battle of Hastings took place there when William the Conqueror so rudely invaded England's green and pleasant land. Today we would be passing the 'Trans-Siberian railway', otherwise known as the Ashford to Hastings railway line, and we would still be in 'Siberia' at 'Omsk', for our second overnight stop, Tunbridge Wells. This took the rally along more enchanting single-track lanes and so Charlie would be taking a long but safer diversion.

It worried me, however, as we would be fairly isolated in Charlie. I reasoned that if Meyton had his eye upon our precious charge, he would gain nothing unless his purpose was to destroy the car, but the worry still remained, so I asked Len to do a thorough check of Charlie as well as the De Dion. 'Clean as a whistle,' was his verdict and I tried to dismiss Meyton from my mind.

Charlie's route was a roundabout one, but it took us through part of Ashdown Forest. I love this forest with its associations with Winnie the Pooh, but as we drove through it I was still anxious about being so far separated from the main rally procession. The roads through the forest are reasonably wide and the wooded areas not so thick that Meyton might be hiding behind every tree, but I was painfully aware that a lot of passions had been stirred up the previous evening and it was difficult to see in which directions they were flying. Add to that the possibility of Pen stomping into the limelight again and I began to wish we were safely back at Frogs Hill and I could hand over responsibility for the car. It would not take long for Pen to winkle out Meyton's story, and right or wrong it would be a first-class one for her. I was surprised that she hadn't followed us, rather than the rally itself, but I saw no sign of her. All was suspiciously quiet. Even so we organized an armed guard around Charlie while two of us had lunch and the other watched the De Dion. The 'armed' ingredient was an alarm whistle.

Eventually I began to relax and enjoy driving this glorious vehicle. Meyton's accusations about the car's authenticity began to fade. 'Does the car feel right to you, Len?' I asked, after I had brought him and Zoe up to date on Meyton.

'Bits of paper – what do they know?' Len pronounced.

I saw his point. This car felt real. She was a De Dion ten h.p. from the right year. Anything else was 'bits of paper'.

Moreover I was with the Major. His grandfather would not pinch any old De Dion. Pascal would want the best. And this was it.

I was reassured to see everyone when we gathered in 'Omsk'. It seemed to be rally business as usual and the De Dion was still with us. There might be unfinished business over it, but I had persuaded myself that that would be for tomorrow, Sunday. Tonight, we could eat, drink and be merry.

Everything on the surface was pleasant enough that evening. There was no sign of Meyton or of Brenda. Helen was talking enthusiastically about the last lap of the rally on the Sunday, and Julian chatted as though the De Dion were already a fixture in Treasure Island and of the money collected for opening the museum to the public. If he was in denial of reality, I didn't care. He was envisaging a fairy-tale ending in which the De Dion would be driven straight into Treasure Island after the finale to the rally and remain there for ever. Let him dream on. I'd dream too. With Helen.

Even the Morrises didn't cause any trouble that evening. I suspected this might be because they were busy with some plan of their own, having heard Brenda's intention to take the car to France sooner rather than later. That seemed a dotty idea which I could not believe Benson had sanctioned and I decided to ring him myself on Monday. Perhaps Brenda saw a fairy-tale ending. I was not so sure. Meyton's threat to tell the world at the finale that the De Dion was not the original rally car still remained, and with it some other question marks.

In the midst of all these differing plans, however, sat this beautifully restored grey De Dion ten h.p. Len always says he has a nose for cars and I do for trouble. It seemed to me that tomorrow both of us might have our powers tested.

'When exactly are you planning to take the car to France?' I asked Brenda curiously as we waited to set off in the De Dion the next morning.

'Soon.'

It was such a short reply that I looked at her sharply. 'Are you sure that's wise?'

She looked at me sternly, as my mother used to do when she thought she had caught me out. 'Why not? The car will be restored to its place of birth. Just as Victoria wanted.'

I was beginning to wonder if 'as Victoria wanted' wasn't becoming a mantra to avoid facing her own secret desires.

There seemed to be more cars joining in the rally for this final day, judging by the full hotel car park, all of them splendid classics. It was looking good and I struggled to put reservations to the back of my mind, including the fact that I knew the press would be gathering for the kill like prairie dogs.

Almost as soon as we had left with the procession, I stopped, and Brenda left me to join Julian again. There had been signs of a leak yesterday and I didn't want to risk it worsening at the vital moment of the 'lap of honour' along the Roman road that led to Harford Lee and Treasure Island.

With the De Dion the star of the show, despite her being on Charlie's flatbed much of the time, we flashed through the rest of 'Siberia' and arrived at 'Moscow' (Tenterden) for a coffee, making rather better time than our predecessors in 1907. We then shot through 'Poland', 'Warsaw', and 'Berlin' (Lympne) and reached the 'border of France', otherwise known as the county of Kent, where we stopped for lunch. On the 1907 rally the two De Dions had had a slow drive back to France suffering breakdowns near the border – with the champagne reception prepared for them being on the far side. Our 'border' was just before the M20 and the Roman road, our triumphal route.

'Ready, Jack?' Len asked.

We pushed the De Dion down from Charlie's floor on to the modern roadway, and turned her around to face her as yet unknown destiny. I felt surprisingly cheerful and ready for the challenge. No matter what it was, no matter whether it was the true 1907 De Dion or not, this was a magnificent car and we would pay her due homage. Surprisingly, Brenda decided not to be my passenger for this last stretch.

'Are you sure you don't want to ride in glory?' I asked her in amazement.

She seemed subdued, not the feisty lady who had tackled the Morrises and Connor Meyton.

'Helen should take my place,' she told me. 'She's done so much for the rally.'

I agreed, but considering that Helen must represent the 'enemy' to Brenda because of her connection with the Major, this was good of her. I handed Helen up like the queen she was and like the Edwardian gent I was pretending to be and we travelled regally along that Roman road towards the finale to the rally. No matter what lay ahead, I exulted, nothing could take the grandeur of this last ride away from us. The De Dion's engine purred, the leak was not obvious, and in any case we were well supplied with water. The sun was out, lifting the grey paint to a sparkling twilight. People were lining the roadside, sparsely I admit in the open country, but they had turned out in their hundreds as we passed Stelling Minnis. Helen developed a regal wave of the hand with great aplomb.

Once past the village however she turned to me. 'What's ahead, Jack?' she asked quietly.

'Whatever it is, we'll come through it. I'm sure Dave's got his men there in case of a punch-up.' I said this lightly knowing full well that punch-up would not begin to describe whatever Meyton had in store.

'And the car's not an impostor?'

'The real thing.' I had a feeling this was significant, and yet for the life of me I couldn't think why. As we approached the turning for Harford Lee, I patted the De Dion encouragingly. 'You can do it, old girl. You can do it,' I told her.

Helen managed a laugh. 'You talking to me?'

'I know we can do it. It's the car that needs encouragement.'

It would be ignominious for the De Dion to have to be driven along here on Charlie. Luckily Julian had repaired the worst of the potholes in his driveway with this in mind, but even so as we turned in at the gates towards Cobba House and Burnt Barn Bottom, trepidation hit me like a punch in the stomach. We were trapped now, with nowhere to go but onwards.

The press, photographers and TV cameramen were lining the drive. I glanced behind me and saw the other cars turning one by one to follow us in, but none of us crusaders knew what lay ahead. I still had a nagging feeling that I had missed a connection. As we chugged towards Armageddon, I remembered Yeats' line about the rough beast slouching towards Bethlehem to be born. What rough beast awaited our arrival? Whatever it was, I knew it had been preparing for this over the past weeks and it was now awake.

FIFTEEN

We made a triumphal entry into 'Paris', Helen, the De Dion and I. The only resemblance to the French city, however, was in the huge blown-up photo posters of the Eiffel Tower, placards and tricolours welcoming us along the driveway. The De Dion had not taken kindly to 'Paris' despite the work on the potholes, so progress had been slow, but she had got us here in the end – just as the De Dions had done in 1907.

We had passed a low-loader on one side of the driveway, which at first I thought was Charlie, but I decided it must be a safety measure for any rally participants whose precious babes were complaining at the thought of the long journey home. It was just as well it was parked there and not at Burnt Barn Bottom because Len was banking on parking in the best spot from which to convey our own precious burden back to its temporary secure home. I noticed at least half a dozen security guards preparing for the worst, eager to defend us both from marauders and casual sightseers. That didn't apply to the press so the Pen Roxtons of this world were to be seen in their numbers, with TV cameras poised for action.

Helen breathed a sigh of relief as we reached Burnt Barn Bottom and Treasure Island. 'Journey's end,' she declared and the De Dion let out a belch of petrol fumes in her support.

'Journeys traditionally end in lovers' meetings,' I told her happily, as I parked in the allotted place she pointed out under a triumphal arch of flags, flowers and photos of the 1907 rally, which framed the De Dion nicely. This was at a suitable distance from Charlie ready for the take-off. Only five or six other cars were to be permitted to park in Burnt Barn Bottom. The rest of the rally cars and press had to drive past it to the field behind, so that this area could be free for speeches, buns and drinks. A dais had been erected at the side of the De Dion and the more mundane needs of sustenance and Portaloos were at the far end by Pompeii and Herculaneum.

Helen couldn't have heard me as there was no reply. We were too busy watching the other cars drive by and then their owners milling with the press. From being populated solely by the media, the place quickly filled up. I saw the Major and Julian arrive, together with Brenda and the Morrises in their wake. Brenda quickly disappeared, a fact of which the Morrises quickly took advantage for their own self promotion to the press.

The other familiar face that had not yet put in an appearance was Connor Meyton. I realized I could well be seeing bogeys where none existed, but not seeing them might be far worse. What had he come on this rally for if not to cause trouble? I'd expected to see him with the press but there was Pen – but no Meyton. And no Dean Warren either.

Nevertheless I felt an instinctive need to remain glued to the De Dion. There was a murderer on the loose, perhaps two, and the probability was that at least one of them was, or would be, here today. The De Dion must surely feature in the saga. That second low-loader lingered in my mind.

Time to cudgel my little grey cells like Poirot. There was nothing I could do about Meyton, but there was something I could do about the De Dion. Mad though it seemed, Brenda claimed to have Benson's approval for taking the car away. Could she possibly be planning to take it *now*? Straight to the Channel ferries? I fought for reason. It was Sunday. There would be no rousing Benson at his office, but I had his full contact details, thanks to Dave, which included a mobile number.

And of course it was on voicemail. I left an urgent message – and hoped. As I switched off, I saw Nick Morris striding towards me.

'Hope you're guarding that car, Colby. You're taking it back to the garage it came from, aren't you?'

'I'm planning to.'

Instant alarm on Nick's face. 'You'll stop that maniac woman driving it away, won't you?'

'If the solicitors have agreed, I can hardly stop her,' I pointed

out. I could see Brenda sitting by herself at a table, and the
dejected slope of her shoulders made me think I was vastly
over-exaggerating the chances of her planning to take the car
anywhere today, let alone France.

'Dad's been trying to get hold of Benson to ask him what
the hell's going on,' Nick said viciously, 'but the office
number's on voicemail all the time and he's made sure he's
ex-directory. Typical. All Dad, I and that Major fellow are
concerned about is that the car is in good hands.'

Nick strode off to join his parents and just as I was wondering
who would end up partnering whom in this merry dance, I
saw Pen come stalking towards me, nose quivering, determined
stride, and eyes gleaming. Ah well, it had to happen sometime,
I thought.

'Heard there was a little fracas at the hotel, Jack,' she said.
'How did I miss that?'

'Unlike you, Pen.'

'Got a great story, though. Guess what. This car's a fraud.
Just any old De Dion, not the one in the—'

I groaned. So Meyton had already struck. 'All unproven,' I
broke in. 'You wouldn't want to print something that could
be discredited at any moment?'

She considered this seriously. 'No . . .' Then she brightened
up. 'If I quote the horse's mouth, that lets me out and gives
me another story.'

'It doesn't let you out if it's libellous, and I, dearest Pen,
am not a horse. As the saying goes, you can take me to the
water, but you can't make me drink.'

'No, but Connor Meyton can. Rang me last night.'

Retreat impossible, advance impossible. Dig in was the answer.
I braced myself. 'Part of what he says about the documentation
might be true, but it does not invalidate the fact that the car itself
is the genuine article. There's a valid bill of sale in existence
which—'

'Oh no there isn't.'

'Pen, I've seen it.'

She looked smug. 'It's a scoop. Meyton told me he's been
holding back on you. That bill of sale from the agent Vaugirard
in Dunkirk – he went out of business in late 1906. The bill's

a fake. And don't say it's Meyton trying it on. I checked it out today. He's right.'

Not only did my heart sink, it hit my boots. *Both* bills of sale were faked. I couldn't wrestle with that now though. Meyton had temporarily won, and this beautiful car was probably not the lady I had taken her for – if he was right. And I feared he was. I pulled myself together to deal with the situation facing me – which did not look good.

'It's not a scoop, Pen,' I said firmly. 'But there might be one for you shortly.'

'Really?' She looked at me narrowly. 'Give me a clue.'

'If I had one, I would.'

A prickly feeling at the back of my neck told me that the story was far from over. Dave must be around here somewhere, but I hadn't seen him – or any police presence, come to that. Just the security guards. Was I wrong? Perhaps this was just the finale to a social occasion.

Pen considered this. 'You've got two hours,' she told me finally. 'And then I file.'

I mulled the whole De Dion story over again. I thought of the Leonardo masterpiece over which there was continuous dispute as to which was the original. The argument didn't seem to have done the contenders any harm, although I had to admit that a De Dion Bouton, however wonderful to car buffs, might be a little further down the line of historic value than a Leonardo. Perhaps not to car lovers, however.

Two hours. Be damned if I was going to be held to ransom by Pen, although none of the cards to play against her were in my hands.

And then my mobile rang. An irate Benson had picked up my message. I'd apparently got it all wrong; he'd told Mrs Carlyle time and time again that until he gave the all-clear the car remained his responsibility and must be returned as arranged to his protection this evening. Why couldn't I get that into my head? Mrs Carlyle had understood that quite clearly, and he had just spoken to her to ensure that she did. She had been most upset at the misunderstanding.

'No misunderstanding,' I told him. 'Worse. *Much* worse.'

Still no Dave when I tried to contact him, though I hoped
he was around somewhere. Another message. The whole world
seemed to be run by message services now. That settled it,
particularly when I could no longer see any sign of Brenda.
I was not going to leave the De Dion's side even if I had to
chain myself to it. No one, but no one, was going to take this
car anywhere but Len and Charlie.

And then Julian appeared to admire the car – or was he
coveting it? His eyes devoured it so greedily I wondered if he
feared this was the last time he might see it. 'Have you seen
Brenda?' I asked. 'It seems she's been holding out on us.' No
reason to keep this secret. 'She's *not* been authorized to take
the car.'

His eyes lit up with joy. 'What are you going to do?'

'Stop her taking it.'

'I'm with you on that. Are the police here?'

'Haven't seen any – must be somewhere.'

'Find them,' he ordered me. 'I'm not going to give that
car up.'

'Even though it's looking as if it's not one of the Peking
to Paris cars?' I told him about Meyton's claim to Pen.

He looked appalled. 'But I know that car. I've worked on
it, I *know* it. It's right.'

I remembered Helen's words, 'It's not an impostor', but
now we had to face the apparent certainty that the odds were
against its being the real thing, and if I knew Pen the
whole world was going to know shortly. It wouldn't stop at
the *Kentish Graphic*.

I warmed to Julian. How does one know 'right'? One might
see a woman across a crowded room and be drawn to her. But
to *know* her needs the quiet of the day and the quiet of the
night. Louise had taught me that. Perhaps cars too need a
solitary communion between owner/driver and machine before
one knows all is 'right' between you. And yet Julian had to
face the fact that in this case it was not right.

The Major was in great form when he came to the dais to
talk about the rally and its 'crowning glory' the De Dion,
which made my news even worse. For once, he chose his
words tactfully, omitting all mention of its ownership. Pieces

of a celebratory cake were then distributed – a cake made by Brenda, so Helen told me, though I still could not see Brenda herself. She had certainly taken the rally to her heart. I remembered the delicious French pastries she had produced and wondered what drew her to France so much. The country? Her marriage? Why was she so set on fulfilling Victoria's apparent wish for the car to live in France?

There was something wrong somewhere, I was sure of it, but I could not fix on it. Something Helen had said; something Pen had said . . .

I could see Julian rounding up people for his tour of Treasure Island. I was sorely tempted to join them but I dared not do so. I tried Dave again without success, and resigned myself to a lone sojourn with the car. Ridiculous really, as nothing could happen to her. Not yet at any rate.

I was nevertheless relieved when the tour ended and the crowd spilled outside again. With a mob of people around I began to relax – until I realized I was shivering, and not just because the sun had disappeared behind the clouds. I glanced up at them – just as all hell broke loose.

Explosion after explosion came from the far corner from where I was standing and behind the cars that had permission to park there. Noise assailed my ears as the crowd screamed and pushed to get away from the point of the explosions of which each seemed louder than its predecessor, filling the air with fumes and smoke. I rushed towards the noise with some of the guards. That sounds weird but I sensed this was not a major bomb attack. Nevertheless the stampede away from the noise prevented our reaching it – and then came more explosions bursting on our ears, this time not from Burnt Barn Bottom but from the field behind it, where the majority of cars were parked. The noise became ever more intense in a crescendo of sound that mercilessly assaulted my ears.

This began a second stampede as some of the crowd tried to reach their cars and others pushed in the opposite direction. I began to head for the field, then changed my mind as another round of explosions began from the first site. I saw the Major and Julian rush inside Treasure Island, obviously to ensure nothing was amiss there, but now that the way was clearer I was able to get to the source of the explosions.

Stupid? Maybe, but as I'd figured out they weren't terrorist bombs it was worth the risk. I was right. The noise ceased and I rushed to investigate. Simply done. The explosions were caused by fireworks that must have been tied together in large groups. So what the—?

The De Dion Bouton. It had to be that.

I spun round and saw to my relief that one of the security guards was cranking the engine to drive her out of danger – no! *Brenda* was at the wheel. This was no safety measure. And that could be no security guard. Brenda had moved over and he was now at the wheel. Didn't I . . .?

No time for reason to catch up with instinct. I had to act *now*. I was pounding across the yard, pushing people out of my way, as I saw the De Dion beginning to move.

So what did I do?

I had some mad idea of stopping it. I rushed to throw myself in front of it – how crazy can one be? Somehow I didn't reach the ground. A tremendous thud in my back sent me stumbling and staggering to the car's far side where I collapsed in a heap, but clear of danger. Even as I struggled to my feet the shouts and yells around me made me realize that the momentum of whoever had thumped me had resulted in their being knocked down by the De Dion. It hadn't been going fast but where people meet car wheels it hurts. I was vaguely aware of several people pulling my saviour free and another two or three pulling the non-security guard down from the car. It was Dave Jennings' team. Sergeant Blake supported me as I hobbled over to see how my saviour was. And *who* it was. He was still lying on the ground, alive though clearly injured.

Sometimes one can be wrong about people. It was Connor Meyton.

I stood back with Helen while the first-aiders checked him over. Dazed, I tried to make sense of this show – or perhaps even in my stupor Helen's and Pen's words dovetailed, ringing all my bells at once, and I reached a staggering conclusion.

'It's my car,' Brenda was screeching at Dave, even while he was arresting her partner for suspected murder. Two of his men had him firmly held. It wasn't Dean Warren and of course it wasn't Meyton. But it was someone I recognized. So did the Major.

'I'd know that scoundrel anywhere,' he roared. 'It's that rotter Robert Fairhill.'

It was Victoria Drake's first husband and, I discovered later, prospective second husband to Brenda under the name of Monsieur Beaumont. I knew him as the impostor Bob Orton.

Arthur Orton, his professional photographer's name as Pen had told me: of course it had rung a bell. Arthur Orton was the name of the impostor in the famous nineteenth-century Tichborne Claimant case.

'Typical of that con-man's arrogance,' the Major grunted. 'Scales fell from Victoria's eyes pretty soon after they married.'

We had managed to hold on until the last of the participants had reluctantly left this never-to-be-forgotten rally finale and then went back to Julian's house to try to work out just what had happened that afternoon. One thing became clear from Brenda's incoherent ramblings about her 'dear Robert' before DCI Fielding took her to headquarters for questioning. We had assumed her 'French neighbour' and prospective husband was French in nationality as well as location, but Beaumont is as much a British surname as a French one. It was he who had persuaded her into this final attempt to seize the De Dion.

'Poor woman,' Helen had said soberly while we were waiting for the ambulance for Connor, who by then was conscious. 'What a shock for her.'

Was she innocent or guilty? I wondered. I couldn't cope with that for a while. Nor with how guilty or otherwise Connor was. No doubt Dave would be seeing a lot of him when he was fit enough.

'Orton's no good, Jack,' Connor had muttered when he recognized me.

I squatted down at his side. 'What did he do to you?' I asked.

'Used me. *Me.* Did his dirty work for him and then he puts me in the frame and does a vanishing act.'

'Alf King?' I said grimly. 'Victoria?'

'Not me, Jack. I steer clear of murder.'

He'd possibly saved my life and he was in great pain, so I had left it at that.

It took a week or two for the dust to settle. Then I met Dave for a pub lunch and he filled me in – provisionally.

'So Meyton was a good guy?' I asked innocently.

'Not so good. No murderer though – at least Fielding doesn't think so.'

'Orton killed Victoria Drake?'

'Sure. Not much doubt there. Fielding says the DNA on the lug wrench will fix him. Put his gloves on a bit too late. She's hoping for a match on glove and footprints too.'

'And Alf King?'

'More of a question mark. Orton denies it, so does Meyton. Mick Smith is the more likely contender, either off his own bat or on Orton's orders.'

'Why though?'

'Meyton's story is that Orton appeared out of the blue early in the year and commissioned Mick to find the De Dion. Said the car would make a killing after the publicity of the rally. When Mick found out that Alf thought the car wasn't the genuine article he tackled the problem of keeping him silent about it rather too enthusiastically, probably on Orton's orders, but tried blackmailing him afterwards. Then you come along asking questions and Bob does a disappearing act, after ridding himself of Mick. Meyton reckons Orton got rid of the body and fired the garage to put Meyton in the frame not him. Meyton does admit to arson – but only for Carter's garage. He was determined to scotch Orton's plans for a happy retirement with the De Dion.'

'Did he know who Orton was?'

'No, but he was pretty sure he was using a false name and lived overseas. That was why he was sure that the rally would be the focal point.'

'Why not during the rally itself?'

'As the Mad Major said, Jack, Fairhill was an arrogant con-man. He wanted max publicity for the De Dion to send the price sky high. The press was saving its powder for that finale – if it had disappeared en route it would have been a minor story, not major.' Dave paused. 'That's Fielding's and my conclusion – how about this Brenda Carlyle though? How does she fit in, Jack?'

I'd had a couple of weeks to put two and two together. 'Rough idea OK?'

'Try me.'

'Fairhill, as the Mad Major puts it, is a scoundrel,' I began. 'Speaks fluent French and gives himself a French pseudonym, Beaumont, which is not only a translation of Fairhill but both a French and English surname. He was divorced from Victoria, but by then knew all about the De Dion. Has the luck to run across Brenda—'

'On a Channel crossing in 2007, he says,' Dave confirmed.

'And discovers that she lives next door to his former wife, whereupon he gets her to find out whether Victoria still has the old car, which he no doubt still believed was the genuine article. Sees a bit of cash to be made, something he is usually short of, as the Peking to Paris rally was in the news again. Sees his opportunity through Brenda and somehow ends up her neighbour.'

Easy enough, I had realized. 'He could have told her he had a house in the same village and then proceeded to rent one under a false name,' I said. 'She only went there intermittently, so wouldn't have known whether he arrived before or after she had met him. He sets Brenda up to urge Victoria to sell the car to her at a knock-down price. Even if she mentions her "French neighbour" it won't be by the name of Fairhill. Victoria refuses to sell, saying, perhaps at Brenda's suggestion, that she'd leave it to her in her will. She knows full well that it's not the genuine article, but good old Bob Fairhill still thinks it is. Brenda immediately accepts, which might have set Victoria back, but she doesn't go back on her word. Chum Bob lets the matter lie fallow – until Brenda happily tells him about the forthcoming rally last autumn when the local councils on the route were first alerted.'

'Odd she didn't want to leave the car to her daughter,' Dave commented.

'Agreed, but that kind of thing happens. Probably Tom got

up her nose. Then the pace must have hotted up, because rumours were flying around about the De Dion, thanks to the dear old Mad Major. Monsieur Beaumont decides that the rally would make the car shoot up in value, and if Brenda was going to inherit, the sooner the better before Victoria changes her mind and sells it. A fortune could be his, thinks Monsieur Beaumont, if he and Brenda marry. They could sell the car for a vast sum; he could get his hands on the loot and disappear at will.'

'Why pull the photographer Arthur Orton trick though?' Dave asked.

I'd thought this out too. 'Maybe it goes like this. Firstly, he hears about the rally from Brenda, and decides the time has come to enrich himself, so as neither he nor Brenda knows where the car is – because Victoria won't tell Brenda – he needs someone to find it. Enter Mick Smith and Meyton. Orton discovers that Alf knows the car isn't the genuine article after all – which implies that Victoria knows that too. So Alf has to be fixed. Secondly, Meyton has found out where the car is and Orton urges Brenda into some good work on the phone with Doris. Once Orton knows that Victoria is planning to move it from Alf's storage barn nearer home, he promptly wines and dines his wife as he did from time to time – ostensibly when he was over from "America" – and kills her.'

'He'd have known where she'd moved the car to, so why not grab it then?'

Easy one. 'He needed the car to run in the rally, in order for the price to go up, so he just had to sit back and wait – as he thought. Only to have the Mad Major raise the stakes by his counter claim.'

'But *two* murders. For the car or the cash?'

'My guess is cash. Murder has been committed for far less than the De Dion would bring, with or without its provenance, and there's nothing rational where money's a motive. Don't forget he probably killed Mick Smith too . . .'

Dave regarded me coolly. 'Don't go painting Meyton as the hero of the hour, will you? It's only his word at present that it was Bob who knocked off Smith and decided to give Dean

Warren a warning by dumping the body in the garage and torching the place.'

I had mixed feelings. It was hard not to feel some fellow sympathy for someone who's saved you from a very nasty experience, such as death.

'If it's any comfort, Jack,' Dave continued, 'I agree with Fielding that Connor's a bad lad, but that he doesn't do murder.'

'And Brenda?'

'Her too. Orton's stooge.'

'That low-loader we passed on the way in to Burnt Barn Bottom, was that Orton's doing?'

'Yup. They had it planned to the minute, reckoning the diversion tactics would keep people busy for fifteen to twenty minutes or so, enough time to get the De Dion out of the yard and fixed up on the low-loader. Typical con-man's arrogance.'

'He conned Brenda too.' She must have seen Orton's plan as a romantic gesture to pick her up in the De Dion and more or less elope with her to Dover. I thought of how I'd seen her at the finale. She hadn't looked excited then, and I wondered whether she had begun to suspect her dashing beau's motives. Then I remembered her screeching at the police when the plan had gone wrong, and felt less sorry for her.

I didn't even have to hunt Pen down to break the news. She walked right into my web by arriving at Frogs Hill in a towering temper. She seemed to think I was responsible for all her troubles. As if.

'What the hell's going on, Jack? You and I were partners on this story, remember?'

'Police work excepted, Pen.'

'*Un*except it then.'

'You really want the gen? Fresh from the horse's mouth?'

'Spit it out.'

So I told her the whole sorry tale, or as much of it as I could. It silenced her. I almost couldn't bear to watch. I'd never seen her so crushed.

'You mean that creep used me, Jack? Just to keep up with the story and keep it running?'

'I'm afraid so.'

'He told me untruths?'

I loved her way of putting it. 'Throughout.'

A variety of expressions crossed her face, but bewilderment won. 'I don't like that, Jack.'

'Don't blame you. What will you do about it running the story – when you legally can, of course?'

Pen considered. Then she brightened up. '*Graphic* journalist first on killer's trail,' she pronounced.

I laughed. 'Go for it, Pen.'

There were a couple of holes in the story that still puzzled me. I couldn't discuss them with Helen and they were not strictly relevant to Dave or Fielding's investigations. Firstly, why the Major hadn't played his ace over the ownership of the car when he had every chance to do so? Secondly, why had Victoria left that car to Brenda, thereby cutting Patricia out? The motivation that Dave and I had come up with seemed weak. It was an expensive bequest to leave to a friend because she didn't want to go back on her word, and yet it seemed she had acted of her own free will. True, Brenda could be a forceful woman when she chose, but Victoria was even more forceful and to leave that car (restored at great cost) to Brenda without good reason seemed out of character.

I decided there was only one person who might settle this for me, and that was the man who had first commissioned me for this crazy venture: the Mad Major. The man had managed to upset Julian, his partner in the museum, although I gathered Julian was now hopeful of buying the car from Brenda (and the Major himself if the legal position worked out that way), and had also upset Helen and me. The Mad Major, I decided, was at the heart of this puzzle and at present he was showing every sign of sliding away from the limelight. It was time to beard him in his den.

I found him at Brooklands race course, the version laid down in his garden. He was sitting in an old-fashioned deck-chair peacefully examining a model Bentley. His peace ended.

'Ah. Morning,' he said unhappily as he saw me. 'Thought you might be over.'

'Just for a chat,' I said cheerily.

'The De Dion's still safe?' he ventured. 'Bad business that.'

'It was. And yes it's safe. Did you *know* that both bills of sale, not just Victoria's, were fake?'

'Thought they might be,' he mumbled. Then he rallied. 'But it doesn't change a thing. Only the documents. The car's the real McCoy.'

'Not according to Alf King. There's no evidence of any damage at the docks bad enough to get anywhere near warranting a write-off. No sign of damage to the chassis, only wear and tear.'

'Perhaps Pascal nicked it on its way back to Paris and made up the whole story?' he tried hopefully.

'I think not, Major. The evidence points up to Pascal buying a used De Dion Bouton, and sending it back to English with Florence with this fairy-tale attached. That's why he never bothered to pick it up.'

I thought he would continue to argue, but he didn't. 'Ah well, still a nice car. Had a word with my solicitors.'

'Are you still challenging the ownership?'

'Maybe. Maybe not. Mrs Carlyle came over to see me. Feels badly about all this. Victoria and that rotter Fairhill and so forth.'

She wasn't the only one. Alf, Doris, Victoria, the Morrises – all victims of one man resorting to murder to achieve his objective.

'Fact is,' he continued awkwardly, 'Brenda's turning her claim over to me, so that the car is mine whichever claim is the better. The Morrises are not going ahead with their claim on it.'

'But that's great news!' I couldn't think of a better way out. 'So why aren't you looking happier about it?'

'It's Pat. Patricia Morris,' he added as if it had slipped my mind who she was.

'You think she should have inherited it?'

'From Victoria, yes. And from me. Fact is . . .' He looked embarrassed.

I was beginning to see the light. 'Nineteen sixty-eight,' I said.

'Right. Pat's my daughter.'

The last piece in the jigsaw. 'Does she know?'

'No. Got to tell her.'

'She'll be pleased,' I said. 'That'll be good news, considering the man she thought was her father is a murderer.'

He brightened up immediately. 'Hadn't thought of it that way.'

I was still puzzled though. 'Why didn't Victoria tell her the truth?'

He was cast back into gloom. 'She didn't want to face it – or me. She was married to that rotter at the time. Wanted to marry her myself when she told me. She wouldn't have it. Said she didn't want to divorce a parasite only to marry a stick insect. Didn't like me being in the military, I suppose. Anyway, she did a runner. Said she never wanted to see me or hear from me again. Not my fault.' He glared at me. 'She said sorry and all that, but this was her life and she was going to live it without me. Never heard from her. False address. Heard she had remarried but didn't know where she was. When this rally idea came up, I thought I'd give it a go. Didn't know her new name but had a hunch she might be in Kent somewhere – her parents came from here. Florence could have been local too. So that's what Victoria and I were talking about that day – Pat. I didn't know she was at Brenda's house, and was fooled when Victoria said she'd take me over to her home to satisfy me. When we got there she was out of course, so she offered to take me to see the De Dion instead. As if that was any compensation. Didn't care two hoots about that, so I said no.'

I stared at him open-mouthed. 'What about Treasure Island?'

'Yes, well, jolly pleased about the car for its sake, if Julian gets it,' he said hastily. 'But Victoria – and my daughter. That's what was in it for me. Chiefly Pat. Getting older, you see. Wife passed over, no other children. But now I realize Victoria didn't want Pat to know anything about me. That's why she left the car to Brenda. Victoria knew the full story about the car and was worried Pat would find out about my rival claim if she inherited the car and the whole story would come out.'

'That must have been hard for you.'

'I wasn't pleased, I can tell you. I've been thinking, though. If Brenda makes the car over to me, I'll give a half share to Pat provided we can keep the De Dion in Treasure Island. Might make her feel a bit better about me as a father. Whether it's the 1907 rally car or not, it's still worth a bob or two. What do you think of that?'

'A really good idea,' I said. 'But given that husband of hers, I'd make it forty-nine per cent.'

He grinned at me. 'Jolly good idea.'

That jigsaw complete, I turned my attention to the other matter worrying me. Helen had been remarkably busy in the last few weeks. I'd only seen her twice and never at Frogs Hill. It was understandable enough with the future of Treasure Island to organize. Even so . . .

So I went over to the museum. Start on neutral ground. 'Where will you put the De Dion when and if you have her for keeps?' I asked her. When we'd finished discussing that and everything else under the sun except the vital matter, I suggested: 'Dinner at Frogs Hill tonight? I'm a dab hand at spaghetti.'

She was silent for a little while, then said, 'You know, Jack. I think I'm busy this evening.'

So there it was on the table, writ clear. No more walks, no more loving, no more Helen. 'Why, Helen?' I asked. 'Can you explain?'

She thought for a moment. 'There's a famous verse about a man who wasn't there. Well, that's you, Jack. You seem to be there, but you're not. Not at present, anyway.'

I knew she was right. I was still out there somewhere, with Louise.

I tried though. 'She'll not come back, Helen.'

'But when will you, Jack?'

'Some day, I will. Some day soon.'

Would I? Common sense told me I would, but how would I know when? I had a brief moment of hope in October. Helen rang me. 'Dinner?' I asked hopefully.

'Sweetheart, not yet. It's the De Dion Bouton. It's all settled.

Probate is through, and the car's registered in Stanley's name
with Patricia Morris owning part of it.'

'How's Julian with that?'

'Content. Now its authenticity has been blown to smithereens, he's not so bent on personally owning it, and we've
thought up a way of displaying it in Treasure Island despite
the question mark over it. Did Len tell you he's already been
over to check it out?'

'No,' I said glumly.

'Good. We were keeping it as a surprise,' she explained.
'We thought you might like to drive the car down here on
Charlie.'

I brightened up immediately. 'Love to.'

And one late autumn day I did just that. Not alone. Len
and Zoe insisted on coming too, and so we drove the De
Dion in state through Harford Lee to Burnt Barn Bottom.
Or, to be correct, I drove Charlie with Zoe while Len drove
my Gordon-Keeble for my return journey.

'Hey! Look, there's a reception party,' Zoe said in glee as
we arrived.

Outside Treasure Island was a table with glasses and a
bottle of champagne. By the open double doors, Helen,
Julian and the Mad Major were waiting to escort the De
Dion in. I drove it in state to its appointed place, and then
we returned to pop the champagne corks. Julian looked
rather wistful as if he would have preferred to have driven
it in himself. Tough. This privilege was mine, even if Helen
remained out of my reach. I had a terrible feeling she might
be turning into a friend rather than my lover. But, hey, what's
so wrong with that?

As I arrived back at Frogs Hill driving in state in my Gordon-
Keeble, I found Charlie had arrived first and saw Len and
Zoe were waiting for me. I took the Gordon-Keeble back to
its home and then invited them into the farmhouse for a
celebratory drink and to chew over the day.

'You know, Jack,' Len said after a while, 'I'm not so sure
about that car.'

Alarm bells clanged. 'The De Dion? What about it?'

'Alf said it wasn't one of the 1907 rally cars, because there was no sign of damage at the docks, right?'

'Right.'

'When I was checking it over, I had a look at it,' he said. 'Careful look. Saw what he meant.'

'And?' I asked impatiently. We'd been over this a hundred times or more.

'Went on looking. Difficult to spot, but inside that butterfly radiator there are a few flakes of old white paint.'

'How do you know it's old?' Zoe countered.

'White lead content. Had it analysed. Also tung oil and soya bean.'

I gazed at him. I thought I saw where he was heading, rustled up my knowledge of the 1907 rally and a wild hope sprang through me.

Len blushed. 'Wanted to be sure before I told you,' he added.

'And now you are?'

'Right for Chinese paint for 1907.'

'And maybe a lot of other years too. So what's so special about that?' Zoe asked.

'Just before the five rally cars set out from Peking in June 1907,' I said slowly, 'two French soldiers painted the words "Peking to Paris" in Chinese script on the radiator of one of the De Dions.'

Zoe's eyes grew as big as the De Dion's hubs. 'You mean . . .'

'Of course a speck or two of white paint isn't conclusive,' I said hastily.

Len cleared his throat. 'Let's get back to the Pits. There's an Alvis to restore.'

THE CAR'S THE STAR

James Myers

Jack Colby's daily driver: Alfa Romeo 156 Sportwagon

The 156 Sportwagon is a 'lifestyle estate', which means that it's trendy, respectable to have on the drive, although it lacks the interior space of a traditional load-lugger. For those who value individuality, its subtle and pure styling gives it the edge over rivals such as the BMW 3-Series. It gives a lot of driving pleasure even with the smaller engines.

Jack Colby's 1965 Gordon-Keeble

One hundred of these fabulous supercars were built between 1963 and 1966 with over ninety units surviving around the globe, mostly in the UK. Designed by John Gordon and Jim Keeble using current racing car principles, with the bodyshell designed by twenty-one-year-old Giorgetto Giugiaro at Bertone, the cars were an instant success but the company was ruined by supply-side industrial action with ultimately only 99 units completed even after the company was relaunched in May 1965, as Keeble Cars Ltd. Final closure came in February 1966 when the factory at Sholing closed and Jim Keeble moved to Keewest. The hundredth car was completed in 1971 with leftover components. The Gordon-Keeble's emblem is a yellow and green tortoise.

Jack Colby's 1938 Lagonda V-12 Drophead

The Lagonda company won its attractive name from a creek near the home of the American-born founder Wilbur Gunn in Springfield, Ohio. The name given to it by the American Indians was Ough Ohonda. The V-12 drophead was a car to compete with the very best in the world, with a sporting twelve-cylinder engine which would power the two 1939 Le Mans cars. Its designer was the famous W.O. Bentley. Sadly many fine prewar saloons have been cut down to look like Le Mans replicas. The V12 cars are very similar externally to the earlier six-cylinder versions; both types were available with open or closed bodywork in a number of different styles. The V-12 Drophead also featured in Jack's earlier case, *Classic in the Barn.*

The 1935 Bentley Silent Sports

In the 1920s, Bentleys enjoyed numerous racing and record-breaking successes, most notably five victories at Le Mans! But the cost of all this was massive losses and the company was bailed out by millionaire adventurer and Bentley racing driver Woolf Barnato, one of the famous 'Bentley Boys'. The Bentley 'Silent Sports Car' series was introduced in 1933. This new model was very different from the previously huge and muscular Bentleys.

1906 10hp De Dion Bouton

This was the most popular car of its time in France and the pride of the nation. It was was small and light – ideal for the gruelling conditions of the 1907 Peking to Paris *raid* (literal translation long-distance trek). The two 10 hp De Dion Boutons that completed the event had the advanced engineering qualities that made these cars such strong contenders in this ultimate endurance test. They both benefited from recently introduced and extremely reliable fast-revving engines, user-friendly three-speed gearboxes and a robust suspension layout. One such model racked up over 80,000 miles of everyday use in England.

Bentley 50s Continental

Bentley used the Continental name on a number of models in the fifties and sixties. The name was reserved for cars with more powerful engines than standard, installed in lowered chassis provided to coachbuilders for distinctive body shapes of specially lightened construction. Continentals have usually been 'coupé' styled two-door saloons intended for high speed. They were named Continental, as with some Rolls-Royces before them, because until the 1960s there were no high-speed roads of any length in their home country.

1930s Bentley drophead

The Bentley 4½ Litre is best known for epitomizing pre-war British motor racing. Created by Walter O. Bentley, the Bentley was a more powerful race car due to its increased engine displacement. In the twenties and thirties prominent car manufacturers like Bentley focused on designing cars to compete in the 24 Hour race of Le Mans, a popular automotive endurance course established a few years earlier. A victory in this competition would quickly elevate any car maker's reputation. The most famous models in this regard – with supercharged engines – were known as Blower Bentleys. A 4½ litre Bentley won the 24 Hours of Le Mans in 1928 and most famously set a top-speed record in 1932 at Brooklands with a recorded speed of 138 mph.

For more information on Jack Colby's cases, see www.amymyers. net and his own website and blog on www.jackcolby.co.uk.